MW00938843

RUN FOR THE
DEVIL

J. J. BALLESTEROS

RUN FOR THE DEVIL

iUniverse books may be ordered through booksellers or by contacting:

iUniverse
1663 Liberty Drive
Bloomington, IN 47403
www.iuniverse.com
1-800-Authors (1-800-288-4677)

Because of the dynamic nature of the Internet, any web addresses or links contained in this book may have changed since publication and may no longer be valid. The views expressed in this work are solely those of the author and do not necessarily reflect the views of the publisher, and the publisher hereby disclaims any responsibility for them.

Any people depicted in stock imagery provided by Thinkstock are models, and such images are being used for illustrative purposes only. Certain stock imagery © Thinkstock.

ISBN: 978-1-5320-1999-9 (sc)
ISBN: 978-1-5320-1998-2 (e)

Library of Congress Control Number: 2017906808

Print information available on the last page.

iUniverse rev. date: 06/22/2017

Other than the historical references made to the colonization of Mexico and other details of generally accepted Mexican history, the contents and characters in this book are entirely fictional. The state of Campeche is among the most tranquil and beautiful in Mexico, with a rich historical and ecological legacy.

PROLOGUE

During daylight, the coast road between Lerma and Punta Morro in the Puuc Hills of Campeche is fairly easy to follow. The winding curves and sudden rises and drops are easily negotiated by sober drivers as long as they aren't in too much of a hurry or distracted by the breathtaking views of the Bay of Campeche. After dark, however, it's a completely different matter, especially on a misty, moonless night when the darkness maliciously unveils every curve, every rise, and every drop at the last possible moment.

Corporal Ramón Muñoz knew the coast road very well and took advantage of that familiarity to test the mettle of the new officer who had only recently reported to the naval zone at Lerma. The hard-jawed corporal had a low regard for officers, believing them soft, self-important, and pampered. He deliberately pushed the olive-drab Ford F-150 Mini Commando through the treacherous road on their way to the mobile checkpoint at Punta Morro, at times coming dangerously close to the edge of the bluff that straddled the rocky beach below.

The other naval infantry officer assigned to the Naval Infantry Battalion, Seventh Naval Zone, Third Naval Region, Gulf and Caribbean Sea Naval Force warned Lieutenant Ramiro Baeza about the corporal's borderline insubordinate behavior, but he chose the dark-skinned corporal with the broken nose as his driver anyway. He rather liked the scrappy corporal, whose battle-hardened facial features and physical condition reminded him of a middleweight boxer.

Lieutenant Baeza distinguished himself in the campaign to end the drug war on the northern border of Mexico. He played a major role in the dismantling of the Frontera cartel and had an intimate knowledge of the workings of their rival, the Norteño cartel. For these reasons, the Armada transferred the young intelligence officer to Campeche, anticipating a drug war between the Norteño cartel and the Comisión, a drug-trafficking organization based in the state of Chiapas seeking to spread its influence throughout the Yucatán Peninsula.

The arrival of such a notable military personage to the naval zone at Lerma, considered a desolate backwater where nothing ever happened, perplexed the other officers assigned there. They did not understand the lieutenant's enthusiasm and his overzealous work ethic, posting nightly mobile checkpoints since his arrival at such forgotten places as Punta Morro. Likewise, the enlisted ranks also had misgivings about his relentless pursuit of an enemy they could not see. To them, the gunrunners and drug traffickers the lieutenant talked about had much in common with the legendary ghosts and witches of Punta Morro.

The lieutenant braced himself as the corporal attempted to take an especially sharp curve at breakneck speed, dropping the wheels of the Mini Commando off the right side of the pavement.

"Punta Morro is not going anywhere, cabo," the lieutenant said calmly.

"Sorry, teniente." The corporal grinned mischievously. "I'm trying to get to the checkpoint before they move it."

The sea fog that had drifted in over the point had thickened, and the corporal flicked the bright lights on and then off, straining to make out the road in the darkness. He suddenly put his weight on the brakes to negotiate another long and treacherous curve.

The lieutenant braced himself to take the turn. "Use your transmission to slow us down, cabo."

"Sí, mí teniente."

Cabo Muñoz downshifted, slowing the pickup, letting his breath out slowly as he eased the Mini Commando into the curve.

"Holy Week is coming up soon," the corporal mentioned. "Some of the men were hoping to go home for Easter."

"That's still some time away, cabo."

"Sí, mí teniente," the corporal responded respectfully. "I was just saying that the men have been pulling checkpoint duty almost every night for the last week."

"The devil never takes a holiday," the lieutenant retorted somewhat harshly.

"Entendido, mí teniente," the corporal acknowledged.

Cabo Muñoz powered the pickup up a hill and around a curve, leaving the sea fog below and behind him as they came into a straightaway. He let off the accelerator when he saw the beam of a flashlight dancing up and down as he approached the checkpoint.

The Mexican marine in full battle dress standing on the road directed the corporal to the right when he recognized the military vehicle. He parked the Mini Commando next to the other military vehicles on the side of the road poised to give chase should anyone try to run the checkpoint. The noncommissioned officer in charge of the checkpoint came to greet them.

"Buenas noches, Teniente Baeza." The marine petty officer saluted the officer.

The lieutenant stepped out of the truck and made a cursory inspection of the checkpoint before returning the salute. The petty officer had skillfully positioned the checkpoint on a short straightaway between two curves with a pursuit vehicle facing in each direction.

"Where's your lieutenant, maestre?"

"The teniente took a patrol to the port at Seyba," the petty officer replied.

"You picked a good spot for your checkpoint."

"Gracias, mí teniente."

The petty officer ran his eyes up and down the lieutenant's neatly pressed uniform as he walked toward the checkpoint. "Fresa," he muttered to himself, using the derogatory term literally meaning "strawberry," used by the common class to refer to rich schoolboys.

"Having trouble sleeping, mí teniente?" the petty officer asked sarcastically.

The lieutenant chuckled and then smiled. "Relax, maestre. I'm not here to run your checkpoint."

"If you'll pardon my curiosity," the condescending petty officer said without looking at the lieutenant, "what brings the teniente out on such an unpleasant evening?"

Lieutenant Baeza glared at the petty officer. He had always held operational security as the most sacrosanct of his intelligence tenets. "You'll understand, maestre, if I don't answer that to your satisfaction." He drew a long breath and exhaled through his nostrils. "Let's just say I'm looking for something … important."

"Just tell me that I'm not out here wasting my men's time."

Before the lieutenant could answer, their attention turned to the sudden appearance of a pair of headlights rounding the curve from the south. The Dodge Ram pickup drastically reduced its speed to a near stop as it entered the straightaway. The marine on the roadway signaled the suspicious pickup to advance to the checkpoint using his flashlight.

The pickup stood with its engine rumbling like a bull glaring at a matador as the petty officer joined the marine in the center of the road. The low rumble of the engine gradually increased its pitch as the pickup advanced slowly toward the checkpoint. Without warning, the driver suddenly gunned the engine, and the pickup charged the two marines. The petty officer pushed his subordinate off the left side of the roadway to keep him from being struck.

The other marines scrambled to board their pursuit vehicles, ignoring the muzzle flash flickering repeatedly from the passenger's side of the pickup as it ran the checkpoint. Lieutenant Baeza went to check on the petty officer.

"I'm all right!" the petty officer yelled. "Go! Go! Go!"

The lieutenant and Cabo Muñoz jumped into their Mini Commando and started after the taillights in the distance, watching the muzzle flash dance back and forth between the pickup and the pursuing marines.

The driver of the Dodge Ram swerved dangerously back and forth across the road while the passenger hung out the window firing his AK-47 rifle at the marines. The armed delinquent pulled himself back into the cab to change magazines.

"Look for a dirt road, and take it," the passenger ordered. "We're going to make a run for it on foot!"

A round pierced the rear window, making a sharp pop and striking the driver in the back of his right shoulder. The bullet made his right arm fall limp, the burning pain disorienting him and causing him to lose control of the vehicle. The pickup careened off the road, sliding sideways into a ravine before rolling over several times and ejecting the passenger. The wreck came to rest in a cloud of dust with its wheels skyward and the cab partially collapsed.

Several marines jumped out of the first Mini Commando to get to the scene. They slid down the ravine toward the jumbled mass of iron and fiberglass. The wounded driver tried to pull himself out of the crumpled cab but was barely able to slide his body out halfway through the shattered window.

Cabo Muñoz had a difficult time seeing through the hazy mixture of fog, dust, and exhaust fumes as he rolled up on the scene, nearly running into the rear of one of the marine pickups. He looked down at the overturned truck and the flashlight beams crisscrossing and slicing through the dense sea fog that had collected along the bottom of the ravine.

Without waiting for the lieutenant, Cabo Muñoz ran down the embankment toward the overturned pickup. The lieutenant made his way down the muddy slope carefully. An enlisted marine came to meet him, holding an AK-47 paratrooper model over his head.

"Look, Teniente!" he called to the intelligence officer. "This fell out a split in the bed of the truck. There must be a hundred of them."

"Put that back where you found it, marinero," Lieutenant Baeza ordered. "The judicial officer and public ministry agent will take it into evidence when they get here."

"Sí, mí teniente!"

Cabo Muñoz followed the young marine to the back of the overturned pickup where he had found the AK-47 rifle. He squatted and shined his flashlight under the bed. Lieutenant Baeza went to join the corporal, squatting next to him and shining his own flashlight under the overturned truck. A score of AK-47 rifles and half as many pistols had fallen out from a split in the bed liner. The corporal pulled on the damaged liner, revealing many more AK-47 rifles.

"Is this what you had us looking for?" Cabo Muñoz asked.

"In part, cabo." The lieutenant looked at the dead passenger, lying facedown a few meters from the pickup. "I was really hoping to talk to at least one of them."

"I think the driver is still alive."

The lieutenant walked to where the wounded driver lay on the ground, the lower part of his body pinned inside the cab. He knelt on one knee by the driver. He felt bad for the foolish young man who struggled to breathe.

"Ayudame," the driver begged. He wheezed and coughed up blood.

"It's best that we don't move you until the paramedics get here," the lieutenant said to the dying man, who began to mutter almost incoherently.

"I like the sound of the waves." He slid his tongue between his lips and swallowed. "Can you hear it?"

Cabo Muñoz looked at the lieutenant and whispered, "You can't hear the surf from here."

"I've always wanted to live by the ocean with all the money I would need to last the rest of my life," he rambled. He closed his eyes and expired.

Lieutenant Baeza patted the man's pockets, looking for identification. He removed his wallet and pulled out a photograph of a young boy, three twenty-dollar bills, and several hundred peso notes. Ironically, all the money he would need to last him the rest of his life amounted to less than a hundred US dollars.

CHAPTER

1

The sheets felt good against Simon Donovan's skin. He lay quietly in the soft morning light, listening to the surf outside his cabaña. A gentle tropical breeze blew through the slats of the wooden venetian blinds over his window, cooling the crisp morning air. He arched his back slightly and stretched an arm over his head to wrap his fingers around the struts of his antique metal bed. She had come to him in his dreams again after a long absence, and so had that feeling he tried desperately to avoid.

It was that bittersweet feeling between the happiness he knew with her and the void that filled the pit of his stomach after she left his life. He sat up and swung his legs over the edge of the bed, staring aimlessly at the horizontal shadows the blinds made on the polished wood-plank floor. The hum of the ceiling fan over his bed lulled him into a trance. The low, rhythmic thumping of the blades reminded him of her heartbeat. The sound of the waves rolling in and then out again reminded him of her gentle breathing as she slept.

She had eyes like obsidian, shiny and black and shaped like almonds. She kept her raven-black hair cut to the shoulder and often wore it in a ponytail that dangled playfully through the back of the baseball cap she liked to wear. She always seemed to have a thick strand of hair falling over the right side of her face that she would brush back to keep out of her eyes. He often lost himself in the glistening pools of her eyes, which seemed to smile at him. He had never known anyone to smile with her eyes like that.

He emptied his lungs, forcing the image of her face out of his thoughts. No good ever came from thinking about her. He stood, stretched his arms and back, and began preparing himself for the day.

He began and ended his days with a quick, cold shower, a practice he'd developed over his many years at sea. Sailors either bathe over the side or take short showers to conserve water when at sea. The clothes he wore were functional, if not a bit unimaginative. He dressed in simple brushed cotton shirts and pants, preferring earth tones and khaki. He never hung or pressed his clothes. He kept his entire wardrobe rolled up in neat bundles either in an antique cherrywood dresser in his cabaña or in the drawer under his bed aboard ship.

On his feet, he wore a pair of seriously distressed roan-colored leather boat shoes. The belt he wore looked like it came from the same piece of leather. He kept his dark but graying hair neatly trimmed. He had near perfect vision, although his gray eyes had lost their ability to read the written word at closer than arm's length. The sun had permanently tanned his face, as one might expect from a man who spent that much time at sea. He had lost the youthful enthusiasm that once dominated his face, the lines and creases of experience having taken its place.

He went to the front of the room and hoisted the blinds to look out the front window. He looked through the tropical growth outside and at the rocky promontory over Morro Point—or Punta Morro, as the locals called it. The locals told stories about the caves at Punta Morro, involving shipwrecked pirates, treasure, and even a hideous witch who fed on the children of the nearby village of Seyba Playa.

His cabaña sat on the high bluff overlooking the Paradise Lagoon. His landlord's family had blasted the harbor out of the limestone a century and a half ago to accommodate the great sailing vessels that came to Campeche to fill their holds with sugarcane and henequen they hauled to New Orleans, Liverpool, Marseilles, or some other faraway, exotic port.

Whether by design or happenstance, the lagoon did not look like man had had a hand in its creation. The coconut palms, banana and mango trees, and other native flora that flourished around the man-made harbor forever masked the lagoon's humble beginning. Now, it is home to a wide variety of birds and marine life that care not how it came into existence. The moss-covered boulders that line the horseshoe-shaped lagoon do not speak of how they came to rest on the fine white sands deposited on the lagoon's narrow beach by 150 years of the relentless rise and fall of the tide.

Indeed, time and tide had made a paradise of this man-made wonder of engineering. Nature's loving hand had also made of the rubble dumped into the ocean to make the breakwater for the harbor into a magnificent reef, teeming with life. Inspired by the way nature had taken man's creation and made it its own, the descendants of the long-forgotten harbor had christened the man-made body of water the Paradise Lagoon.

His cabaña and several others once housed the crews of the Clyde steamers and schooners that put into the harbor. They had all fallen into ruin with the decline in the henequen market. A hurricane had stripped the palm-leaf roofs from the hardwood pole rafters long ago, and the jungle tried to reclaim the faded white, moss-stained stucco walls. The heavy hardwood floors, made from the planks salvaged from a shipwreck off an island in the Arcas cays, had also fallen to the ravages of time. His landlord had resurrected the cabañas, fully restoring their facades and updating them with electricity and indoor plumbing.

Across the lagoon stood the palatial Hacienda Laguna Paraiso, built by Don Manuel Barrera López for his beautiful wife, Doña Marta Moreno Velles in the latter half of the eighteenth century. For decades, the family had harvested copra from the vast coconut groves that surrounded the hacienda. After a hurricane destroyed much of the coconut groves, the family switched to sugarcane for their cash crop and later henequen. With the expanding trade brought by the Industrial Revolution, the head of the Barrera family made the momentous decision to build a harbor by their seaside plantation.

The harbor flourished for the better part of the next century until technology and the changing times had made the harbor at the Paradise Lagoon obsolete. The family closed the hacienda after another great hurricane ravaged Campeche nearly a century ago. Only recently did the last remaining descendant of the Barrera family return to resurrect the hacienda and turn it into a five-star hotel, which he named the Hacienda Laguna Paraiso, or the Paradise Inn as it was known in the tourist brochures circulated in the United States, Canada, and Europe.

He stepped out the front door and stood on the porch made of stone and mortar. The sun had yet to rise above the hills, and the low morning light soothed his troubled thoughts. Since he lost her, he had looked for something to fill the void that consumed his existence, something that could give him some measure of happiness and meaning to his life.

He believed, or at least he had hoped, that he had finally found that something. He walked toward the edge of the bluff and looked down at his two-masted schooner. It ran sixty-five feet along the deck and drew six feet of water. He had bought her at a US Marshals' auction in Galveston, Texas. The Justice Department had seized her after the US Coast Guard intercepted her south of Bolivar Point in Texas with a load of cocaine in her hold. She sailed as the Moonlight Runner then, and her captain and crew had worn her down.

She needed a complete refitting. Her engine teetered on the verge of disrepair, her deck needed refinishing, and she needed a new set of sails. The sea and neglect had made of her a floating eyesore, but he saw in her a sleeping beauty desperately waiting for a kiss to rouse her from her sleep. Old ships like her, built the old way with classic lines, reminded him of the writings of James Michener and Ernest Hemingway. It took nearly six months of pouring his heart, his soul, and his bank account into her to resurrect her great beauty.

He ignored the belief that changing the name of a ship brought bad luck and did it anyway. She needed to have her demons exorcised as much he did. So he set off to perform the necessary ritual to cleanse her of her nefarious past and took her to the center of the Gulf of Mexico, where he rechristened her the Siete Mares, "the seven seas," after a Mexican song about a man's ill-fated love and his destiny to sail the seven seas.

"Skipper," he heard a familiar voice call.

He saw his partner, his first mate, walking up the stone path leading to his cabaña. Duncan Augustus Fagan, the name given to him by his mother, didn't seem fitting for a man of the sea, so he went by Augie. He kept himself lean and in good shape for a man his age. He had chiseled good looks and wore his hair cropped close to his head "to keep the seagulls from nesting in it," as he put it. His attire fit his personality. He wore an old pair of faded blue denim jeans and a chambray shirt when ashore. When at sea, he preferred cutoffs and loose-fitting vintage rock-and-roll

T-shirts. His idea of dressing up involved a pair of poplin pants and a tropical print shirt.

"I thought you were on your way to Campeche City," Donovan said to him.

"I forgot to tell you last night to see if the new crewman you're going to interview knows anything about working on internal combustion engines." Augie went to stand next to him. "If he does, I could sure use his help to overhaul the engine."

Getting the ship back in shape had taken more money than he anticipated. He had put off performing the costly overhaul as long as he could, and as Murphy would have it, the engine gave out just as they had gotten a new charter.

"We'll be lucky if he knows how to work the sails," Donovan remarked. "He's a panga fisherman," he pointed out, referring to the fiberglass launches. "I doubt if he knows how to work anything more than an outboard motor."

"We can always teach him how to work the sails." He turned to Donovan and grinned. "I could use the help if he can do more than turn a wrench."

"Hey," he said defensively. "I know how to remove water pumps, carburetors, and alternators and remove the heads with a little help."

"Yeah," Augie scoffed, "but can you put them back?" He chuckled. "I'd better get going. The job is gonna to take most of the day, and we can't get started until I get the parts we need."

"I should be done with the new crewman by the time you get back."

Augie looked over his shoulder as he headed down the stone-covered path. "Don't forget to get the money to pay back Don Macario." Their landlord, Don Macario, often bailed them out in emergencies.

"The bank's my first stop."

Arturo Farías, the head of the Campeche Growers Association, always took breakfast on the patio behind his lavish home east of Campeche City. He built it to resemble a Spanish castle erected during the reconquista, the period when the Spanish drove out the Moorish invaders from Iberia. Like those imposing edifices, it had tall stone walls and formidable parapets but with a red-clay tile roof his wife insisted he include. He took great pride in his Spanish heritage. His ancestors helped conquer the Maya in Campeche and defend against the ruthless pirates who ravaged the Spanish settlements in the name of other European crowns. The patio, made of an expensive Italian-clay tile sat on a precipice overlooking a narrow, tree-covered canyon with a small stream flowing through it.

The narcotics trafficker had aged gracefully. His face did not betray the pressures endured by a man in his position. His hair retained most of its color, and his hazel eyes still glimmered with the determination of a much younger man. He had worked hard all his life to build on what his grandfather started so many years ago.

His family once owned a vast hacienda, awarded to his ancestor by the king of Spain for his service to the crown. For almost two centuries, the family enjoyed a lifestyle befitting royalty, made off the backs of first slaves and then mestizo péones. The land reforms that followed the Mexican Revolution whittled the hacienda down to its current size. The family still managed to make a good living growing hemp. His father established the Campeche Growers Association to maximize the profits made from the export of henequen. Like his family, all the members of the association descended from military families who came to Campeche during the Spanish Colonial era and established large haciendas. They all prospered until the decline in the henequen market.

To compensate for the decline in the market, his grandfather bootlegged Mexican liquor hidden among the henequen he shipped to the mob in New Orleans. In time, the members joined him in this illicit business venture. Their bootlegging enterprise ended with the repeal of the Volstead Act, and the association struggled for a time until the Second World War boosted the demand for henequen. This short-lived boom only postponed the inevitable. Artificial fibers dealt the henequen market a deathblow, and the association had to look for another cash crop.

His grandfather passed the chairmanship to his father to make the transition. At the time, cannabis had grown in popularity in the United States. He looked to his grandfather's example for inspiration, and the association went from processing henequen into cordage to processing it into its narcotic form. Marijuana plants gradually replaced the hemp plants, and the Campeche Growers Association slipped from a legitimate agribusiness to a continuing criminal enterprise. They shared their good fortune with the community, earning for them the name of Los Campechanos, as much for their generosity as being from Campeche.

After taking his normal breakfast of a plate of fruit, a bowl of bran, and glass of juice, Arturo Farías settled in to read the newspaper with his first cup of coffee. The front page that day featured the results of the game of the local baseball team, the Campeche Pirates, who beat the Ciudad del Carmen Dolphins two to one. The lead story related to the lifting of the travel advisory to Tamaulipas by the American State Department in response to the end of the war between the Norteño and Frontera cartels. He scoffed when he read the headline about the successes of the governor's counternarcotics task force.

The governor's so-called counternarcotics task force contributed to rather than countered the narcotics trade by selling the drugs they seized to a band of corrupt police commanders in the nearby state of Chiapas, known as La Comisión, the Commission. The leader of that rising drug-trafficking entity started off as a jailer in the penitentiary in Tuxtla Gutiérrez where he made contacts with and learned about the drug trade from mules doing time for transporting drugs for the Norteño cartel. Believing that the Frontera cartel would prevail in the northern border drug war, the jailer persuaded a particularly greedy band of state police comandantes to join him in a scheme to hijack drug loads destined for the Norteño cartel and sell them to the Frontera cartel. His error in judgment only recently came into the light.

Many in the law enforcement community believed that the head of the governor's task force, a disagreeable state police commander named Sánchez, struck the deal with the Commission to emulate their success and possibly join that emerging drug-trafficking cartel. However, Comandante Sánchez entered into the arrangement solely to line his pockets, never intending to imitate or join the Commission. He personally selected the police comandantes in the task force to help him with his scheme on a commission basis, keeping the share normally reserved for the lion for himself.

Arturo continued to scan the morning headlines, glancing at a fatal accident on the libre road, a new construction project in Lerma, the hijacking of a pleasure boat near Holbox Island, and a gun seizure at Punta Morro. The latter headline caused him to put his cup down and turn to the police section.

The police section abounded with pictures of the wreck on the libre road, a bricklayer detained for beating his wife, and a picture of a fleet of new vehicles delivered to the state police. He glanced briefly at the story regarding the hijacking of a sailboat bound for the Mayan Riviera west of Holbox Island.

The twelve-meter sailing cruiser, captained by a James Cohan of Newfoundland, came under attack by a group of men with AK-47 rifles aboard two high-speed launches. The men robbed the Canadian pleasure boater at gunpoint and brutally raped his daughter while the defenseless man watched.

"Animales," Don Arturo said to himself as he shook his head in disgust. He looked at the bottom of the page where he found the article about the gun seizure at Punta Morro.

The brief article sat below a poor picture of an overturned pickup in a deep ravine with several marines standing around the wreck. The article did not include much detail, only that the pickup ran a checkpoint, resulting in the accident that killed both occupants and the discovery of a hundred automatic rifles and pistols hidden within the truck.

He folded the paper in half and set it aside when he heard the housekeeper opening the french doors to the patio for his wife. Arturo had met Elena Gámez Eguia while on business with her father at his finca outside of Medellin. The former Colombian beauty queen fell immediately for the distinguished Mexican grower, despite the difference in their age. Recognizing the benefit of sealing their partnership by bringing the dashing Mexican into the family, her father gave their union his blessing. The auburn-haired, blue-eyed beauty kept fit by playing tennis three times a week and took pride in the fact that she hadn't gained a kilo since they met over a decade ago.

Elena sat in the chair across the table from her husband, resting her tennis bag on the floor, the handle of her racquet protruding at a thirty-degree angle. The right strap of her tennis outfit had fallen off her shoulder, and she tugged it back into place. The bright lime-green fibers of her outfit glowed like fluorescence against her bronze skin. He liked the way she looked when she dressed in that particular tennis outfit and the way she pulled her auburn hair tightly behind her head in a ponytail. She wore very little makeup. She didn't need it.

The housekeeper put the pitcher of juice at the center of the table after filling Elena's juice glass.

"Gracias, Imélda. Es todo," she said, dismissing the housekeeper.

Elena looked past her husband at the hills surrounding their home as she sipped from her juice glass. She looked at Arturo and then at the folded newspaper by his side. She set her glass down and got her smartphone from her gym bag. She stared intently at the screen as she ran her thumb across it until she found what she wanted to show her husband.

"Did you see the article about the governor's counternarcotics task force?"

"I glanced at it."

Elena cocked her head to the side when she noticed him clenching his jaw. She smiled playfully. "Did I hit a nerve?"

Indeed, she had and rarely could Arturo hide that from her. Now that the drug war on the northern border had ended, the Norteño cartel would begin getting its house in order. The thefts of their drug loads by the Comisión, who had so egregiously interfered with a crucial supply line, topped the list of their priorities.

"I told Rodrigo we should have just paid Sánchez off and been done with it, but no, that idiot had to put him and his task force commanders on the payroll."

Elena set her smartphone down. "On the bright side"—she took a sip of juice—"at least you're getting something for your money."

Arturo huffed the air out of his lungs. He adored his wife and knew that she did not intend to upset him. He took a slow, deliberate breath before responding to her uninformed comment. "By hiring Sánchez, he's put us in a precarious position with the Norteño cartel."

Elena cocked her head. "I don't understand."

"When the Norteños learned that the governor's task force was stealing our loads and selling them to the Comisión, they proposed an alliance to eliminate them." Arturo scoffed. "What they really wanted was for us to eliminate the Comisión. All their resources were tied up fighting the Frontera cartel." He inhaled sharply. "When I explained that we didn't have a military wing, they offered to send us a few advisers to help us raise one."

"What did you tell them?"

"I turned them down, of course." Arturo put his hand on the newspaper. "I told them that our problem was with Comandante Sánchez's task force and not the Comisión." He wiped his brow with the back of his hand. "I explained that we have never needed a military wing and that we would handle Sánchez and his task force the way we have always settled our problems—through negotiation." He turned his head to gather his thoughts. "Now that the war on the northern border is over, the Norteños have made it clear they intend to go after the Comisión." He looked at Elena. "By hiring Sánchez and his people to be our security force, Rodrigo not only made me look like a liar," he sighed. "He made it look like we've sided with the Comisión."

His wife frowned. "How was Rodrigo able to hire a security force if you're supposed to be the chairman?"

Don Rodrigo De León, the current patriarch of the De León family, had long challenged Arturo for the chair of the association. The Farías family had always held it, and none of the other members had ever considered changing that. The association had always prospered under his family's leadership and even expanded into the cocaine market under Arturo's guidance. However, recent events had made many within the association uneasy.

"All matters coming before the association are put to a vote," he explained. "Rodrigo was able to convince the majority that the

Norteños are using their problem with the Comisión as a pretext to take Campeche and the whole of the Yucatán by force."

"Is there a chance that the Norteños will do that?"

"No," Arturo said, shaking his head. "Force is normally used as a last resort. If the Norteños wanted to expand into Campeche—and I'm not saying that they do—they would offer us an opportunity to join their cartel first." He raised his head. "If they sense that we intend to resist, especially using force, they will respond accordingly."

"I understand why you were against hiring them," Elena remarked. She lowered her eyes in thought before looking at her husband. "What chance would they have against the Norteños?"

Arturo glared at her. "Have you ever heard of the Thunderbolt—El Rayo?"

"El Rayo?" Elena briefly shifted her eyes to the sides and then shook her head. "No."

"His name is Aníbal Barca Rayos." He took a sip of coffee. "He used to be a colonel in the special forces. The Norteño cartel lured him away from the army to break the stalemate in the drug war. He brought with him a cadre of highly skilled, combat-hardened special forces soldiers who fought with him in the Michoacán drug war to counter the Frontera cartel's own elite paramilitary unit."

"You mean Los Demonios," Elena interjected. "They got their name from their leader, Fausto López, alias El Demonio."

Arturo raised his brows, surprised that she knew about the notorious vigilante. "The colonel wiped them out. Well, almost. López got away." He took another sip. "Sánchez's people wouldn't stand a chance."

"What if we were absorbed by the Norteño cartel?"

"We wouldn't be absorbed, per se," he explained. "There would be a few subtle changes, but in the long run, it would be business as usual." He dropped the corners of his mouth. "In some ways, it might even be beneficial." He looked up and smiled at his wife. "But I wouldn't worry about it. I don't believe the Norteños are interested in expanding. The only thing they have on their minds right now is crushing the Comisión."

Elena sat quietly for a moment, digesting what they had discussed. She picked up her smartphone and continued to scan the news as she sipped from her juice. "Um," she swallowed as she set down her glass. "Did you see the story about the pirates at Holbox Island?"

Arturo chuckled. "Well, I don't know if I'd call them pirates."

"Look at what they did!" She obviously disagreed, raising the pitch her voice. "They robbed that poor man on the high seas and violated his daughter. How can you say they're not pirates?"

"I know, I know," Arturo backtracked his dismissal of the savage marauders. "It's just that when I think of pirates, I think of Henry Morgan and Lorencillo in big ships. Not a bunch of bandidos in pangas."

The housekeeper bailed him out of the discussion when she announced the arrival of his associate and best friend. "Don Casimiro is here to see you."

Elena turned around in her chair to greet him. The man stood well over six feet and had a massive chest and broad shoulders. She smiled at the big man. "Buenos días, guapo."

Casimiro Mendiola chuckled at her playful compliment. He had no illusions about being a handsome man. He enjoyed life and didn't mind being overweight. The only reservations he had about his appearance concerned his balding head.

Elena glanced at her tennis watch and quickly finished her juice. "I have to go."

"Who are you playing with today?" Arturo asked his wife.

"Carmen Zepeda," she said, rising to her feet. She grabbed the tennis bag and gave Arturo a peck on the lips as she started to leave.

"Try not to humiliate her," Arturo said to her.

"She's been taking lessons again." She stopped to give Casimiro a kiss on his cheek. "Her game is much improved."

The housekeeper followed Elena into the house, closing the french doors behind them. Casimiro sat next to Arturo. He took a handkerchief from his back pocket and blotted the perspiration off his prominent forehead, taking care not to disturb the few strands of hair he had strategically arranged on the top of his head. He glanced at the newspaper sitting on the table next to Arturo and set it aside.

"You saw the article about the guns at Punta Morro."

"I did." Arturo pulled his newspaper toward him and glanced at it. "Very troubling."

"Is that all you have to say?" Casimiro picked up the newspaper. "Fifty semiautomatic pistols and as many Romanian AK-47 semiautomatic rifles." He dropped the paper on the table. "It's more than just troubling." He reached for a jelly-filled doughnut from the pastry basket on the table. "This confirms my suspicions. El Demonio must be here."

"All it confirms is that your information was correct about the gun shipment," Arturo disagreed. "It doesn't mean that Fausto López is here."

"How do you explain the way the Campeche gangs have taken over all the street crime?" He bit into the doughnut and began chewing, spilling jelly on his shirt.

"Simple." Arturo handed a napkin to Casimiro. "After the comandantes organized them to get the drugs they stole from us to the Comisión, they simply took the next step."

15

"Not on their own." Casimiro swallowed. "They're extorting protection money from the pimps and whores." He poured himself a glass of juice. "Now I understand they've started collecting from the legitimate businesses as well." He downed the juice in one gulp, "Someone had to show them how to do that, and I know it wasn't the comandantes. It has to be someone like López."

Arturo watched his friend down the rest of the pastry and pour himself another glass of juice. "Even if by some coincidence López was here, Sánchez wouldn't stand for him interfering with his control over the comandantes."

"It's not up to Sánchez anymore. Not since we paid him off and Rodrigo hired the task force to work for us. Since Sánchez no longer pulls on the purse strings, the comandantes listen to Rodrigo and not to him." Casimiro took a cookie from the basket, "Rodrigo obviously wouldn't soil his hands with the gangs. He has to have a go-between."

Arturo clenched his jaw as he listened to his friend. He drew a deep breath. "What makes you think it's López?"

The big man set the cookie down and began making his argument with his fingers. "First, my informer tells me that a mysterious man, possibly a cocaine trafficker, just moved into the plantation house she works at in Lorenzo." He moved to the next finger. "She describes him as a large man with satanic tattoos who always wears sunglasses to hide his eyes."

"What makes her say that?" Arturo crunched his brows. "A lot of people wear sunglasses."

"At night?" Casimiro retorted. "The one time she saw him without his sunglasses, he quickly turned away to put them on before she could see his eyes." Casimiro picked up the cookie. "El Demonio has a blue eye and a brown eye." He bit into the pastry. "I've heard it said that people with different color eyes are witches and consort with the devil."

"Silly superstitions," Arturo dismissed the myth. "What concerns me more is what makes your source believe he's a cocaine trafficker."

"She overheard him telling his people to force some poor panguero to use his launch to bring a load of cocaine ashore." Casimiro took another bite. "That coincides with the rumors about cocaine being smuggled by somebody working on the Arcas platforms." He took a sip of juice. "That would explain the sudden appearance of basuco being sold on the streets."

Arturo scoffed. "Superstitions, rumors. Nothing you've told me convinces me that Fausto López is in Campeche."

Casimiro finished his cookie. "Rodrigo told one of the members that he has someone training the gangs to fight like an army, someone who knows how to fight El Rayo." He looked down at a stain on his shirt and began rubbing on it, making it worse. "Somebody showed the gangs how to extort money. Probably to buy those guns the marina got at Punta Morro." He dipped the tip of his napkin in a glass of water and tried to remove the stain from his shirt. "The informer was right about the guns taken by the marines at Punta Morro." He continued rubbing fervently. "The satanic tattoos. The eye thing. The military training. Knowing how to fight El Rayo." He looked at Arturo. "All that tells me it's El Demonio." He set the napkin on the table. "What more do you need?"

After taking breakfast at a popular taqueria in Seyba Playa, Mexican Naval Infantry Corporal Santiago Bosquez and Second Petty Officer Miguel Ángel Meza headed back to the Seventh Naval Zone in Lerma. They had spent the previous day in Champotón rekeying the radios with the new codes at the Fifth Naval Sector. Corporal Bosques, who grew up in Campeche, and his immediate supervisor, Second Petty Officer Meza, who hailed from the heart of the Chihuahuan desert in the north, disagreed about which state had the best cuisine. In particular, they argued about who made the best taquitos.

"So what did you think?" Cabo Bosquez asked the second petty officer.

Maestre Meza rolled his head to look at the corporal, who sat behind the steering wheel. "Are you referring to the taquitos or to the waitress who served us?"

Cabo Bosquez chuckled. "Both."

The second petty officer turned his head and stared at the road ahead as they left Seyba Playa. "She was very pretty."

"What about the taquitos?"

Maestre Meza smiled at Cabo Bosquez. "Who cares?"

The "libre," the road taking the two marines back to the Seventh Naval Zone, did not have any toll booths on it, hence its name, meaning "free." Libres followed the old routes established centuries ago, taking advantage of the natural contours of the terrain, making the roads slow, curvy, and a bit treacherous. The modern, much faster multilane roads, known as cuota roads, charged a toll to use them, giving them their name. Unlike the libre roads, the cuota roads cut through the terrain rather than following it, bypassing the smaller towns like Seyba Playa.

No one uses the libre road unless they have plenty of time, are not in a hurry, or simply don't have any money. Buses, large and small, and all manner of trucks carrying goods or rubble use the libre to avoid paying the costly tolls. They lumber through the countless curves that wind around the quiet countryside, slowly climb every rise, and descend every drop carefully, making it impossible, or at the very least, extremely dangerous for anyone to pass them. The fields of small white wooden crosses and funerary arrangements situated all along the libre stand as a silent monument commemorating the foolhardy who, because of impatience or daring, took that ill-advised risk.

The wilderness lines both sides of the road, waiting patiently to reclaim the narrow ribbon of asphalt as it did the once great cities of the Maya. If not for the road crews who tend to the encroachment of the vines, roots, and the fallen limbs, many places would be impassable. Where the jungle is dense and the thicket high, Old Federal 180, as the libre is known officially, is dark long before the sun sets and well after it rises.

A group of men sat aboard two sports utility vehicles parked side by side on the east side of the libre just south of the San Lorenzo pedestrian bridge, waiting patiently in the shadows under the thicket, hidden from view. The men all dressed in clothing approximating the uniforms of the federal police down to the patch of the Mexican flag traditionally worn on the shoulder. Each man had an AK-47 rifle, paratrooper model, either sitting on his lap or with the muzzle on the floorboard between his legs.

Their leader, a callous man of little humor and cruel intensity, went by the pseudonym of El Perro for good reason. He was like a vicious dog, and his facial characteristics were not unlike those of a short-haired, jowly pit bull with dark, cold, unpredictable eyes. No one ever called him by his Christian name, Rafael Escalante Yanez. They referred to him as either El Perro or comandante, the rank appropriated by the leaders of a paramilitary cell like his. The men with him were known as sicarios, the Spanish word for assassins but used in Mexico to refer to foot soldiers in a criminal organization. Though they did commit assassinations in the true sense of the word, they amounted to armed thugs, plain and simple.

The comandante sat in the front passenger seat of the black GMC Yukon, smoking a cigarette with his window intentionally left unopened to annoy the other men in the vehicle. None dared to complain.

"They should have been here by now," his driver remarked. He opened the window to adjust his rearview mirror, letting the smoke out. "Maybe that waitress was mistaken about the direction the marinos took after they left."

"Patience, Tomás. You have to believe in your halcón," El Perro responded.

Halcón is Spanish for a falcon or hawk, used by criminal organizations to refer to people hired to watch for any activity of interest, especially involving the police, the military, or rival organizations. Shopkeepers, waiters, shoeshine boys, taxi drivers, and even corrupt municipal policemen often serve as halcónes because of their ability to watch a given place on a daily basis.

"She's just a stupid waitress."

"She was not hired because of her brains, Tomás. Only to watch and report."

"Maybe they took the cuota, jefe," the sicario sitting behind him suggested.

"The halcón saw them take the libre after they left the restaurant." El Perro noticed that the driver of the Dodge Durango parked next to him had trouble keeping awake. "They told her they were heading to their base in Lerma. They have to come this way." He rolled down his window and flicked his cigarette butt at the driver sitting in the Durango, striking him on the side of his head. "Stay awake, pendejo!"

"There's a dark-green truck coming this way," El Perro's driver announced. "It might be them."

Several people waited at the bus stop at San Lorenzo in the shade of the overhead walkway for the morning bus to take them to Seyba Playa or Villa Madero. Among them, women dressed in powder-blue housekeeper uniforms, schoolgirls dressed in plaid skirts and white blouses, and the schoolboys dressed in khaki pants and white short-sleeved shirts. An old man dressed in a white Mexican guayabera shirt and khaki slacks shifted his weight on his bamboo cane slightly to look for the much-anticipated bus as the rumbling sound of a large vehicle approached from the north. No one saw the vehicles approaching from the south.

Corporal Bosquez did not notice the two sports utility vehicles approaching from behind, maneuvering to flank his F-150 pickup as he neared the San Lorenzo bus stop. He failed to notice the black Yukon leaving the roadway on the right as he watched the Durango trying to pass him drive directly into the path of an oncoming bus.

The bus driver put all his weight on the brake pedal to avoid colliding with the Durango, tossing his passengers against the seats in front of them.

"Watch out!" Maestre Meza exclaimed as he braced himself.

The marine's F-150 skidded off the road, striking a tree. The people at the bus stop ran in a panic, looking for a place to hide. Only a nine-year-old boy stayed to watch El Perro's men surround the wrecked truck, pointing their AK-47 rifles at the injured marines.

"Fuera! Fuera!" one of the sicarios barked, ordering them out of the wreck.

"Manos arriba, cabrones!" another sicario yelled frantically.

Corporal Bosquez lay unconscious in his seat while Petty Officer Meza, dazed from the impact, stepped out of the passenger's side, holding a Beretta pistol.

Comandante Escalante walked toward the injured petty officer, holding his AK-47 rifle by his side. "Drop the gun, pendejo!" he ordered.

The dazed petty officer did not immediately respond, standing unsteadily by the side of the pickup. Blood ran from his ears, his nostrils, and the corners of his mouth. He coughed as he wheezed with every breath.

"I said drop the gun, pendejo," El Perro repeated. "Don't be a hero."

Maestre Meza raised his pistol slowly in the general direction of where the comandante stood. El Perro laughed as the dazed marine's knees buckled and he put his free hand on the pickup for support.

The ill-humored comandante took a lead-filled leather strap out of his pocket and walked up to the injured petty officer, who dropped his pistol and lowered himself to sit on the ground.

"He's hurt bad, jefe," his driver commented.

El Perro put the slapper back in his back pocket and picked up the Beretta dropped by the wounded marine. He pulled back on the slide and ejected the round in the chamber.

"Did you see him point this gun at me?" He showed his men the bullet and smiled cynically at them. "This bullet was meant for me."

Comandante Escalante stepped back and gawked at the wheezing marine. The wounded petty officer, sitting with his back resting against the pickup, looked up at him. El Perro aimed the pistol at the petty officer's forehead and pulled the trigger.

The gunshot resounded in the still morning air.

"I thought El Demonio wanted them alive?" El Perro's driver commented.

Comandante Escalante slipped the marine's pistol into his waistband.

"He was going to die anyway," he said callously. "We still have one who can tell us how the marina knew about the gun shipment."

CHAPTER

2

By midmorning, most of the pangueros had already returned to Seyba Playa with the day's catch. The artisanal fishermen beached their long fiberglass pangas on the narrow beach only a few feet below the malecon, the seawall that protected the town from the rising waters of a storm surge. From the street side, the two-foot-high wall appeared to only stand two feet high. However, it stood a good six feet above the water's edge and could easily handle a moderate storm surge. Some of the pangueros liked to tie their pangas to one of the white concrete balls that sat spaced evenly on top of the wall.

A passing shower had dampened the sidewalk that meandered lazily along the malecon like a slimy concrete snake. Across the street, a few residents swept the water from the walks in front of their homes. Most of the houses stood only a single-story and were made of cinder block, finished in stucco, and painted in an array of pastel colors. Among the modest homes located two blocks south of the port stood a light-blue two-story building that had once served as the fishermen's community center before a new, more spacious facility replaced it near the centro, the downtown district.

The bottom floor of the old community center had a small kitchen, a long diner-style counter, and a large room for the fishermen to gather in. A dormitory took up most of the second floor for the bachelor fishermen to sleep. The old building stood unoccupied for several years until a married couple from Ciudad del Carmen bought it. The wife, who specialized in Mayan cuisine, started a restaurant she called the Cocina Maya, the Mayan Kitchen, on the bottom floor. The husband, an ordained minister of the Church of the Good Fisherman, used the large dining area to minister to the pangueros of Seyba Playa, his lifelong dream. During the rest of the week, he also worked as a panguero. The couple remodeled the dormitory upstairs into a comfortable three-bedroom apartment.

The long plate glass windows on either side of the front of the restaurant gave the diners an ocean view. The wife used her well-developed artistic ability to paint the restaurant's name arched over the image of a Mayan pyramid on one of the windows. On the other, she painted a simple white cross with the words "Iglesia del Pescador Bueno," the "Church of the Good Fisherman" humbly below it.

A jogger running along the malecon past the Cocina Maya did not pay any particular attention to the men sitting in the black sports utility vehicle just up the street from the restaurant. Behind the tinted windows sat four men. The ones sitting in the front, although different in dress and demeanor, shared the same murderous occupation. Both worked as sicarios, hired guns, for the criminal mercenary who employed them.

The driver, a small-framed, clean-shaven man in his twenties, approached his work with cool, calculated resolve. He had a refined and courteous manner and an even disposition. Despite these traits, he could be ruthless, and although he didn't especially take to killing, he had no compunction about doing it. Educated as a abogado, a lawyer, he had left that lucrative profession for the better-paying job as a sicario for the Frontera cartel before its demise. He wore his dark hair trimmed neatly and paid close attention to the way he dressed. He preferred dressing in dark, well-pressed clothing and black ankle-high boots, despite the tropical heat.

The man sitting next to him had a much different disposition and fashion sense altogether. He had the nature of a rabid dog, acted impulsively and recklessly, and overall was an entirely disagreeable human being. Tall and thin, with long, stringy hair and a beak nose, Beto didn't seem to care about how he dressed. He tended to favor dressing in tropical print shirts he refused to button and baggy shorts and wore tennis shoes without any socks.

In the backseat sat the former leaders of the Frontera cartel's paramilitary wing, Los Demonios. Neither started out to work for drug traffickers. On the contrary, they both got their start fighting against the drug traffickers in the Mexican state of Michoacán as vigilantes. Now, they had become what they had fought so hard to destroy.

The vigilantes were lauded as heroic at first for standing up to the ruthless drug traffickers ravaging the people of Michoacán. They gradually lost their popular appeal when their bloody vendettas made the front page of the national papers. Most vigilante groups had fought tit-for-tat, killing only in battle, turning those they captured over to the military. Their paramilitary organization, however, fought a psychological campaign, using the bodies of their fallen enemies to send gory messages to their compatriots and killing their captives after torturing them and then mutilating their bodies, suggesting ritualistic sacrifice and forcing the government's hand.

The government's offer of amnesty and incorporation into a rural defense force to the various vigilante groups operating in Michoacán did not include their band. The government regarded them as much as enemies of the state as the very drug traffickers they fought. Hunted to near extinction, the surviving members of their band went to the northern border to fight for the ill-fated Frontera cartel. The men sitting in the backseat represented the sole survivors of the original vigilante force turned narco-paramilitaries.

Behind the driver sat Dario Robles López, a large man known for his brute strength and soft-spoken temperament. He might not have joined the vigilantes if his parents and only brother had not been brutally murdered by the traffickers. He had fought valiantly and nobly to avenge the murders of his family but had grown weary of killing long before he followed his cousin to the state of Tamaulipas on the Texas border to fight for the Frontera cartel.

Next to him, talking on his cell phone, sat El Demonio, the head of the once powerful paramilitary band that served the now defunct Frontera cartel. By all accounts, Fausto López had much in common with his evil namesake. He had earned that infamous sobriquet not so much for the evil deeds he perpetrated against combatant and bystander alike, but for his dedication to the powers of darkness. López demanded unwavering loyalty from his men and earned it through fear and intimidation, except in the case of his faithful lieutenant and cousin, Dario Robles.

El Demonio closed his eyes and pinched the bridge of his nose, "There was no way to avoid it?" He listened for a while and then sighed. "Take him to the finca. I'll be there after I'm done here." He ended the call and put the phone in his pocket.

"Something wrong, jefe?" Felipe asked his boss.

"Escalante killed one of the marineros." He looked out the windshield at an old maroon convertible driving up to the Cocina Maya. "Who's that?"

Felipe watched the tall man in a white cotton shirt and khaki pants step out of the maroon Delta 88 Royale convertible. "I think his name is Dónovan, jefe." He looked back at Fausto. "He owns that big sailboat at the Laguna Paraiso."

"Donovan?" El Demonio removed his sunglasses from his hardened face, revealing his odd-colored eyes: one blue and one brown. "I know that name."

Unlike other drug traffickers, El Demonio dressed like a man going to dinner at a country club. He often wore a sports coat, dress slacks, and penny loafers instead of western-style shirts, cowboy hats, and boots.

"Let me handle the panguero, primo," Dario said to his cousin.

"I want Beto to do it." Fausto watched Donovan walk into the restaurant. "He knows what to do."

"Are you going to give him a chance to pay for the outboard?"

"Why should I?"

"You already have a panguero meeting the ship. Why do you need another?"

"I don't." Fausto turned to his cousin. "He interests me as a fisher of men. Not as a fisherman."

The skinny sicario with long, stringy hair put his left elbow on the top of his seat to look at his boss. "Do you want me to wait until the gringo leaves, jefe?"

El Demonio put his sunglasses back on his face. "I don't think he'll interfere." He eased back into his seat. "Not if he is who I think he is."

"Why don't we wait a few minutes to give him a chance to leave, jefe?" Felipe suggested. "No sense in leaving a witness if Beto has to get rough with the old man."

The tiny brass bell hanging over the door chimed subtly as Donovan walked into the Cocina Maya. He looked around for a moment and then stepped toward the right side of the counter to look down the short hallway leading to the back.

"Hola," he called. "Hello."

He heard the sound of someone hurrying down a staircase he could not see before a short, bald, heavyset man emerged from the hallway. The clothing he wore reminded Donovan of the assistant principal at his junior high school. The full-faced man had a bulbous nose and combed back what little hair he had on the sides of his bald head.

"Buenos días," he said meekly.

"I'm looking for a man named Benício," Donovan said. "He was supposed to meet me here about a—"

"I'm Benício."

Donovan tried to hide his disappointment. "I'm Captain Donovan."

"Please sit down, Capitán. Can I get you a cup of coffee?"

"No, thanks." Donovan looked at his watch as he sat on a stool at the counter. "I've got to get back to the ship to help my partner overhaul an engine." He looked at Benício. "You don't by any chance know how to overhaul an engine?"

"I'm afraid not." Benício chuckled. "But I can change the oil and fill it with gas."

Donovan scoffed. "I can't do much more than that myself."

"If you don't mind my asking, Capitán ..." Benício pointed at the white cross on the front window. "Does the job require us to work on Sunday? I'm the minister."

"Sometimes." The question caught Donovan off guard. "You're a minister?"

"I have a small congregation," he explained. "I'll need at least a week's notice so that I can find someone to stand in for me." He sensed Donovan's discomfort. "Is something wrong, Capitán?"

"I'm sorry." Donovan squirmed uncomfortably. "I was expecting a much younger man. Working the deck of a schooner is hard work and requires a lot of stamina."

Benício hung his head. "I see."

Donovan felt bad for the old man. "Have you ever sailed before?"

"Not really," he replied glumly. "When I was little, my father and uncle would take me out in their fishing boat. It had a sail on it. Sometimes they'd let me work it."

"I need a crewman who can handle the demands of the job. Preferably someone who knows how to work the sails."

The bell over the door jingled, causing Donovan to look over his shoulder. A young woman wearing a white, loose-fitting cotton blouse opened gloriously down to the third button walked toward them. Her blouse, like the dove-gray slacks she wore, accentuated her impossibly narrow waist.

"What did they tell you at the bank?" Benício asked her as she came to the counter. She glanced warily at Donovan. "You can talk in front of Capitán Dónovan," Benício reassured her. "He's a friend."

She looked at Donovan apprehensively before answering. "They said they couldn't lend us any more money." The woman took another nervous glance at Donovan and then whispered to Benício, "Did you get the job?"

He shook his head slightly as the bell over the door again jingled. The color left the old man's face when he saw Beto standing in the doorway.

"Perdoname, Capitán," Benício excused himself to go meet with Beto, not that Donovan heard him.

The woman's beauty enthralled Donovan. The soft gleam in her green, almond-shaped eyes radiated like emeralds. She had flawless skin like velvet and hair as black as a raven's wing that rested on her delicate shoulders, the ends curling under in a pageboy hairstyle. Something about her eyes and the way her hair framed her high cheekbones and face seemed familiar to him, even more so when she brushed back a thick strand of hair that had fallen across the right side of her face.

"What's your name?" Donovan asked.

"Itzél," she replied, obviously more interested in watching Benício than in talking with him.

Donovan looked at the stringy-haired young man with the beak nose. "Who's the beach bum?"

Itzél hesitated before responding. "A bill collector."

"He looks more like a spring breaker than a leg breaker," he quipped. "Who's he collecting for?"

"A man named Fausto López," she said reluctantly, her brow wrinkled with concern.

Donovan had heard of the name but wasn't sure she was referring to the same man. "He doesn't by any chance go by another name, does he?"

Itzél didn't seem to know what he meant.

"Like El Demonio."

"I-I think so."

"The very devil himself," Donovan muttered under his breath. He took a closer look at Beto. "What's Benício doing borrowing money from a man like that?"

"He didn't borrow it," she explained. "Señor López put a new outboard motor on his panga without telling him."

"Why did he do that?"

"He wanted Benício to get something for him on the other side of the reef."

"I can imagine what that something was."

"He wanted to give back the new motor, but someone damaged his old motor."

"He couldn't get it fixed?"

"It was too damaged."

Donovan dropped his head for a moment. "How far on the other side of the reef does he want him to go?"

"I don't know," she said softly. "Somewhere between the reef and the Arcas."

"The cays?" Donovan whistled in disbelief. "In an open launch?"

"Señor López gave him a choice. Either get the package or pay him five thousand pesos for the motor in cash." Her voice began to quiver. "He saw your flyer and hoped he could get the job to pay the debt."

As much as he wanted to help the woman, Donovan didn't feel he could hire the little old man. "I'm doing your father a favor by not signing him on," Donovan explained. "Working the deck is a young man's job."

"He's not my father," Itzél corrected him. "He's my husband."

Her words blindsided him like a well-placed punch to the jaw. He just stared at her, dumbfounded by what she had said. A young boy in his early teens with jet-black hair burst out of the hallway behind the counter and went to stand by her.

"Buenos días, Mamá." The boy kissed her on the cheek. He smiled at Donovan. "Buenos días, señor."

Itzél put her hands on the boy's shoulders. "This is Capitán Donovan, Poli."

"Mucho gusto, Capitán Donovan." The boy held out his hand. "I'm Hipolito Garza Canek."

Still dumbstruck by the blow, Donovan didn't seem to hear him.

"Poli is my son," Itzél said.

"Your … son?" The second blow further affected his balance. He shook it off and turned to the boy. He had his mother's eyes, and his olive skin made his teeth seem especially white. He took the boy's hand and shook it. "Mucho gusto."

"Are you in the army?" Poli asked.

"No, mijito," Itzél said to her son, using the usual endearment Mexican mothers used to address their sons. "He's the captain of a boat."

"Ship," Donovan corrected her. "I'm the captain of a ship. The schooner Siete Mares."

"Wow," Poli marveled. "A real schooner captain."

He grinned at the boy as he regained his balance. "Do you know what a schooner is?"

"Of course," he said proudly.

She fussed with his hair. "Poli's been fascinated with sailboats since he was a boy in Ciudad Carmen."

The boy took his mother's hand from his hair. "I'm going to be the captain of my own ship someday."

Donovan nodded slowly and mussed his hair. "I'd put money on it."

Itzél gasped suddenly when she saw the stringy-haired sicario grab her husband by his shirt. Donovan turned just as Beto slapped the fat little man with the back of his hand. Donovan grabbed Poli as he started to dart to help Benício.

"Let me handle this." He handed Poli to his mother and walked briskly to where Beto continued to slap the little old man. He grabbed the skinny sicario by his free hand and twisted it until he let go of Benício.

"That'll be enough of that." He shoved the sicario to one side and stood between him and Benício. "Mind your manners, junior."

"Don't interfere, gringo," Beto said menacingly.

The stringy-haired sicario pulled back on his shirt tail, revealing the automatic pistol he had in his waistband. Without warning, Donovan put his hand on the pistol and took it from him. He ejected the magazine almost in the same motion, kicked it to one side, and tossed the gun over his shoulder.

"You were saying?"

Beto stood motionless with his mouth open. Itzél gasped in horror when she saw El Demonio and Felipe through the plate glass window, walking toward the door. She wrapped her arms around her son to keep him from going to help.

Felipe held the door open for his employer and then followed him into the Cocina Maya. A few moments later, Dario Robles walked into the restaurant. Fausto glanced briefly at Donovan and then turned to Beto.

"Is everything all right, Beto?"

His humiliated minion stared helplessly at his master. Felipe picked up the magazine and went to get the gun. El Demonio removed his sunglasses and glared at Donovan with his odd-colored eyes.

"Your name is Dónovan."

"Captain Donovan," he corrected him. "And you are?"

El Demonio smirked contemptuously. "You may call me Señor López, Capitán Dónovan," he replied. "Is that big sailboat docked at the Laguna Paraiso yours?"

It irritated Donovan to have his ship characterized as any kind of boat. "I have a ship at the Paradise Lagoon."

Felipe offered Beto's gun to his employer. Dario took the gun instead and started to slip it into his waist when his cousin took the gun from him. Fausto turned to Beto, chuckled, and tossed the pistol to him. "Try not to lose it again."

Beto pointed it at Donovan, glaring bitterly at him. Donovan scoffed, unimpressed by the menacing gesture.

"Put the gun away," El Demonio ordered. He glared acrimoniously at Benício before turning to Donovan. "Who is this man to you?"

Donovan looked back at the little old man. "He's a friend."

"Your friend refused to do me a simple little favor after he accepted a new outboard motor from me."

"I don't know if I'd call making a run to the other side of the reef in an open launch simple," Donovan remarked.

"Pangueros do it all the time," Fausto retorted. "I've even seen them as far as Los Arcas."

"Why don't you get one of them to do it?"

"I already have," El Demonio scoffed. "But there's still the matter of payment for the outboard motor."

"Why don't you take back the motor?"

"The motor's no good to me, especially since he's been using it," he said dryly. "I'll lose money if I try to return it."

"What choice did I have?" Benício looked at Beto, not daring to accuse him. "Someone damaged my motor."

"And how does that make me responsible?" Fausto retorted bitterly. "You know Seyba Playa is plagued by vandals." He grinned with pleasure when he saw Donovan staring at the woman standing behind the counter with her arms around her son.

Donovan felt his heart flutter as he looked at Itzél. He wanted to make the anxiety on her face go away and hold her in his arms. He thought about the money he had just withdrawn from the bank to repay Don Macario for the parts Augie needed to overhaul the engine. It amounted to just over five thousand pesos. Without thinking any further, he reached into his pocket and pulled out a roll of pesos.

"Five thousand pesos?" He counted out the money.

Fausto looked at Dario and then at Donovan. "What are doing?"

"Let him finish counting," Dario interjected.

After he finished counting out the five thousand pesos, he put the few remaining hundred peso notes back in his pocket. He held the money out to El Demonio. The man with the odd-colored eyes glared nefariously at the little old panguero.

"This man is not worth your sympathy," he said to Donovan.

"You gonna take the money or not?"

Irritated by his tone, El Demonio glared at Donovan malevolently. Dario took the money and offered it to Beto, who snatched it from his hand.

"That should conclude your business here," Donovan said to El Demonio.

"I'll decide when my business here is concluded," he chided bitterly. He shifted his eyes to look at Itzél and her son.

"Oh?" Donovan retorted pretentiously. He looked through the plate glass window at a municipal police car slowing down almost to a stop outside of the restaurant. Donovan had parked his convertible in a loading zone. For once, he hoped that the policeman would do something about it.

"I'd better move my car."

"Don't bother." Fausto waved off the policeman with his eyes. The policeman tipped his head and slowly drove off, ignoring the violation. He smiled at Donovan. "You're right about the run being dangerous in a small boat. A larger vessel would be better suited." He looked at Donovan through his brows. "Perhaps you'd like to make the run yourself?"

"No, thanks."

"Is your ship not for hire?"

"I only accept charters that are legal."

El Demonio looked at Felipe and chuckled. "Why would I ask you to do something illegal?"

"I know the kind of business you're in, Señor López." Donovan was direct. "I won't haul anything illegal."

"Really?" He raised his head. "That's not your reputation."

"You have me mistaken for someone else," Donovan responded.

"I don't think so." He inhaled deeply and let the air out slowly. "Correct me if I'm wrong." He took two steps toward Donovan as if to get a better look at him. "Are you not the same Dónovan who ran cargo out of Panamá?"

"I ran a tramp service in Panama, if that's what you mean."

"I heard that you were especially good at being discreet." He cocked his head and looked at him through the corner of his eye. "I heard that you weren't above closing an eye to see that the cargo got delivered."

"I had paper for everything I delivered."

"I would expect that you did." El Demonio snickered sarcastically. "I have a need for someone with your skills."

Donovan didn't appreciate what he was implying. "Regardless of what you may have heard, all the cargo I delivered was legitimate."

"I'll pay you well."

"No, thanks."

"I'll make you rich beyond your wildest dreams."

"I said, 'No, thanks.'"

"What's the matter, Capitán?" He grinned diabolically at him. "You don't seem like a man who's afraid to take a bite of forbidden fruit?" He looked lasciviously at Itzél. "Especially such a juicy one."

Donovan felt his face get warm at the thought that his attraction to the little panga fisherman's wife was that obvious. "I don't know what you're talking about."

El Demonio chuckled sarcastically. "Of course you don't." He glared bitterly at Benício. "There's a lesson in this for you, little man." He glanced at Itzél. "Nobody does anything out of the goodness of his heart." He turned to Donovan. "Tell me when you change your mind, Capitán. I have a house on the beach in San Lorenzo. I'll be waiting to hear from you."

"You'll be waiting until hell freezes over."

El Demonio looked at him curiously and then laughed sinisterly. He put on his sunglasses and turned to his men. "Vamonos." Felipe held the door for him and then followed him out behind Beto. Dario looked apologetically at Benício and then glared at Donovan before leaving the restaurant.

Overwhelmed by the excitement, Benício began to sway until his knees buckled.

"Benício!" Itzél called to him.

Donovan lunged toward him, barely catching him before he collapsed. Poli rushed over to help him sit Benício at the nearest table. Itzél brought a glass of water and gave it to her husband. Donovan couldn't help but stare at her as she attended to him. He felt his heart flutter when she looked up and their eyes met.

Benício raised his eyes and saw his wife gazing into Donovan's eyes. He set the glass heavily on the table, breaking the moment between them. "Gracias, Capitán Dónovan, for your help. I didn't mean to involve you."

Itzél raised herself and looked at him. "That was very kind of you."

The sparkle in her eyes made him feel like a starry-eyed teenager mustering the courage to ask a pretty girl to dance. His silence and the way he couldn't break his eyes away from her made her uncomfortable, and she turned away to loosen her husband's collar.

"¿Como te sientes?" Itzél asked her husband. "How do you feel?"

"I'll be fine." He lifted himself off his chair. He waited until he caught his breath before he turned to Donovan. "It'll take me a little time to pay you back. I'll pay any interest you feel is just."

Itzél started for the cash register. "I have some money I can give you right now."

"No, wait." Donovan took her by the arm. He felt his chest tighten and his breath leave him when she looked back at him. His heart ached for her, and he found it difficult to speak. He swallowed the lump in his throat. He needed a reason to see her again, and a thought came to him to almost certainly guarantee it.

"¿Sí, Capitán?"

He released her and turned to Benício. "I came here looking for a crewman." He looked at Itzél. "That little fainting spell convinces me that your husband is in no condition to crew on a schooner." He looked at Poli. "Your son, on the other hand, should be able to work the deck without any problem."

"But he's just a boy," Itzél objected.

"I'm almost sixteen, Mamá," Poli asserted.

"I was younger than he was when I first went to sea." Donovan smiled. "I have another boy not much older than Poli crewing for me now."

"Will the work be dangerous, Capitán?" Benício asked.

"As long as he listens and follows orders, he'll be all right." He turned to Poli. "I'll take a little out of his paycheck until the loan is repaid."

Itzél clicked her tongue and stroked Poli's hair. "I don't know."

"Don't worry, Mamá." Poli took her hand off his head. "I'll be all right."

"He'll need to be at the marina at daybreak," Donovan said.

"He doesn't have a way to get there," Itzél said, obviously looking for a reason to keep Poli from taking the job.

"He can use the truck," Benício suggested. "He knows how to drive."

"Sí, Mamá," Poli said enthusiastically. "I drive better than Señora Gutiérrez," he said, referring to a notoriously bad driver they knew.

Her eyes widened. "But you don't even have a permit."

"I can get one."

She glanced at Donovan, her eyes full of apprehension. She turned to her husband. "What if I need something in town?"

"I'll get it for you when I get back from the reef."

"What if there's an emergency?"

Donovan looked at his watch. He had to get back to the lagoon to help his partner overhaul the engine. He already dreaded having to explain that he not only drained their bank account but that he gave the brunt of it away. He didn't want to add to it by getting there after he started overhauling the engine.

He could understand a mother's reluctance to let her son go off to sea. It had been a scene played over time and again since man first left the shore to venture over the horizon. She had to let her son go, if not to fulfill the boy's dreams, to further his own. He couldn't imagine not seeing her again, even if just to admire her beauty like an aspiring artist admires a masterpiece at an art museum.

"He can stay on the ship," Donovan suggested. "I'll pick him up on Sunday night and drop him off on Friday."

Itzél could not hide the distress in her eyes. She took her son's hand and pulled him close to her. She gazed at Poli lovingly as she brushed his hair back. This time, he let her.

She let out a nervous sigh. "I'll go pack a bag for him."

CHAPTER

3

Getting the gaskets, rings, and other parts he needed to overhaul the engine took Augie longer than he expected. Fortunately, getting the heads reworked didn't take as long, making up for the lost time. After leaving the machine shop, Augie took the libre instead of the cuota only because his last stop had been in Lerma and he didn't want to have to go back into Campeche City to get on the toll road. He told himself that taking a drive along the coast would help him prepare for the job he had ahead of him.

He winced at the sound of the gears grinding as he downshifted the old drop-top Volkswagen Safari to take a sudden drop on the old coast road. He found that by gently swirling the stick, he could find a sweet spot that allowed him to make the shift smoothly. However, it didn't always work. With every unsuccessful shift, the grinding seemed to get just a little worse. It wouldn't be long before the transmission would make its last shift.

He bought the Safari from a hippie couple from Mexico City he met one summer when he went surfing in the treacherous waters off Mexico's middle Pacific coast. The body of the odd-looking convertible lacked the rounded features of its more familiar counterpart. It had an angular shape that made it look like a box on wheels. Even the fenders looked like the flaps of a rigid metal box. The owner had painted it beige, making it look like a miniaturized version of a German Africa Corps staff car. He repainted his "wonder wheels," as he liked to call it, to its original orange and replaced the rag top. The orange paint had long faded, and the rag top had succumbed gradually to rot.

The Safari emerged from the thicket into an open stretch of road, giving him a view of the ocean. In spite of the blue sky, the water had an emerald hue to it with patches of aquamarine near the coast. As would be expected for that time of the year, a squall churned off the coast, creeping relentlessly over the horizon.

He lost sight of the ocean as he descended the steep slope outside of the hamlet of San Lorenzo, nearing the stop known as the San Lorenzo paradero. He rounded a particularly long curve and had to apply his full weight on the brake to keep from rear-ending a long column of cars that had slowed to a near stop. He lifted himself, using the door and his seat, and craned his neck to see what was causing the problem. As the traffic inched forward slowly, he gingerly rotated the stick until it slipped into a lower gear and carefully advanced his wonder wheels behind the column of cars.

As he approached the San Lorenzo pedestrian bridge, he saw the reason for the problem. A headless body in a military uniform hung upside down from the footbridge over the highway with a sign over it addressed to the marina that read "learn to respect." Several state and municipal police cars lined the side of the highway as a group of people dressed in plainclothes hustled about the crime scene, taking photographs of the wrecked marine Ford F-150 pickup or the corpse.

After finally getting past the paradero, he came to a slow winding curve where a Mexican marine in full battle dress uniform, wearing a dark blue flak jacket with the word Marina on it stood in the center of the road with an M16 rifle slung on his shoulder. He was holding a small stop sign. As he drove closer, the marine directed him to the side of the road where a group of similarly dressed marines had just released the car ahead of him.

"Documentos," the petty officer in charge of the checkpoint ordered.

He reached into his wallet for his driver's license and immigration card. The petty officer ran his eyes over the thin gringo with the salt-and-pepper hair.

"Abra la cajuela." He ordered him to open his trunk as a marine walked to the back of the Safari.

"It's in the front." He put his wallet on the dashboard and reached for the trunk release. "Está en frente."

The marine walked to the front of the Safari and inspected the contents of the trunk as another marine ran a mirror attached to the end of a pole under the car, searching the undercarriage. A tall lieutenant wearing a perfectly blocked cap and dressed in a well-pressed, form-fitting uniform with the sleeves rolled neatly above his elbows walked up to the petty officer. He handed the officer Augie's documents and stepped aside.

The officer looked at the picture on his driver's license and compared it to his face. "Duncan Augustus Fagan?"

"That's right, teniente," he responded respectfully.

It had always rubbed Augie the wrong way to have someone call him by his Christian name. He considered it far too formal and not befitting a man of the sea. He had the sea in his blood and not just because his mother had given birth aboard his father's shrimper but because he came from a long line of seafarers. Although he selectively excluded parts of the family history during the retelling, he was proud that his great-great-great-grandfather served as an able seaman aboard a warship during the Civil War before settling near present-day Aransas Pass, Texas. Never mind that the ship was a Yankee sloop and that his great-grandfather came there during the Union blockade of the Confederacy.

The lieutenant walked to the front of the car and examined the license plate and the import sticker on the windshield. He walked around the passenger's side of the vehicle, stopping to look at the cardboard boxes stacked in the backseat.

The lieutenant pulled back on the flap of the box nearest him. "What are you carrying?"

"Parts to overhaul an engine."

"You don't have any guns or ammunition hidden in any of these boxes, do you?"

Augie put his elbow on the top of his seat to look sternly at the lieutenant. "You're welcome to go through all the boxes if you want." He pointed to the front of the Safari. "I've got more in the trunk."

"That won't be necessary." The lieutenant released the flap on the box. "Where are you going today, Señor Fagan?" the lieutenant asked dryly.

"To the Laguna Paraiso."

"What are you doing in Campeche?"

He looked at the lieutenant's name above his left pocket. "I own the Paradise Dive Shop at the Laguna Paraiso, Teniente Baeza."

"I didn't know there was a dive shop there."

"Unfortunately," Augie scoffed, "not many people do."

The lieutenant stood silently for a moment as he took another look at Augie's documents. "Are you familiar with the Moonlight Runner?"

Augie scrunched his brow. "Moonlight Runner?" He opened his mouth and raised his brows when he realized what he meant. "You mean the Siete Mares."

"Excuse me, the Siete Mares," he corrected himself.

43

"I'm the first mate."

"Then you know Capitán Dónovan."

"He runs Seven Seas Adventure Cruises. I'm his partner."

"How well do you know him?"

"Well enough, I guess," he responded apprehensively. "What's this about?"

"Do you know what he did before he came to Campeche?"

What his partner did before coming to Campeche had never really mattered to Augie. They had briefly discussed their lives over a beer but hadn't shared much detail. It didn't seem that important to either of them.

"He was some kind of shipping agent in Panama, I think."

"Were you aware that he's been arrested by the authorities in a number of countries in Central America and the Caribbean?"

The disclosure obviously unsettled Augie, momentarily tying his tongue. "Uh, no." He felt his face turn red. "Arrested for what?"

The lieutenant studied the Texan's face with unflinching eyes. "Fraud, misrepresenting cargo, undocumented cargo, and theft to name a few of the charges."

"I didn't know all that." Augie put both hands on the wheel and stared straight ahead. After a moment, he turned to the lieutenant. "Did he go to jail for any of those things?"

The lieutenant seemed reluctant to answer. "Perhaps detained is a more accurate word."

"So he never went to jail?"

"Obviously, he was able to talk his way out of jail."

"So these detentions could have just been misunderstandings," Augie retorted.

"He seems to be misunderstood with a great deal of frequency."

Augie shrugged his shoulders. "Things like that happen all the time down here."

"Things like that happen to smugglers."

"Are you saying that my partner is a smuggler?"

The lieutenant gazed at him before continuing, "Capitán Dónovan has been investigated for attempting to illegally introduce medical supplies, communications equipment, and articles of war without the proper import documents."

"But he was cleared in every case."

"Smugglers are very clever," the lieutenant commented. "They're masters at manipulating import and export documents, and … the truth."

"But he was cleared after the paperwork was straightened out. Right?"

"More likely after a bribe was paid."

"Or extorted," Augie countered.

The blunt insinuation brought the lieutenant's grilling to a sudden stop. He dropped his eyes to look at Augie's documents. "Don't you think it's a little suspicious that a man like him suddenly shows up in Campeche in a smuggler's ship, especially in these troubled times?"

"Whoa, whoa, whoa," Augie said abruptly. "Say that last part again, the part about the smuggler's ship."

"You didn't know that the Moonlight Runner was seized by the American government with a half ton of cocaine in her hold?"

For the second time that morning, the lieutenant succeeded in rattling Augie. Again, Donovan's lack of detail had put him in the uncomfortable position of having to defend him. "He told me it had been seized by the IRS."

The lieutenant looked at Augie like government officials often do when evaluating the veracity of what they're being told. He shifted his attention to the boxes in the backseat and stared at them as if trying to decide whether to inspect or not.

"I don't mean to suggest that Capitán Dónovan is involved in anything other than what he says he is, but you can see how it looks."

"Well"—Augie fidgeted uncomfortably in his seat—"you should never judge a book by its cover."

The lieutenant looked at the blown-out knees of Augie's worn-out blue jeans and the frayed ends of his faded shirt. He smirked as he handed back his documents. "You make a very good point, Señor Fagan."

After leaving the Cocina Maya, El Demonio's Ford Expedition made a left turn off Federal 180 and drove up a narrow road into the hills east of Seyba Playa. The drive to the finca had been a quiet one, each man occupied with his own thoughts as they waited to get to the secluded country house. The finca took full advantage of the difficult landscape. Except for the occasional outcropping of limestone, the trees lining the road hid what lay in the low, rolling hills behind them.

"Jefe," Beto said to El Demonio over his shoulder. "What do you want to do about the panguero?"

"He already paid for the motor," Dario interjected. "We don't need him."

Felipe cocked his head to the right, keeping his eyes on the road as he drove. "You mean Dónovan paid for the motor."

"It doesn't matter who paid for it," Dario argued. "The debt has been paid."

"Pinche gringo," Beto cussed. "You should have let me shoot him, jefe."

"You had your chance." Felipe chuckled. "He took the gun away from you."

"He won't do that again."

"Hah," Felipe scoffed. He glanced briefly at his boss. "What do you want done about Dónovan, jefe?"

"Nothing." He sat quietly for a moment, watching the road ahead through his dark glasses. "I have plans for the famous Capitán Dónovan."

"What about Benício?" Beto asked. "You're not really going to let him off so easy?"

"Our business with him is done," Dario insisted. "Leave him alone."

Fausto looked harshly at his cousin. "I'm not done with the fisher of men," El Demonio said nefariously. "But for the time being, I don't want either him or Dónovan bothered. "¿Estamos?"

Felipe and Beto looked at each other. "Sí, jefe," both men replied almost simultaneously.

"Right now, all I'm concerned with is how the marina knew about the guns so that it doesn't happen again."

"You're not thinking of using the same people again?" Felipe commented. "They took a big chance getting these guns for us. They won't be able to do it again now that they've been absorbed by the Norteños."

"José Luis is working on another supplier," Fausto responded.

"Where is José Luis anyway?" Felipe asked.

"He's back at the house in Lorenzo." El Demonio inhaled deeply, "He's waiting on the beach for Chucho to bring the cocaine to him after he picks it up from Capitán Santos this morning."

"I don't know how much longer we can use that Pemex ship." Felipe glanced back to his right. "His people have been asking him why it's been taking him so long to make the supply run to the Arcas platforms. They're starting to get suspicious."

"He's just getting a little nervous." Fausto looked out the window. "After he gets me the last fifty kilos, I'll think about giving him a break."

"Maybe he can talk Dónovan into making the runs," Felipe suggested.

Fausto looked at Felipe. He sat quietly staring at him through his dark glasses without responding. Felipe squirmed in his seat as he waited for a response. Fausto finally turned away and looked out his window. "That's not a bad idea."

The sunlight breaking through the gaps in the treetops along the east side of Old Highway 180 flickered intermittently on Donovan's convertible as he drove back to the Paradise Lagoon. The woman he just left dominated his thoughts, especially her eyes. It was not just that they gleamed like the most flawless emeralds he had ever seen—and he had handled the best Colombia had to offer—but the way she spoke with them in a language more melodic than anything penned by the legendary composers of the nineteenth century. He could not fathom how a woman of her magnificence could be married to a man he equated to a troll lurking in the dark recesses under a bridge.

He glanced over at Poli, who had his elbow on the door and his eyes glued to the road ahead. He could see a lot of the woman in the boy. He shared her emerald eyes and smooth raven hair. The boy's youth barely masked the rugged contours of his face in contrast to the smooth angelic features of his mother's. He wondered if he had inherited those traits from Benício. If he had, he wondered how long before he would begin to lose his hair and morph into the creature Benício had grown into with age.

"You said you had another boy my age working for you?" Poli asked.

"His name is Sandy." Donovan put his right elbow on the top of his seat. "He's about three years older than you."

"Where's he from?"

"Texas." Donovan put his hand back on the wheel and looked up the road. "He's taking a break from college. His uncle, my partner, brought him down to give us a hand with the ship." He looked back at Poli. "He's a good sailor. You stick with him, and he'll show you the ropes."

"The ropes?"

"The job." Donovan chuckled. "You'll like him. He's a good kid and a hard worker."

"Does his uncle work on the boat?"

"Ship," Donovan corrected him. "The Siete Mares is a ship, and yes, his uncle is the first mate. He runs the ship. He'll be the one telling you what to do."

"Is he like the captain?"

"I'm the captain. He's the first mate. I make the decisions. He carries them out." He put his eyes back on the road. "Mr. Fagan is tough. If he tells you to do something, you jump, and don't worry if you don't know how to do what he tells you. Just ask him and he'll show you." He smiled at Poli. "He's tough, but he's fair." He turned his eyes back on the road. "You'll like him."

Poli drew an apprehensive breath. "I hope so."

Donovan chuckled and then frowned when he saw that Poli seemed troubled. "Don't worry about Mr. Fagan. He'll take some getting used to, but like I said, you'll grow to like him."

"I'm not worried."

Donovan continued driving, occasionally turning to look at Poli, who hadn't said a thing for a while. Until he told him about his first mate, he had been rather chatty. "I didn't mean to scare you about Mr. Fagan."

"I'm not worried about him," Poli said, crossing his arms as he stared at the road.

The concern on the boy's face told him that something did bother him. He had something on his mind that appeared to trouble him. Donovan had to know the reason behind the worried look.

"First time away from home?"

"I've been to retreats in Carmen," he replied. "Sometimes as long as two weeks."

"Then what's bothering you?"

Poli looked at him, "Do you think those men will be back?"

Donovan looked at the road ahead. "I don't know."

"Do you think they'll hurt my mother?"

"Not if I can help it." He smiled to himself as an idea came to him. He turned to Poli. "If it makes you feel better, I'll check in on her from time to time."

"Gracias, Capitán."

Neither spoke as they continued toward the Paradise Lagoon. Their talk seemed to reassure Poli, although he did sit quietly, obviously still thinking about what had happened at the restaurant. Donovan also sat quietly, thinking about Itzél and how if the engine had not broken down, Augie might have been the one who had gone to the Cocina Maya to interview the prospective crewman. His mind then drifted to another chance meeting.

SALA DE URGENCIAS MÉDICAS, COATZACOALCOS, VERACRUZ
JUNE, TEN YEARS EARLIER

At two o'clock in the morning, the emergency room at the regional hospital in the port city of Coatzacoalcos is as lonely as a West Texas bus station at midnight. Donovan opened the door for a Korean seaman, bent over in serious distress, the front of his shirt covered in vomit. He moaned as he staggered ahead of Donovan into the empty reception room. The odor of alcohol mixed with sweat and vomit hung over the man like a thick cloud. Donovan turned his head to catch a breath before gently rapping his knuckles on the intake window. The Plexiglass window thudded to a stop as the woman behind the counter slid it open.

"Aye, Señor Dónovan," the round-faced receptionist gasped as she pinched her nose. "Charge this one to the company too?"

"Please." He pulled up the ailing seaman to keep him from falling to the floor. "His name is Pak. First name Soon." He pulled an envelope out of his back pocket and handed it to the receptionist. "You'll find everything you need in there."

As the receptionist entered information on her computer, the municipal policeman working security at the emergency room shook his head and walked up to Donovan. "You've been busy this week," he said.

"Tell me about it," he responded dryly. "Luckily, his ship is pulling out tomorrow, and I'll have a week to recharge before the next one comes in."

The policeman lowered his head to look at the ailing man's face. "What's wrong with him?"

"He bet he could eat a live octopus." Donovan put his hand on the beleaguered seaman's forehead and pulled his head back. "The octopus decided it didn't want to play and jammed a tentacle up his nose."

The receptionist raised herself in her seat to look. "¡Aye, no!" she gasped when she saw the protruding tentacle. She covered her mouth and turned away.

The municipal officer's face contorted with disgust. "Why would anyone want to eat a living octopus?"

"The Koreans consider it a delicacy."

"How do they eat them?"

"Well ..." Donovan released the man's head. He used his free hand to show the officer. "You're supposed to swirl it in a bowl of dipping sauce really fast until the tentacles wrap themselves around its body. Then you toss it in your mouth and eat it before it can uncoil itself."

"Have you ever eaten one?"

Donovan shook his head. "Never could get up the nerve."

"What did he do wrong?"

"Mr. Pak obviously forgot what his mother told him about not playing with his food."

The double doors to the treatment area opened suddenly. A young woman dressed in blue hospital scrubs and a white lab coat held the door open and looked at Donovan. "Mr. Donovan?"

The woman brushed a lock of hair that had fallen over the right side of her face, covering her eye. Dumbfounded by her beauty, Donovan felt a chill run through him. Her full-bodied raven hair hung on her shoulders in a neat pageboy, cupping her face. Her almond-shaped eyes, dark like coal, seemed to smile at him as she waited for him to bring the ailing man to the door.

The little Korean man put his hand on the small of Donovan's back and pushed him forward as he followed him toward the treatment room doors. Unlike the others, the woman did not react with disgust at the sight of an octopus's tentacles protruding from the Korean man's nose. She put her dainty hand between the stricken man's shoulder blades and bowed her head to look into the hunching little man's face.

"That's a nasty problem you have, Mr. Donovan."

"I'm Donovan." He pointed at the Korean. "That's Mr. Pak." Donovan glanced at the name tag on her lab coat. "Doctor ..."

"Tonatzin," she said as she led them into the treating area, brushing back the lock of hair that again fell out of place. She drew back the curtain around a cubicle across from a bathroom and patted her hand on a gurney, inviting Mr. Pak to sit. She inspected the tentacle that was firmly wrapped around the bulbous part of his face as she slipped on a pair of rubber gloves. "I didn't know the local Korean restaurant served sannakji?"

Impressed, Donovan raised his brows. "You know about eating live octopus?"

"I know you're not supposed to try it when you're intoxicated." She left the cubicle and returned shortly afterward, rolling a small stainless-steel table with various medically related items, including a pair of forceps and a pair of scissors on a neatly folded white towel fitted perfectly to the bottom of a stainless-steel tray. "I'm surprised they served it to him," she said as she arranged the items on the tray. "He's obviously intoxicated."

"Oh, he didn't get the octopus at a restaurant," Donovan said. "Pak bought it off a boy selling crabs on the beach." He chuckled. "He bet he could eat it in one gulp."

She rolled her eyes and looked at him. "What fool took that bet?"

Donovan turned his eyes briefly to the side. "I think he just wanted to show off to his crewmates."

"Being a sailor, you would think he should know better than to eat anything that comes out of the water around a busy port without cooking it first." Doctor Tonatzin put her hand on Mr. Pak's chin and raised his head. "He could ingest an amoeba and develop dysentery." She turned to Donovan. "Hold his head up for me."

She pulled on the octopus's protruding limb with a pair of forceps as Donovan held Mr. Pak's head steady. She took the scissors off the tray and snipped off the tentacle, causing the octopus to draw the injured limb back into the intoxicated man's nose. She readied her forceps and prepared to extract the cephalopod from his mouth, "Open your mouth, Mr. Pak."

Instead of opening his mouth, the little Korean sailor drew back his shoulders and made one long, protracted swallow. After passing the octopus, he put his hand on his chest and smiled.

"One swallow." Donovan chuckled. "You did it, Pak."

The little man grinned at Donovan and held his hand out for his winnings. The doctor looked sternly at Donovan.

Mr. Pak suddenly stopped smiling, and his eyes widened. He bent over and folded his arms around his stomach, groaning miserably. He raised his head, breathing heavily, and stared helplessly at the doctor. He slapped one hand over his mouth and grunted. He then bent over, wrapping both arms around his midsection.

"Uh-oh." Donovan stepped back.

Doctor Tonatzin pulled the curtain back and calmly pointed to the bathroom across from the cubicle. Mr. Pak hopped off the gurney with one hand firmly over his mouth and the other pressed against his stomach as he raced for the bathroom.

"Looks like you were right about that amoeba."

The little man waddled unnaturally toward the bathroom and slammed the door behind him. Donovan sighed with relief and grinned widely.

"I'd better keep him here for a little while to make sure he's all right," she said to Donovan.

"Thank you, Doctor." Donovan gave her the once-over with his eyes. The scrubs and lab coat didn't completely hide the petite woman' feminine attributes. He completed his survey by looking at the white jogging shoes she wore. He smiled at their diminutive size.

She noticed that he was staring at her feet. "What?"

"Nothing." Donovan raised his head and tried to suppress his smile.

She looked down at her feet. "We're on our feet a lot." She looked up at him. "That's why we wear comfortable shoes."

"That makes sense." Donovan looked down at her shoes. "I was just admiring the size."

She wrinkled her nose and blushed. "They're not very big."

"I used to hang a pair just like those on the rearview mirror of my car when I was in high school."

She slapped him on his arm and giggled. "Stop it."

Donovan looked at her name tag. "Tonatzin. You never hear that name bantered about."

"It's Náhuatl," she explained.

"That's interesting." He looked into her soft charcoal eyes. "Is your first name Náhuatl also?"

She looked away and smiled. "You want me to tell you my name?"

"If I may be so bold."

She looked up at him coyly. "Xochitl," she said softly.

He threw his thumb back toward himself. "I'm Simon. Simon Donovan."

"How do you know Mr. Pak?"

"I'm a shipping agent. My company in Houston sent me to Coatzacoalcos to facilitate the transfer of cargo being shipped to the United States from China. Part of my responsibilities include providing for the needs of the ships and their crews. Mr. Pak is a crewman aboard one of the ships my company is using to transport the cargo."

Dr. Tonatzin scrunched her brow. "If the cargo is coming from China, why is it stopping here?"

"The company decided it was faster and cheaper to unload the containers at Salina Cruz on the Pacific coast, ship it across the isthmus by rail, put it on a ship in Coatzacoalcos, and take it to the port of Houston."

"Why not use the Panama Canal?"

"The canal is not always the cheapest or the fastest way to get goods from the Pacific to the southern United States. The Salina Cruz to Coatzacoalcos route is an old route that was used before the opening of the Panama Canal."

The doctor, mesmerized by either Donovan's explanation or his voice, gazed absently into his eyes as she listened. He paused and smiled at her. She blushed and turned away. She began fumbling with the items on the tray.

"So," she said as she nervously rearranged the items on the tray. "Do you live in Houston?"

"No." Donovan walked around the gurney. "I live in Panama. I manage a shipping subsidiary for the company in Panama City."

The sound of Mr. Pak retching and vomiting interrupted their conversation. She looked toward the bathroom.

"He's going to be dehydrated." She started to leave the cubicle. "I'd better get an I.V. ready."

Not wanting to lose momentum, Donovan looked for a way to keep the conversation on a personal level.

"What about you?"

Doctor Tonatzin either didn't hear him or chose to ignore his question as she hurried out of the cubicle. Donovan felt he had lost the connection he had made with her and wanted desperately to keep her talking. She returned shortly afterward with a clear plastic bag containing the intravenous fluid and went to fetch the I.V. tree standing in the corner of the cubicle.

"Do you live Coatzacoalcos?" he asked her as she rolled the tree toward the gurney.

"Hmm? Oh." She looked back toward the bathroom, anticipating Mr. Pak's return. "For the moment."

He wanted to keep the conversation going, having lost the connection. "Can I buy you a cup of coffee?"

She gazed into his eyes, saying nothing as he held his breath in anticipation. Her pupils broadened as she looked at him, the lock of hair again falling across her eye. He felt a tingling deep within his chest, and his throat became dry as he watched her slowly brush it back behind her ear.

"No," she said, delivering her response with the suddenness of a torpedo strike in the dead of night as she hung the I.V. bag on the tree.

CHAPTER

4

No one in the Seventh Naval Zone in Lerma could recall the last time such a large seizure of guns like the ones taken at Punta Morro had occurred. Since first light, a platoon of enlisted men hurried to prepare the outdoor reception area next to the headquarters building for the media event scheduled for nine that morning. A passing shower drenched the military base, soaking the metal chairs assembled on the raised stage to seat the dignitaries attending the presentation, including the governor. Like ants on a fallen insect, the marines swarmed the stage armed with towels and push brooms to dry off the chairs and push the water off the stage.

The rain shower rushed inland, leaving in its wake a cloudless sky and a sun obsessed with reclaiming the moisture, thickening the morning air into a vaporous shroud of misery. The puddles dotting the parade ground gleamed like the pieces of a broken mirror as the reporters and photographers trickled in, taking their seats in front of the podium, anticipating the press statement by the base's information officer, Teniente de Fragata Raúl Suárez. The section behind the podium also began to fill with naval officers and comandantes of the Federal Preventive Police, the directorate of public safety, and the state police. Only the section reserved for the governor and several local elected officials on the right side of the podium behind a red cordon remained unoccupied. Moored within view of the assembly sat the Azteca-class coastal patrol boat commanded by Capitán de Corbeta Martín Mendiola.

The marines arranged the impressive number of captured weapons on three tables in front of a temporary wall under an oversized logo of the secretariat of the navy. The petty officer in custodial charge of the weapons arranged the pistols in five rows of ten on the center table. On each of the two outer tables, he displayed the captured AK-47 rifles in two rows of ten and one row of five. He stationed two marines in full battle dress and armed with M4 rifles at the ends of the tables, each concealing his face with a black balaclava.

The corporal charged with escorting the official visitors to their seats looked over his shoulder and slowed his pace to wait for the two Campeche state police commanders, who made no effort to keep step with him. Both men stood over six feet tall but looked entirely different in the way they wore their uniforms. Comandante Sánchez, the larger of the two men, had an undisciplined waistline, and he wore his white uniform shirt with the collar open. It lacked the crispness and taut fit of the shirt worn by his associate, Comandante Prieto, who wore a uniform tie with a polished brass tie clip. Both comandantes wore white pancake hats with Prieto's being well formed and Sánchez's hat looking more like a U-boat commander's with the sides and top pulled down.

The rear admiral commanding the naval zone stood patiently behind the podium, waiting for the arrival of the governor and his entourage, smiling occasionally at the photographers and reporters sitting in front of him. Behind him, carefully reviewing his notes, sat Teniente Suárez, the information officer who politely tried to ignore the comments being made by the senior officer sitting next to him, Capitán Martín Mendiola.

"Look who just showed up," Captain Mendiola whispered to the nervous junior officer.

Lieutenant Suárez raised his head in time to see the two state police commanders ignore the frustrated petty officer who tried to show them their seats. After conferring silently, Sánchez and Prieto sat at the end of the row behind the naval officers, apart from the other distinguished invitees.

Comandante Sánchez looked over the heads of the other guests through his bushy eyebrows. He grinned when he spotted the two municipal police commanders in his task force standing behind the section in front of the podium. The two comandantes made for an odd pair. Comandante Briones, the taller man, had a distinctive Asiatic visage and a thin frame, while the much shorter comandante, Tápia, looked like a broad-faced toad. Neither saw Sánchez watching them from the podium as Briones gazed pensively at the captured cache of weapons while Tápia, his lower lip rolled out and his arms folded across his chest, glared viciously at anyone who looked their way.

"Look at Briones and Tápia," Sánchez whispered to Comandante Prieto.

Prieto scoffed derisively. "Pinche Tapón," he said, using the diminutive comandante's nickname, "the drain stopper." "Who does he think he is? Mussolini?"

"I thought they might show up." Sánchez grinned. "Chino didn't want to believe that their precious cargo had fallen short." Comandante Briones had been known as "El Chino" since childhood because of his Asiatic appearance.

Prieto looked at his giddy associate. "How did you know the shipment wouldn't get through?" He squinted his eyes. "You didn't alert the marina? Did you?"

"Of course not." Sánchez frowned. "The guns were bound not to make it. I'm surprised they got this far." He looked at the display of captured weapons. "They had too far to go to get here. Too many chances to get noticed. Too many people involved." He chuckled contentedly. "Perhaps the others will listen to me now."

"Hmm," Prieto mumbled.

"You don't agree?" Sánchez glared at his associate.

"I don't know." Prieto adjusted his seat. He had always been loyal to Sánchez, despite his cantankerous and often hateful ways. "Resuming the deal with the Comisión is asking too much from them."

"What do you mean too much?" Sánchez whispered angrily. "They need guns. The Comisión can get all they need."

"The others prefer to wait for the guns Fausto said he can get them."

"This proves López can't deliver," he argued. "They're better off sticking with me and renewing our relationship with the Comisión."

"They won't see it that way," Prieto retorted. "Fausto has them convinced that they're better off distancing themselves from the Comisión."

"Why? Because of the Norteños?"

Prieto nodded. "It's only a matter of time before the Norteños go after the Comisión." He leaned closer to him. "They believe if we do business with them, the Norteños will think we're allies. They're afraid the Norteños will see us as a threat."

"I have news for the others." Sánchez muffled his bark. "The Norteños already believe we're a threat." He turned in his chair. "You don't think they know we've taken over the gangs? You don't think they know we're turning them into an army?" He chuckled sarcastically. "What do you believe they're going to think when they read about this seizure? One hundred guns?" He scoffed. "If anything, we're better off working with the Comisión. Together, we'll have more men than they do and an endless supply of guns and ammunition. The Norteños will think twice before they tangle with us."

"I wouldn't bank on numbers alone," Prieto remarked. "Los Demonios had much greater numbers than Los Rayos, and the Norteños still prevailed over the Frontera cartel." He sighed. "As far as the endless supply of guns you're talking about … they have a lot to be desired."

"I'll agree that the guns they gave us last year weren't exactly top shelf."

"Top shelf?" Prieto scoffed, "It's probably been forty years since they've even seen a shelf. Most looked like they'd been buried for who knows how long."

"They weren't that bad. With a good armorer, we could get them back into shape. The point is that the Norteños are coming and we're better off facing them together with the Comisión." He folded his arms and looked back toward Briones and Tápia. "All we have to do is renew our arrangement with them."

"Well, uh …" Comandante Prieto balked. "Don't you think the arrangement was a bit one-sided?" he said. "You were the only one making any real money. The rest of us only made a fraction of what the Comisión gave you."

"Why shouldn't I get paid more?" Sánchez whispered angrily. "Who persuaded the governor to set up the counternarcotics task force to begin with?" he added, shaming Prieto. "Who handpicked each of you to be on that task force? Who struck the deal with the Comisión to buy the drugs we took from the Campechanos?"

"You did," Prieto responded meekly.

"I was working to get each of you a bigger share of the profits," he lied. He followed that with another lie. "Alejandro was thinking about inviting us to join his organization."

Alejandro Pelayo Diaz, the jailer who founded La Comisión had no expansion plan. The shortsighted basis for organizing the Comisión centered on selling the drugs they seized from the Norteño cartel to the Frontera cartel. His arrangement with Comandante Sánchez never included any possibility of membership in his organization.

Prieto looked skeptically at Sánchez. "I happen to know that's not true."

"Well"—he rolled his eyes at him—"I'm sure the prospect of facing Colonel Barca and the Thunderbolts will make him reconsider."

Prieto turned to Sánchez. "What about El Demonio?"

"What about him?"

"Are you forgetting that it was he who organized the gangs for us?" He turned to his friend. "Thanks to López, we make much more money selling protection than we ever did helping you sell drugs to the Comisión."

"Are you forgetting that it was me who brought the gangs under our control in the first place?"

Prieto hissed as he cringed. "We didn't exactly have control over them."

"But it was me that got them to agree to listen to the comandantes. There wouldn't be anybody to organize if I hadn't done that."

"They listened only because you gave them money," Prieto pointed out to him. "If Fausto hadn't trained the comandantes how to set up a protection racket, we would've lost what influence we had over the gangs after we stopped paying them to take the drugs we stole to the Comisión for us."

"What about the security jobs I got us with the Campechanos?"

"Nobody took the jobs seriously, except for Comandante Garza in Ciudad del Carmen." Prieto shrugged. "To them, it was just a payoff. With what they make off extortion, the others couldn't care less what the Campechanos give them at the end of the month."

"That's the gratitude I get." Sánchez lowered himself into his chair. "If it wasn't for me, the comandantes would still be taking hundred-peso bribes from the gangs instead of having them under their thumbs."

"That may be true, Heriberto." Prieto raised a brow and inhaled deeply. "But things have changed. The comandantes have grown into powerful plaza bosses with their own sicarios." He hesitated. "They believe their future lies with El Demonio and not the Comisión." He folded his arms and sighed. "It's like I said. It's only a matter of time before the Norteños send Colonel Barca to adjust accounts." In the drug trade, "adjusting of accounts" is synonymous to "evening the score." "None of them want to be in his crosshairs when El Rayo deals with the Comisión like he dealt with the Frontera cartel."

"Are they so naïve to believe that Colonel Barca doesn't already have them in his crosshairs? What makes them think that the Norteños will stop with the Comisión?" Sánchez looked up at the governor and his entourage as they walked around the corner of the administration building and onto the assembly stage. "They've eliminated the Frontera cartel and mean to dominate the market. The Campechanos and the Campeche gangs are in the way."

"¡Presenten!" the petty officer in charge of the detail guarding the weapons ordered as the governor and his entourage made their entrance. The marines snapped to attention, bringing their rifles smartly to a vertical position in front of them and stomping their right boots in unison. The assembly rose to their feet as the admiral greeted the governor and personally escorted him to the section set aside for him and his aides. Lieutenant Suárez left his seat and stood by the podium, waiting for the admiral to introduce him.

Comandante Prieto leaned closer to Sánchez. "There might be a way to persuade the others to agree to work with the Comisión as long as it means a fairer share of the profits and a guarantee of a steady supply of quality weapons."

"That's all I'm asking," Sánchez lied.

At the end of the pier where it tees near the center of the Paradise Lagoon sat the Siete Mares, basking in the sun. The rays bouncing off the lagoon danced playfully against her white hull like the wings of a thousand butterflies. The teak in her masts, cabin tops, and bowsprit glistened like freshly polished furnisher, and the polished brass of her fittings shimmered like mirrors. The Jacob's-ladders stretching from the gunwales to the top of her masts pulled on those stalwart structures like the strings of a violin, and like a violin, she made music when the wind blew through her rigging as she wandered restlessly from port to port. At anchorage, the restless wanderer rested, waiting to make music again.

While the restless wanderer rested, her crew worked to keep the ravages of the wind, the sea, and the sun in check. Sandy Trelis came out of the main cabin with a bucket of soapy water in one hand and a heavy mop in the other. The thin, blue-eyed young man, not yet twenty, with blond, shaggy hair and long limbs, rested the mop against the steering box and poured the contents of the bucket on the afterdeck. He rolled up the ends of the short sleeves of his red T-shirt like a fifties tough guy. He wiped his hands on his cutoff blue jeans as he looked down on his old worn-out canvas boat shoes. He had just cut off the laces and knotted the ends at the topmost eyelets to make them easier to put on and take off like his uncle had shown him. He put the bucket aside and began gliding the heavy mop across the deck in long, sweeping strokes.

"Ahoy on the afterdeck," a venerable old man called from the top of the gangplank. In his hand, he carried an old instant camera.

Sandy rested the mop against the steering box. "Come aboard, Don Macario."

The old gentleman had the grace of a movie star of the Golden Age of Mexican cinema and dressed just as stylishly in a white silk shirt, buff-colored linen pants, and a Panama hat. He had piercing gray eyes and a heroic nose and square jaw with a well-defined cleft on his chin.

"What have you got there?" Sandy asked.

"It's an old instant camera." He handed it to Sandy. "I thought your uncle might want to add it to his museum pieces he has at the dive shop."

"He does own some pretty old junk, especially that coffeemaker." Sandy chuckled. "He's the only one who can get it to work."

"It's called a percolator." Augie stepped through the hatch of the main cabin. "And that junk you're referring to still works." He took the camera from his nephew.

"I thought it would look good next to that old metal oscillating fan and the Smith Corona on your desk."

When Don Macario gave Augie the old typewriter and oscillating fan, neither worked. He got them running in no time at all, surprising the old gentleman.

"Thanks." He looked the camera over and then showed it to Don Macario. "Do you have any film for it?"

"I think it has a few shots left in the cartridge." Don Macario looked at the counter. "Um-hmm. Five left." He handed it back to him. "I may have a couple stored in the library."

Sandy turned his head as Donovan and Poli came up the gangplank. "The skipper's here."

Poli followed Donovan to the afterdeck, holding an overpacked suitcase in one hand and grinning like the Cheshire Cat.

"Who do we have here?" Augie noticed Poli's unusual green eyes. "Looks like he swallowed a bucket of algae."

"This is our new crewman, Poli."

"He looks kind of young," Augie remarked. He glared warily at his partner. "I thought you said that the guy you were going to talk to had a wife and kids."

"That guy didn't work out."

Augie looked skeptically at the boy. "How much sailing have you done?"

"We're taking him on as a trainee," Donovan answered for him. He turned to Sandy. "I'd like for you to show him the ropes."

"Sure thing, Skipper."

"I don't know about this," Augie said under his breath. He always paid attention to the way a man dressed—not in a fashion sense but in a practical way. He ran his hand through his hair. "He's going to have to change his clothes, especially those shoes."

"He's right," Donovan said to Poli. "Did you bring a pair of tennis shoes? The deck of the ship gets pretty wet."

Poli shook his head.

"What about clothes? He can't work dressed like that."

"All the clothes my mother packed are like this," Poli commented.

"Your mother packed your bag?" Augie rolled his eyes and glared at Donovan.

"What?" Donovan snapped. "Didn't your mother ever pack a bag for you?"

Augie drew a long, deep breath and exhaled. "How old are you?"

Poli's eyes gazed at the first mate nervously. "Sixteen?"

"Sixteen." Augie rubbed his chin as he sized up the boy. He scoffed and then smiled. "I was twelve when I first went out to sea."

"I thought you said you were born on your father's shrimper?" Donovan remarked.

"That was the first time I came back from the sea," Augie retorted. "My mother went out to sea with me in her hold." He turned to Poli and rubbed his head. "Do as you're told, and you'll be fine."

Relieved, Poli grinned. "Gracias, Señor Fagan."

"Mr. Fagan, if you please, aboard ship," he corrected him. He showed him the bottom of his well-worn canvas boat shoes. "You're going to need shoes with soles like mine with good traction." He pulled on his shirt. "Wear loose-fitting clothes like mine or Sandy's, but not so loose that they can get caught in a winch."

Donovan glanced at the blown-out knees on his partner's blue jeans, the backs of the cuffs frayed from years of stepping on them.

"I think those jeans are ready for the cutoff drawer."

"These are the last of my dress pants," he commented. "Jeans are like boots. It takes time to break 'em in."

Don Macario smiled, amused by his friend's simple fashion sense. He cocked his head to the side as he looked at Poli. "Isn't Itzél Canek your mother?"

"Sí, señor," Poli said respectfully.

"You know him?" Donovan asked.

"I often eat at the Cocina Maya," Don Macario replied. "His mother's food is the best in Seyba Playa, if not all of Campeche."

"Gracias, Don Macario." The boy smiled proudly. "I'll tell her you said that."

"Wait a minute. The owner of the Cocina Maya is your mother?" Augie studied Poli's features. "That explains the green eyes." He glared at his partner cynically. "It might explain a lot more than just that."

"What are you getting at?" Donovan resented the insinuation.

Don Macario winced at the unintended outcome of his question to the boy. He changed the subject. "Did you see the camera I donated to Augie's museum?"

Augie handed the camera to Donovan. "Like everything else I have in there"—he looked at his nephew sternly—"it works."

"It may still work," Donovan said as he fiddled with the camera, "but the question is, do they still make film for it?"

"It has film in it," Don Macario said, taking the camera from him. He held the camera up and pointed it at Poli.

"Wait!" Donovan stopped him, remembering what Poli told him back at the restaurant about wanting to steer the ship. He grabbed Poli by the sleeve and stood him by the steering box, putting his hands on the ship's wheel. "Now take your picture."

"Let's make it a group picture, commemorating Poli's first day as a working sailor." As Don Macario held the camera up, he waved his free hand to move everybody into place. "Everybody gather around Poli." He waited for them to get into place and then snapped the shot. The camera whirred, and the old gentleman pulled the picture out of the slot.

"I'll be damned," Donovan remarked. "It still works."

"Like everything else in the shop," Augie added.

Don Macario fanned the picture until it developed and handed it to Poli. "Give that to your mother."

"Gracias, Don Macario." His eyes widened as he gawked at the picture.

Don Macario looked at his watch. "I have to be going." He handed the camera to Augie. "Pablo's coming in early to talk to me about another advance." He chuckled. "He must have a new girlfriend."

"That reminds me." Augie turned to his partner. "Did you go by the bank?"

Donovan felt his throat tighten. "About that ..." He swallowed. "I had an unexpected expense." He turned to Don Macario. "Is it all right if we pay you back after we get paid for the next charter? It shouldn't be more than a couple of days."

"Of course." Don Macario rubbed Poli's hair as he walked past him on his way to the gangplank.

"Sandy," Augie called to his nephew, "bring the parts in the back of the Safari and the trunk to the ship. And take the new guy with you."

"Yes, Uncle Augie."

"And stop calling me that when we're at work."

"Aye, aye, Mr. Fagan."

Sandy tapped Poli on the shoulder. "Come on."

Poli put the picture in his shirt pocket and followed Sandy toward the gangplank where they waited for Don Macario to leave the ship. After running down the gangplank, their feet stomped on the heavy planks of the pier like beating drums as they ran toward the Safari.

Augie turned to his partner. "So, what happened to the guy you went to talk to?"

"For one thing, he's too old, and I think he has a weak heart. There's no way he could handle the work."

"What made you decide to hire this kid?"

"The kid's his son. He seemed eager and jumped at the chance to learn how to sail."

"I don't know." Augie looked at the boys unloading the Safari. "The kid doesn't even have the right kind of shoes."

"He's as good as anybody we could expect to find on such short notice. Maybe better. This kid's smart, eager, and willing to learn."

"I suppose you're right." He exhaled. He turned to Donovan and squinted. "What about the unexpected expense you mentioned."

"About that." He cleared his throat to stall for time. "You know how his father was the only one to put in for the job?"

"What's that got to do with it?"

"Well, the reason he was looking for work was to pay off an outboard motor he bought from this creep." He coughed into his hand. "I mean, the jerk sent a leg breaker to collect while I was there."

Augie looked angrily at his partner. "So you paid it off."

"Think of it as an advance. I'm taking a little out of Poli's paycheck until it's paid back."

Augie sighed, gazed at the sky, and shook his head. He looked at his partner. "Do you at least have enough to pay for an oil plug?"

"Sure." He chuckled nervously. "Why?"

"We're gonna need one by the end of the day. You'd better go into Campeche and get it."

"Do you mind if I take Poli? I'd like to get him a pair of boat shoes."

"You have enough for that?"

He scoffed. "I didn't totally blow our bank account."

Augie sighed deeply. "Why not?"

"I'll be back in a jiff to help you with the engine, if I don't run into any checkpoints. They've been hitting hard lately."

"I know what you mean. I was stopped at one not far from here." He looked dubiously at his partner. "There's a Lieutenant named Baeza that's taken a big interest in you."

"Me?"

"He asked me if I knew that the Siete Mares was seized with a load of cocaine." Augie folded his arms. "I thought you told me she was seized by the IRS."

"She was," Donovan retorted. "The IRS seized her after it was proved she was bought with untaxed proceeds. The ship was passed from the coast guard to the DEA and then to the IRS." He scoffed. "Does it really matter?"

"It seems to matter to Lieutenant Baeza."

"Look, I only found out she was a drug runner after I took possession from the marshals in Galveston." Donovan wiped his brow. "Frankly, I would've never known if the property master hadn't told me when he gave me the ship's papers." He sighed. "I didn't mention it to you because I didn't think it was important."

Augie clicked his tongue and looked at the cabañas on the bluff. He drew a breath before turning to his partner. "He also told me you had a criminal record."

The color washed from Donovan's face.

"He tried to convince me that you're some kind of smuggler," Augie added.

Donovan's face hardened. "He's just probing."

"I get that, but for what?"

"Don't tell me you've never been shaken down by the cops?"

"That's beside the point."

In the time that the two had been partners, they had never doubted each other's integrity. They may never have shared the more intimate details of their pasts, but they had trusted each other. Donovan brought the brunt of the infrastructure into the partnership, and it stung that Augie should question his honor. The two looked at each other, waiting for the other to throw the first punch.

"Tell me again just what it was you did before you retired?"

Donovan bowed his head, partly in frustration, partly in disappointment. He drew a long, slow breath, suppressing the urge to raise his voice. "Like I told you, I ran a subsidiary in Panama for a Houston-based shipping company."

"What about the criminal charges?"

"Look, Augie." He paused. "Don't let that lieutenant get you worked up."

"What about the charges?" Augie insisted.

"Sometimes paperwork gets lost or isn't prepared correctly or completely. I worked in Latin America," Donovan explained calmly. "You've lived in these parts long enough to know that the law here works differently. You're presumed guilty until you prove otherwise. In the meantime, you're locked up until the paperwork clears."

"What about bribes? Did you pay any bribes to keep from being thrown in jail?"

The question irritated Donovan. "What about you? Haven't you ever paid off anybody since you've been here? You know that's how things get done south of the border. To answer your question"—Donovan looked at him through his brows—"I've never paid a bribe to keep from going to jail or to avoid inspection."

"The lieutenant said that some of the cargo you were caught with were articles of war," Augie continued to press. "What does that mean?"

It was clear to Donovan that the lieutenant had gotten to his partner. "The articles of war is a list of items considered to be war material. That includes airplane parts, fuel bladders, and an assortment of other commercially available items most Americans don't think of as articles of war."

"Who were you taking the 'articles' to?"

Donovan had to think how best to answer his question without complicating the issue further. "Sometimes we did contract work for the government. We were asked to deliver the goods quietly and to avoid media attention. It was all quite legal and sanctioned by both our government and the client government." He sighed sharply. "Customs guys always get shaky around heavy hardware, even when they're just parts."

His explanation seemed to dull the edge of his partner's suspicions. However, it didn't seem to him that his doubts had been completely alleviated by the way he turned his head to the sides, obviously troubled by some imagined inconsistency.

"That sounds reasonable, I guess."

Believing he had quelled his partner's misgivings, Donovan smiled and started for the gangplank. "I'll be back with your plug in an hour or so."

"The lieutenant also said that you were charged with theft," he added.

Donovan dropped his head and emptied his lungs. He turned to face him. "My company sent me to Costa Rica to repossess a fifty-four-foot cabin cruiser and bring it back to Houston. I had all the paperwork and a set of keys. A Costa Rican police boat came after me and took me and the cabin cruiser back to Limón. I was back underway that afternoon after the repo order was verified." He glared at his partner. "Satisfied?"

"What was the name of the company you worked for?"

The question taxed his patience, making it difficult for him to keep from becoming agitated. "Are you interrogating me?"

"I just want it to be clear in my mind. The lieutenant pressed me hard. Every time I answered his questions, he'd hit me with another I couldn't explain." Augie shook his head. "I don't think he's through with us."

Donovan went to the main cabin and stood by the hatch. "Are you coming?"

After a moment, Augie followed him down the companionway. He could hear his partner rummaging around in his stateroom as he walked toward it. He stood in the doorway and quietly watched his partner as he sat on his bed sorting through the various envelopes he had in the metal box on his lap. He opened one of the envelopes and began sorting through several documents.

"The name of the company I worked for is Century Shipping." Donovan removed a document from the others and stood, dropping a photo on the deck. He handed the document to his partner. "The home office is in Houston. We had a fleet of eight ships, varying in size, two of which were the large container types."

74

Augie picked up the picture on the deck and looked at it. He glanced at the woman in the photo and started to hand it to Donovan before snapping it back to take a second look. "How long have you had this picture of Poli's mother?" He squinted and drew the picture closer and then gazed at his partner. "This isn't Poli's mother."

Donovan snatched the picture from him and laid it, facedown, on the bed. He glared at his partner for a moment before sitting back on the bed to continue shuffling through the documents. "We moved all sorts of goods. I started off doing advances to make sure that the cargo went through smoothly. I filed the appropriate import or export documents, double-checked the bills of laden, manifests, licenses, certificates, et cetera." He looked at his partner. "We also handled government contracts, but I can't go into that." He lowered his eyes to look at other documents he intended to show him. "I handled Latin America and the Caribbean basin. The company eventually moved me to Panama to run their subsidiary there."

Augie stood silently in the doorway, watching his partner shuffle through the papers. He selected a couple of documents and held them out to his partner. "The document on the top refers to my retirement benefits. As you can see, I took a cash payout to buy this ship." He looked at another pair of documents before holding them out for his partner. "Here's the bill of sale and the title for the ship."

"I don't need to see them." He sighed and turned away in shame.

"Sure, the Siete Mares used to be a drug runner, and yes, I have been detained by the authorities on more than one occasion until my paper cleared, but I'm no smuggler," Donovan insisted. "I came down here to run a sailing charter, and that's what I'm going to do. I'm not gonna worry about some naval infantry lieutenant. He's barking up the wrong tree."

Augie nodded softly. "You've made your point." He slapped his hand on the doorjamb and pushed himself off. "I'll be in the engine room."

After his partner left, Donovan put the documents back in the metal box and reached for the photo on the bed. He stared at the faded picture with the worn edge of a velvet-skinned, ebony-eyed woman wearing a lab coat, and sighed deeply.

COATZACOALCOS, VERACRUZ
SEPTEMBER, TEN YEARS EARLIER

The dawn had yet to fully break, and the lights of Donovan's rental car gleamed off the wet pavement. He drove by the regional hospital near the malecon as he always did on his way to the office he rented near the port. Out of the corner of his eye, he noticed a woman wearing a white lab coat standing in the small parking area outside the emergency room entrance. Her jet-black hair hung over her face as she stared at the tire on the left rear side of an old pickup. He slowed down to take a closer look and then smiled when he recognized her. He turned around and drove into the parking area. He felt a tingle run through his chest when she brushed back a thick strand of hair from her face as she raised her head.

"Do you need help with that?" he asked as he rolled down his window.

Her dark, somber eyes brightened suddenly. She smiled timidly. "I haven't got a spare tire."

"Are you sure?" Donovan turned off the engine and stepped out of his car. "Have you looked under the truck?"

She wrinkled her nose the way she had during their first meeting. "Under the truck?"

Donovan walked behind the truck and looked under it. "Where's your jack?"

"I, uh," she stammered and then blushed. "I don't know."

"You ..." Donovan let out his breath as he smiled.

He walked to the right side of the truck, opened the door, and reached behind the seat to get the scissor jack under the backseat. He took it to the rear of the truck and laid it next to the flat tire and then went to get the spare.

"I don't know much about cars," she said as she watched him lower himself to the pavement to remove the spare tire from under the truck.

"I'll have you on your way in a little while."

"Thank you, Mr. Donovan."

"Call me Simon."

She chuckled softly. "All right, Simon." She looked musingly at him as he removed the tire. "I haven't seen you bring anybody to the emergency room in a while."

"The last couple of crews have been different from the others," Donovan said from under the truck.

"Do sailors always get drunk when they're not at sea?"

"Well ..." He grunted as he loosened the nut holding the tire in place. "Some do like their rum. Others like to fight." Donovan dragged the tire from under the truck. "But not all of them. Most of the last two crews I handled were teetotalers." He rolled the tire to the left rear side of the pickup and began removing the punctured tire.

"When will you be going back to Panama?"

"Not for a little while yet," he replied as he removed the lug nuts. "When will you be completing your internship?"

His question surprised her. "How did you know I was an intern?"

Donovan lookup up at her as he removed the flat tire. "Who else would they stick on the graveyard shift?"

She chuckled. "I'll be done by Christmas."

"Where will you go next?"

She sighed as she watched him put the spare on the wheel lugs. "Veracruz."

"Is that home?"

"Close," she said.

After Donovan finished replacing the tire, he took the truck off the jack and rolled the flat tire to the back of his car.

"What are you doing?"

"I'm gonna take your tire to get fixed." He threw the tire into his trunk.

"Don't bother with that."

"It's no bother." He slammed the trunk shut. "Do you think we can get that cup of coffee now?"

The question seemed to startle her, and she looked away. "I don't think that's a good idea."

"Why not?" Donovan chuckled. "I'm just asking you to have coffee with me."

"Why do you want to have coffee with me?" She looked up at him. "So that we can get to know each other? Make plans to go to dinner later?"

He looked into her eyes and the soft features of her face as she waited for his response.

"I think you are a fascinating woman, and yeah …" He nodded. "I'd like to get to know you better."

"All right." She looked away. "My father is a doctor. When I was a little girl, he would sometimes take me with him when he visited the Indian villages around Veracruz to care for the sick."

She glanced at him briefly. "I couldn't believe how poor they were. Many had never seen a doctor and relied on the local curandero for medical care."

"A witch doctor?"

"A shaman. A faith healer," she said to him. "Ever since then, I've wanted to be a doctor to care for the people living in the margins of society."

"Like the Indians."

"I'm an Indian," she retorted. The troublesome strand of thick hair fell across the right side of her face. "I've worked very hard to get where I am." She brushed back the hair from her eye. "I know what I want to do with my life. I can't afford to be distracted."

Donovan lost himself in her gaze. He had never been so taken, so bewitched by so simple a thing as the way she looked at him with her almond-shaped eyes.

"It's just a cup of coffee."

CHAPTER
5

The toll road between Campeche City and Seyba Playa may not be as picturesque as the coast road. However, the rises and drops between the valleys and limestone hills do provide for an interesting drive that can seem like a roller-coaster ride if taken at high speed. That's not to say that the drive through the Puuc hills is not scenic, for there are many breathtaking overlooks to marvel at for those who stop. Even so, people don't take the toll road just to marvel at scenic overlooks. They take it because they're in a hurry and can afford the tolls.

The body of the antique Oldsmobile convertible rose noticeably as Donovan topped the hill at eighty-five miles an hour. The breeze whipping through the old open-top car blew through Poli's hair like the north wind blowing through a field of tall grass. Poli smiled and braced himself with every curve as they sped down the toll road toward the Paradise Lagoon. Donovan looked over at the kid and chuckled to himself when he saw him comparing his new leather boat shoes to his own weathered pair.

"I've never been to Campeche City on the cuota before," Poli commented.

"We would have taken the libre if we didn't have to get back with Mr. Fagan's oil plug," Donovan explained. "It's a much nicer drive, especially at this time of the day."

The boy rested his head on the headrest and gazed at the hills as they raced past them. He sat up and took the picture Don Macario gave him out of his pocket.

Donovan glanced at him and grinned. "That's a good picture of you at the helm." He winked at him. "You look like a real sea captain."

"Do you think I'll ever be able to drive the boat?"

Donovan winced. "That's part of the job."

Poli sighed and took another glance at the picture before putting it back into his pocket. He stretched his feet out and looked at his new boat shoes. "I really like the shoes you bought me." He bounced the toes off each other. "They look … awesome," he said, using a word he just learned from Sandy.

"They're more than just for looks," Donovan remarked. He rested his left elbow on the door. "If there was time, we'd drop by the restaurant to get you some work clothes."

"Too bad," Poli mused. "My mother could have made us some cochinito taquitos," he said, referring to the Mayan delicacy of shredded steamed pork wrapped in a hot corn tortilla. "They're my stepfather's favorite."

"Stepfather?" Donovan scrunched his brows and turned to look at Poli. "I thought Benício was your father?"

"Oh, no." Poli shook his head softly. "He's my stepfather. My real father died working on an oil platform when I was five years old."

"I'm sorry to hear that."

"It's okay. I hardly remember him," Poli commented unsentimentally. "My mother still misses him. She's always telling Benício how much I'm like him."

"Doesn't that bother your stepfather?"

"I think he understands that she misses him." Poli looked out to the side, "Sometimes, when she thinks she's alone, she still cries for him. I don't understand it. He's been dead for eleven years." He looked at Donovan. "She should get over it."

Donovan stared at the road ahead and sighed. "You never get over the people you love."

"I tell her she's married to Benício now and that she should forget my father." He shook his head. "She treats him more like an uncle than a husband."

His remark intrigued Donovan. "How so?"

"They almost never kiss, and when they do"—he tapped his index finger on the side of his face—"it's on the cheek."

Donovan chuckled. "That's how married people kiss."

"It's more than just that. They never do anything together." He let out a long sigh. "I kind of feel sorry for Benício. Maybe that's why he spends so much time with Lázaro."

"Who's Lázaro?"

"Benício's cousin. He's a panguero like him." He put his hand out and watched it catch the wind like the wing of an airplane when he cupped his hand slightly. "They're together right now, mending one of Lázaro's nets."

"What happened to his net?"

"I don't know. I think he got it caught on something. Sometimes, he isn't very careful about what he's doing." Poli turned to Donovan, dipping his head slightly as if to confide some dark secret. "He used to be an alcohólico." He looked back at his outstretched hand. "He doesn't drink anymore."

Donovan looked at him. "What made him stop?"

"Benício." He brought his hand back inside. "I think that's why Benício's with him so much. To keep an eye on him."

"What does your mother think about that?"

He stuck his hand out again to play with the wind. "I think she likes being by herself." He changed the angle of his hand, allowing his hand to rise slowly. "She spends a lot of time alone in her bedroom with her things." He changed the angle again and watched his hand slowly drop. "She doesn't like for anyone to go into her room when she's in there."

A thought came to Donovan, and he had to consider carefully before he posed his next question. "Doesn't Benício have to go in there at bedtime?"

"Benício has his own bedroom."

Suddenly, stopping by the restaurant to get work clothes for Poli didn't seem like such a bad idea to Donovan. He ran his eyes over Poli's clothes and then put them back on the road. "Are those your school clothes?" He slowed the convertible down when he saw the sign marking the approach of the Seyba Playa exit. "They look pretty new."

Poli pulled on his shirt with both hands. "My mother just bought them for me."

"They're too nice to work in." Donovan reached into his shirt pocket to get some pesos to pay the toll. "We'd better stop by the restaurant to get you some work clothes."

His face lit up. "All right! Cochinito tacos!"

The few people who lived near the house nestled in the thicket in the hills east of Seyba Playa dared not talk openly of their new neighbors. Only the foolish would speak of what they thought went on in the old shack and then only in half whispers. The wise paid no attention to the men behind the dark-tinted windows of the sports utility vehicles and pickup trucks that went up the winding dirt road, like the black Ford Excursion that raised a thick, spiraling cloud of dust behind it.

The rolling cloud of dust made one last spiral behind the black Ford Excursion as it came to a stop in front of the wood-framed house in need of paint and a new roof. The guard posted outside the house opened the door slightly and announced the arrival of their boss, Fausto López.

Felipe opened the door for El Demonio, who removed his sunglasses to walk into the two-room house, deliberately kept dark with black trash bags taped over the windows. Two of El Perro's men sitting on an old couch stood immediately, while the three sitting at a small round table at the back of the room made an effort to stand. Fausto gestured for them to keep their seats as Dario and Beto followed Felipe into the house. The oldest sicario sitting at the table stood anyway and went to stand by an old, rust-stained refrigerator by the table.

"Bienvenido, jefe," the old sicario said. "Can I get you something to drink?"

"Where's Comandante Escalante?" El Demonio demanded.

A gut-retching scream rang out from the back room, answering his question. "El Perro will be with you shortly," the old sicario replied.

After a moment, the door opened slowly as the leader of Los Perros walked into the front room, wiping his hands on a bloodstained towel. He rubbed the spots of blood and sweat from his bare chest and then did the same with his face.

"Did you find out how the marina knew about the guns?"

Comandante Escalante looked at the men standing around Fausto, taking his time to finish drying the sweat from his face. "He didn't know anything." He tossed the towel aside. "He was just a stupid corporal."

"Was?"

El Perro nodded his head subtly. "I had to make sure he told me everything he knew." He inhaled sharply and raised his brows. "I guess even a lemon only has so much juice to give."

"Very amusing," Fausto remarked. "If you hadn't been so eager to kill the petty officer, you might have learned how the marina knew about my guns."

"He was practically dead when I shot him." He glared at him sternly. "He probably didn't know any more than that pinche cabo anyway."

Fausto pinched the bridge of his nose, closed his eyes, and expelled his breath through his nostrils. "Did the corporal say anything that might be helpful before he died?"

El Perro turned to the old sicario reclining against the refrigerator. He snapped his fingers repeatedly and then held out the palm of his hand. The sicario opened the refrigerator to get a bottle of water and handed it to Comandante Escalante.

"He said that a teniente named Baeza ordered the checkpoint."

"Baeza?" Fausto drew back. "Not the same Baeza that gave us trouble in Tamaulipas?"

"Baeza is a common name." El Perro shrugged. "I don't think it's the same man. Why would they send him here?"

"You're probably right." Fausto looked to the side. "Nobody knows I'm here." He sighed and then turned to El Perro. "Did he say anything else?"

Comandante Escalante twisted the top off the bottle. "Only that he's had the infantes out almost every night for the last month." He took a sip. "I think the marineros just got lucky."

Two subtle knocks on the front door interrupted the conversation. The guard stuck his head in. "José Luis is here."

José Luis Ortega made his reputation working for the Domínguez brothers and the Frontera cartel as a transporter. He came to work for Don Rodrigo and the Campechanos in a swap with the Domínguez brothers, trading his expertise as a transporter for a referral to a trusted Colombian supplier. The slender Mexican had a taste for stylish clothing, favoring light-colored, tropical-weight sports coats; linen pants; and Italian shoes. When the weather permitted, he wore dressy leather sports coats and matching ankle-high boots. He kept his hair stylishly full and sported a thin Errol Flynn–style mustache. He fancied expensive silk shirts he liked to wear with the collar open to show off the gold mariner's anchor cross and the figure of a small panga dangling at the ends of two thick gold chains.

"Did you get it?" Fausto asked José Luis.

José Luis looked at the men in the room as the guard closed the front door behind him. His eyes stopped when they got to Dario. He looked at Fausto. "We need to talk."

The apprehension on his face disquieted El Demonio. He turned to Comandante Escalante. "Clear the room."

"You heard el jefe," El Perro said to his men. "Andale, cabrones. ¡Vamanos!"

As Comandante Escalante's sicarios filed out the front door, José Luis watched Dario out of the corner of his eye. After the last man shut the door behind him, Fausto walked up to José Luis.

"Did something happen to my cocaine?"

The transport specialist drew a breath and then exhaled. "Chacho was picked up by a patrol boat."

"¡Chinga su madre!" Fausto cursed the panguero's mother. He began to pace like a caged lion.

"Don't worry. Your cocaine is safe. Capitán Santos spotted the patrol boat before he got to the rendezvous."

"Why was Chacho picked up?"

"The pendejo had a gun on him."

"Pinche buey," Fausto cursed.

"You were lucky, Fausto." Dario tried to calm his cousin. "At least you still have your cocaine."

"Lucky?" Fausto muttered to himself. "Lucky that the marines stumbled on my guns or lucky that I didn't get my cocaine?"

"The Armada is always inspecting catches off the Seyba Reef," Dario added. "You're lucky that Capitán Santos spotted the patrol boat before he met the panguero."

José Luis turned an eye to Fausto, the other he kept on Dario. "Santos said that the patrol boat weaved through a group of fishing boats to get to Chacho."

"They must have been targeting the panga," Felipe commented. "If they were out inspecting catches, why did they ignore the fishing boats? They're always getting caught snaring turtles with their nets."

"I spoke with our friend at the naval zone," José Luis interjected. He glanced at Dario before continuing, "She said that a new intelligence officer is the one who sent the patrol boat to look for Chacho's panga west of the Seyba Reef."

"Did she give the intelligence officer's name."

"Baeza," he responded. "Teniente Baeza."

"Baeza?" Fausto looked at El Perro. "Do you still think it's not the same man?"

Comandante Escalante took a sip of water and then shrugged his shoulders. "You worry too much. We can handle him, if it is him."

"Why don't we send him a message?" Felipe suggested.

"I've already taken care of that." His suggestion offended Comandante Escalate. "At the Lorenzo paradero."

"I mean a personal message," Felipe added. "One just for him."

"Yes," Fausto said softly. He turned to Escalante. "Send him a personal message."

The ruthless comandante sneered at Felipe. He went to the refrigerator and took out a plastic shopping bag. The bag sagged like it had a head of cabbage in it. He glanced viciously at Felipe before handing the bag to El Demonio.

"Will this do?"

Fausto looked in the plastic bag. The petty officer's cold, dead eyes gazed emptily at him. "Maybe the petty officer can be useful after all." He chuckled fiendishly.

"I can cut the cabo's head off and put it with this one and leave them on the marina's doorstep in Lerma with a personal message for Baeza."

Fausto's odd-colored eyes narrowed. He twisted his face into a fiendish grin as he gave the bag back to Escalante. "Do it."

"Are you sure that's a good idea?" Dario said to his cousin. "Do you think it's wise to antagonize the marina any further?"

Despite his distrust and lack of respect for Dario, José Luis had to agree with him. "He's right, Fausto. Why stir a hornet's nest? The message at the paradero is enough."

"He has to learn respect," El Demonio said through his teeth.

"The teniente is not the problem." José Luis turned his head subtly toward Dario before looking at Fausto. "How Baeza knew where to find Chacho is. He was way beyond where the pangas usually go to fish. I don't understand why they ignored the fishing boats?"

"What are you suggesting?"

"I would think it was obvious." He put his hands in the pockets of his trousers and stepped toward the center of the room. He looked at each person there except for Dario before turning to El Demonio. "We have an informer among us."

"That's insane," Fausto dismissed the suggestion.

"Then explain how the marina just happened to be at Punta Morro at the precise time your guns were coming through?"

"Comandante Escalante said it before you got here," Dario interjected. "The marina just got lucky."

"Lucky?" José Luis took a step toward Dario. "It's a big ocean." He approached Dario like a prosecutor cross-examining a witness. "Teniente Baeza knew when and where to send the patrol boat. How do you explain that?" He looked at the others. "There is an informer among us."

"It's not any of my people," El Perro retorted. He looked at Fausto. "If there is an informer, it has to be one of yours."

"Impossible." Fausto turned to José Luis. "If there was an informer, why did the Armada jump Chacho before he could meet the Pemex boat? Hmm?" He glared at José Luis. "It's because they didn't know about the Pemex boat."

"Maybe Chacho told somebody where he was going?"

"I don't think so," José Luis disagreed. "He's a poacher. Poachers know how to keep their mouths shut about what they're doing."

"What about the Pemex captain?" Felipe added. "He is a dog. He might have let it slip to one of his viejas." He chuckled. "Remember, if he wasn't such a lady's man, he wouldn't be working for us."

"If Santos had let it slip to one of his viejas, why did the patrol boat jump Chacho and not him?" José Luis glanced at Dario and then turned to Fausto. "Somebody in this room is talking to Teniente Baeza."

"There's no informer." Fausto glowered at him. "You're just being paranoid."

"Maybe I am." José Luis stared contemptuously at Dario. "Maybe not." He rolled his eyes to Fausto, "In the meantime, how are you going to get the merchandise from the Arcas cays?" He scoffed. "Chacho's no good to us anymore."

"I already have one in mind." Fausto grinned nefariously.

Felipe squinted his eyes dubiously. "You don't mean that fat little preacher in town?"

"Why not?" Fausto's grin turned even more sinister. "He owes me."

"For what, primo?" Dario interjected. "Dónovan paid off the outboard motor."

"That's not what I mean," he responded angrily. "Nobody turns me down."

"How do you plan to get him to make the run?" José Luis asked. "He made it clear he won't do it."

"He would have done it if Dónovan hadn't interfered," Fausto retorted.

"Why not use the same approach we did with Capitán Santos," Felipe suggested.

"I doubt you'll be able to get the reverendo into bed with a prostitute," José Luis remarked. He scoffed. "Who are you going to find more beautiful than the woman he's married to?"

"I don't mean him. I'm talking about Lázaro. His cousin. The borachín," Felipe explained. He used to be quite the cantinero." He chuckled. "Como le gustaba las gorditas. He was always trying to screw fat girls."

"Do you think you can do with him what you did to Santos?" Fausto asked Felipe.

"If I can get him drunk"—Felipe rolled out his lower lip—"it shouldn't be any problem."

"He no longer drinks," Dario remarked.

Felipe put his palms up and shrugged his shoulders. "So we make him have a relapse."

"How does that get the Reverend Benício to make the run?" José Luis asked.

"The reason Lázaro no longer drinks is because of Benício. He pulled him out of the gutter and showed him how to fish." Felipe dipped his head to reassure Fausto. "He'll do anything to help his cousin."

"I should have thought about that to start with," Fausto remarked. He snickered wickedly. "We were using the wrong bait to hook the fisher of men." His face grew cold as he turned to Felipe. "Make it happen."

By late morning, the breakfast rush had come and gone, and business at the Cocina Maya gradually dwindled to a trickle. Even though she had the food already prepared and ready to serve, breakfast always taxed Itzél. It came in spurts, so she had little trouble managing the hungry hordes and used the downtime in between to catch her breath. That morning, however, the rush wore her down like a herd of stampeding wildebeests.

As a matter of practice, she dressed in traditional clothing worn by Mayan women in keeping with the theme of the restaurant. She had her raven hair wound into a tight bun behind her head, and she wore an embroidered white blouse with a wide neck tucked snugly into a red skirt. By the end of the rush, the bun had lost its integrity and her blouse had lost its tuck.

By eleven, the breakfast rush had come and gone, giving Itzél two hours to freshen up and prepare for la comida. At times, a straggler or two stopped by for a cup of coffee and a pastry or a breakfast taquito. She never turned a customer away and gladly waited on them all without it interfering much with her routine.

Itzél raised her eyes when she heard the bell over the door jingle sharply as she poured coffee into the cups of an old couple sitting at a table near the entrance. It surprised her to see her son burst through the door. Her surprise turned to absolute horror when she saw Donovan through the window, walking a few steps behind him.

"Hola, Mamá," he greeted her.

"Poli," she said nervously. "What are you doing here?" She brushed an unruly lock of hair out of her face and pulled awkwardly on her clothes as she finished pouring coffee into the old man's cup. Poli dashed past her without answering.

She glanced briefly at Donovan before walking briskly behind the counter to return the coffeepot to its warmer. She tried to fix her clothes, covering her exposed shoulders and tucking her blouse back into her skirt. She raised her hands to put her hair back into place as she turned around. She gasped when she saw Donovan standing across the counter from her.

"Capitán Dónovan." She turned her head. "I didn't expect to see you until this weekend."

The toilet flushing distracted him before he could answer. A few moments later, Poli walked out of the bathroom and joined his mother behind the counter.

"Sorry, Mamá, for not answering your question. I had to go to the bathroom."

"I thought you weren't coming home until this weekend." She brushed a speck of lint off the front of his shirt and noticed his new boat shoes. "Where did you get those funny-looking shoes?"

Donovan glanced briefly at his own shoes and then cleared his throat. "The soles on the shoes he was wearing were too slick to work on a wet deck."

She shook her head at her son and clicked her tongue. "He has tennis shoes he could have used." She went to the cash register and opened the drawer. "How much for the shoes?"

"That's all right." Donovan held up his hand. "It's a work expense."

The bell over the door chimed as the old couple left the Cocina Maya.

"Gracias," Itzél thanked them cheerfully as they walked out the door.

"Capitán Dónovan brought me here so that I can get some clothes for work," Poli told his mother.

"What's wrong with the ones I packed for you?"

"Um …" Donovan swallowed. "He needs something more comfortable and a little less dressy to work the deck."

She looked at him curiously and then turned to her son. "Don't keep the capitán waiting. Go get your old clothes."

"Sí, Mamá."

Poli darted down the hallway and up the stairs, leaving his mother alone with Donovan. As she walked toward the hallway to wait for her son, he looked at the soft contours of her body and the way her disheveled hair dangled across the side of her head. He couldn't imagine her looking unattractive under any circumstance or any kind of light. She had bewitched him since he first saw her. However, like a magic charm, her marriage to Benício and the belief that she had a child with him had broken the spell. What he had learned that morning had taken the charm from its magic.

The restaurant seemed a lot smaller now that he had her to himself. He thought he knew exactly what he wanted to tell her, but he couldn't find the words. His tongue felt thick and a thousand thoughts bounced inside his head. He had to talk to her and he searched desperately for how to begin.

"He's really a good-looking boy."

She looked over her shoulder at him. Her eyes had a soft, melancholic glow as she smiled dolefully at him. "He's looks just like his father."

"Poli told me about his father," he said reverently. "I'm sorry for your loss."

"He's so much like him." She sighed and looked away. "It scares me sometimes."

He remembered what Poli told him about crying for her late husband. He wondered if he could live in his shadow, like Benício apparently did. He could hear Poli rummaging upstairs, and he didn't want to spend what little time he would have with her talking about her dead husband.

"I like the pattern on your blouse," Donovan said, hoping to redirect the tone of the conversation.

She smiled at him and daintily put her fingertips on the intricate pattern around the collar. "I embroidered it myself."

"It's beautiful." He looked into her eyes. "It really brings out your eyes."

"Gracias," she said coyly. She lowered her head to keep him from noticing that she was blushing.

"Where'd you get that pattern?" Donovan asked. "Did it come to you in a dream, or does it represent the village you're from?"

Itzél looked at him curiously. "How do you know so much about Indian culture?"

He did not want to explain to her how he knew that. He looked for a way to answer her question without compromising the secret he wanted to hide. "I had a friend a long time ago who knew a lot about indígenas."

"Was she an Indian?" Itzél asked perceptively.

Again, she had set him back. "What makes you think my friend was a she?"

"It's in your face." She walked to him and gazed into his eyes. "She must have been very important to you."

He felt a tingle run through him, and he inhaled deeply. "It scares me sometimes," he muttered, almost inaudibly as he released his breath.

SIERRA DE SANTA MARTA, VERACRUZ
SIX YEARS EARLIER

He left the city of Veracruz just after taking breakfast in a rented Chevrolet Suburban headed south along the coast toward Coatzacoalcos, bound for a village on the side of an extinct volcano known as El Cerro San Martin Pajapan, high in the Sierra de Santa Marta. The coast road took him past rustic fishing hamlets and unspoiled beaches known to few outside of the locals. At times, the road would ascend the side of a mountain to overlook rocky points and the indigo-blue waters of the Gulf of Mexico. After a relatively short forty-mile drive, he reached the picturesque port city of Alvarado, driving over the long bridge over the wide mouth of the Papaloapan River. He felt that at his current pace he would reach his destination sooner than the hotel concierge had told him. When he turned off the coast road to begin his drive toward the volcano, he understood what the concierge meant when he told him that it would be unwise to get in too much of a hurry.

The road to San Martin Pajapan immediately transported him to a time he thought long past. Never had he seen such sheer beauty as he saw that day. In his travels, he had seen many amazing and wondrous, if not baffling, things. It defied his sense of understanding how there could still be areas so underdeveloped existing in the shadows of the modern world. He weaved through jungle, at times so dense that it seemed he would be devoured by it, and broken terrain with precipitous drops, looking down upon angry streams that meant certain death for the unsure of foot.

As he drove along the narrow road that wound around the side of the mountain, he glanced briefly across a wide chasm over a particularly steep drop. He took a second look when he thought he saw a child pressed against the far rock wall, standing precariously on a narrow trail. The child snapped his head to glare at him, giving him a start. His face, withered and wrinkled like that of an old man, glared at him malignantly.

Donovan felt the left front tire leaving the road and jerked the wheel sharply to the right to keep from falling into the deep gorge. When he looked back across the chasm, the childlike being had disappeared. He slowed the Suburban to a near stop, unsettled by both what he thought he had seen and his near calamitous fall. He felt his heart in his throat and could hardly catch his breath.

He finally reached the village, emerging out of a cloud of white dust trailing behind the Suburban as he pulled in front of a white cinder block building, apparently the largest building and the only one in the tiny hamlet that did not have a thatched roof. A group of small children gathered around the driver's side, waiting for him to step out of the monstrous vehicle. They looked on in awe at what must have seemed to them a giant when Donovan stepped out of the Suburban. They stood silently, staring at him with their mouths agape and full of wonder.

"Hola, niños," he greeted them.

The oldest child, perhaps six or seven, let out a playful shriek and led the band of screaming little urchins around the side of the cinder block building. Donovan chuckled to himself as he walked toward the rear of the Suburban. He pretended not to notice the children as, one by one, they stuck their heads from around the corner to sneak another glance at him. Without warning, he jumped from behind the Suburban and held his hands out like claws, growling ferociously. The smallest one let out a scream, followed by the others as they snapped their heads back behind the side of the building.

"You have to forgive them," a young Mexican man dressed in a black short-sleeved shirt with a clerical collar said to him. "The children are not used to seeing tall people."

"You probably don't get many foreigners coming around here." Donovan winked at the littlest girl, who dared sneak another peek at him.

"Actually, more than you'd think," the priest said as he walked toward him. "There are volcanologists from all over the world coming to study the volcanos of the Los Tuxtlas volcanic field. From time to time, one strays into the village." He offered his hand. "I'm Padre Fernández. You must be Señor Dónovan."

"Mucho gusto. Pleased to meet you." Donovan shook his hand. He gazed aimlessly at the distant hills he had driven earlier.

"Is there something wrong?"

"No, nothing's wrong." Donovan turned to look at the priest and hesitated. He drew a deep breath and exhaled sharply. "I thought I saw what I thought was a strange-looking child walking on the side of a cliff."

The priest looked at him warily. "Was the child bald?"

He nodded his head softly. "Yeah."

"His face twisted or withered like a prune?"

His eyes widened. "I thought it was an old man."

"Did he have any clothes on?"

Donovan rolled his eyes briefly to the side. "Come to think of it, I don't think he did."

"Hmm." The priest dropped his head. "What you saw was a chaneque." He looked at Donovan. "A sort of goblin."

"I thought priests didn't believe in that stuff."

He chuckled. "It's our practice to be familiar with the local folklore." He smiled at Donovan. "According to myth, the chaneque are the guardians of the hills, the streams, even the wind. They resent intruders and often attack them by scaring them, forcing their souls from their bodies without killing them."

Donovan swallowed hard. "How do you know if your soul has been forced from your body?"

"It is believed that an affected person will become listless. If the soul is not recovered, that person will become ill and die." He raised his brows and sighed. "Some Mexicans believe that the chaneque are the souls of unbaptized children who turn into harmful demons that prey on the living, luring them into an early death."

"How do they do that?"

"They play tricks on you, trying to confuse you so that you make a fatal mistake."

"Like driving off a cliff?"

The priest looked curiously at Donovan. "Is that what happened to you?"

Their conversation was suddenly interrupted by a woman dressed in a lab coat calling from the entrance to the building. "Have you been scaring the children?" The precocious little girl who had dared to sneak a second peek at Donovan stood behind the woman, hiding behind the tail of her lab coat.

"Your medical supplies are here, Doctora Tonatzin," the padre said.

Xochitl walked up to Donovan, leaving the little urchin standing in the doorway. She looked sternly at him. "Why are you scaring the children?"

"I was just having fun with them." He looked at the precocious little girl and winked at her. She threw her hands over her head, screamed, and stutter-stepped behind the building.

The stern look left Xochitl's eyes as she laughed at the little girl's playful flight. She smiled at Donovan and threw her arms around his neck. "It's good to see you, Simon."

Donovan leaned over to kiss Xochitl but stopped when he heard the children giggling. The children had abandoned the side of the building and stood in the open staring at them. Padre Fernández shooed them away. Xochitl released Donovan's neck when she saw a young woman helping an older one walk up the hill toward them.

"Who are they?" Donovan asked.

"A couple of my patients."

"By the way you ripped your arms away from me, I thought one of them was your mother."

"Shut up." Xochitl snickered as she slapped him on the arm. "The younger woman is bringing her mother-in-law in for a physical examination."

The two women both wore white blouses that were colorfully embroidered with a rainbow of colors in a pattern approximating a waterfall. They both wore a red wrap-like garment around their hips and legs. The young woman was pretty and apparently cared for the old woman as she lovingly helped her up the hill. The old woman smiled pleasantly at Donovan as she whispered something in the younger woman's ear. They both looked at Donovan and smiled at him.

"Buenos tardes, señoritas," he greeted them, turning his head to the side and bowing slightly.

Neither woman said anything, politely bowing their heads in response as they walked toward the building. The clothing the women wore interested Donovan. "I've always wondered why the native women dress in those clothes."

"Tradition." Xochitl took Donovan by the hand. "They make the blouses themselves."

"Really?" Donovan commented. "I thought they all got them at some native outlet mall. They all seem to wear the same thing."

"If you look closely, you'll see that they are all quite different. Every village more or less adheres to a basic pattern. Here, it's a waterfall. In the next village, it's a tree. Some women claim that the designs come to them in a dream."

After shooing the children away, Padre Fernández went to guide the old woman into the clinic. Her advanced age caused Donovan to wonder.

"Are you sure that's her mother-in-law?" He whispered to Xochitl as he smiled at the old woman. "She looks more like her grandmother."

"Mamá Tlalli had thirteen boys." Xochitl whispered. "She married the youngest one."

Padre Fernández glanced briefly at Xochitl and Donovan as he helped the older woman through the door. The younger woman, her face nearly expressionless, raised her eyes to look at Donovan and then quickly averted them as she followed the padre and her mother-in-law into the building. The priest said something in Náhuatl to the younger woman, who shook her head as she followed him through the door.

"Do you understand their language?"

"A lot of it," Xochitl replied. "The variation of Náhuatl they speak is different from the one I know."

He scrunched his brows. "I thought Náhuatl was Náhuatl."

"Mmm, mmm." She shook her head. "Their dialect has been influenced by the Popoluca, who share these mountains with them and Proto-Maya." Xochitl looked at him. "So, what did you bring me?"

"Just a few things I was able to scrounge around town," he said to her as he led her behind the Suburban. "Gauze, bandages, Q-tips. Things like that."

She pulled out a cardboard box and opened the flaps. "Penicillin! Epinephrine!" She looked suspiciously at him. "Where did you get these?"

"I did some trading with the people I know."

"How did you get them into the country?"

"That's what I do." He chuckled. "Don't worry. I didn't break any laws. The way I got them in was perfectly legal ... sort of."

"Mamá," Poli called down the stairs, "where's my swimming things?"

Donovan looked up at him. "Swimming things?"

"He means this thing he puts on his face with a plastic tube he uses to swim underwater."

"You mean a diving mask and snorkel." Donovan chuckled.

Itzél put her hands on her hips. "What's so funny?"

"Nothing." Donovan put his hands up and shook his head. "Finding swimming things is serious business."

"Never mind," Poli called back down. "I found them."

Itzél glared at Donovan intensely. The grin on his face faded as the two gazed into each other's eyes. She snickered, and they both began to laugh.

"You have a wonderful laugh," Donovan said to her.

"It's just a silly laugh." She dismissed the compliment.

"You deserve to laugh all the time," he said boldly. "A woman like you should never be sad."

They gazed at each other silently with the same intensity they had on the day they met. Donovan could see her chest rising and falling gently as she breathed. He felt his own chest want to burst. Neither heard Poli running down the staircase, nor did they take notice of the subtle jingle of the bell over the door.

Benício walked through the door with a smile on his face like he normally had after a good day at the reef. The smile left his face when he saw his wife gazing deeply into Donovan's eyes. He watched them for a moment, neither aware of his presence. They looked at each other like two lovers about to kiss, and they might have had they not been standing so far apart. He cleared his throat to get their attention. Itzél's eyes widened with surprise while Donovan turned away to hide the guilt he knew showed on his face.

Poli burst through the hallway, unknowingly coming to Donovan's rescue.

"I'm ready," he told Donovan.

"Good." He glanced briefly at Benício. "You ready to go back to work?"

"All set." Poli held out his sports bag. Part of the snorkel protruded through the zipper.

"Time to shove off, then."

"Adiós, Mamá." Poli kissed his mother on the cheek.

"Vaya con Díos, mijo," Benício said as he watched him go to the door.

"Gracias, Benício." The bell chimed once as Poli pushed the door open with his behind. "Oh, I almost forgot." He let the door shut as he walked briskly back to his mother's side. He handed her the picture Don Macario had taken of him with the crew. "This is for you."

She looked at the picture and smiled. "Thank you, mijo." Itzél handed the picture to Benício, who looked at it before handing it back to her.

"Capitán Donovan says that I'm going to drive the boat," Poli announced proudly.

They both looked at Donovan, who cringed at Poli's choice of words. "He means steer the ship."

"Do you believe that's wise, Capitán?" Benício asked.

"By this time next year, he'll not only be able to steer the ship," Donovan looked proudly at Poli, "he'll be able to do it in the dark."

"Let's shove off, Skipper?" Poli said as he headed for the door.

Donovan tipped his head to Itzél and then at Benício before heading out the door. While Benício went to the front window to watch the big red convertible drive away, Itzél went to the cash register and opened it. She stared at the picture, smiling proudly at the image of her son at the helm. She turned her eyes at Donovan standing next to him and subconsciously rubbed her thumb on his image.

"Capitán Dónovan is a very handsome man," Benício commented as he watched the convertible disappear around the curve by the entrance to the port.

Itzél slipped the picture under the tray and closed the drawer. "He's okay, I guess."

CHAPTER

6

The carrack dwarfed the sloop sitting next to her in the tranquil waters off Siho Playa Point. The carrack had beautiful lines and her rigging artistically balanced compared to the sloop's functional design. The sails on her square-rigged fore and main masts and lateen-rigged mizzenmast fluttered gently in the light wind, her masts reaching higher over her deck than the single bare pole jutting from the center of the smaller vessel. Her deck ran twice as long as the sloop. It had three levels with a two-tiered afterdeck and a raised foredeck. Her heavier crossed bowsprit reached out three times farther than the simple spar projecting ahead of the sloop.

It had been an hour since Mr. Brown had led the landing party beyond the tree line of coconut palms to gather provisions. The captain stood on the beach a few feet from the water's edge above where the landing party had beached the launches. As the captain trained his spyglass to the north on the rocky precipice rising above the point, the cox'n and his mate waited by the boats in ankle-deep water, each armed with a blunderbuss, watching his side of the beach for trouble.

The cox'n brought his weapon to the ready. "Movement in the palms, Cap'n."

The captain lowered his glass and tucked it snugly into his bucket-top boot. He put his hand on the hilt of his cutlass as he turned to look across the narrow belt of white sand at the coconut palms. Wary that the movement could be a Spanish patrol or a band of their feathered allies, he slowly drew the short sword from its scabbard, waiting to see what would emerge.

He released a long sigh and slipped the cutlass back into place when he saw the first group of men come out of the palms. In their hands, they carried heavy casks of water, sacks of fruit, and firewood. The captain smiled when he saw two mates carrying a large, rudely dressed pig tied by its feet to a stick on their shoulders between them.

Some of the men went shirtless and bare of foot, wearing only the knee-high breeches common to them all. Others wore loose-fitting shirts made of linen or a coarse cotton fabric, stockings, and straight shoes or crudely made sandals. Many wore scarves tied behind their heads or long knitted caps knotted at the end. One wore a floppy, wide-brimmed hat, the front of which folded back with the wind as he balanced a log on his shoulder.

A boatswain covered the crew's flanks, armed with a musket and a sharp tongue to hurry the crew along. The man leading the landing party, the quartermaster, covered the rear with a cutlass in his hand and two flintlock pistols tucked into his waist. Unlike the crew, the boatswain dressed in the uniform of the Royal Navy from which he had deserted, while the quartermaster, a ruggedly handsome man, dressed in a bright cross-tucked blue linen shirt; buff-colored breeches; and black bucket-top boots.

As the captain, a large man not yet thirty years of age, waited for his second-in-command to join him, he looked over his shoulder to admire the prize awarded to him by his mentor, Christopher Myngs, for his part in the successful raid of San Francisco de Campeche up the coast.

"Have you ever seen a sight more beautiful, Mr. Brown?"

The quartermaster looked on the merchant ship resting gracefully on the gently lapping emerald water offshore. The dying rays of the setting sun glowed softly around the contours of the ship's oaken hull like a halo. The carrack's rigging pierced the brilliantly colored vertical walls of the thunderhead rising quickly behind it.

"I still prefer the sloop, Captain," he commented. "She's faster and more maneuverable in battle."

"Aye, Mr. Brown, she was a good ship, but she has no real firepower." He returned his eyes to the merchant vessel. "The carrack is much bigger and can handle the cannons we took from the Spanish in Campeachey. They'll give us greater range and more punch than the puny two-pounders aboard the sloop. Her hold can carry much more provisions and ammunition and still have plenty of room to store the spoils we take."

"At a price, Captain," Mr. Brown pointed out to him. "You'll be sacrificing speed in battle."

"She'll be fast enough," the captain responded. The tail of his white linen shirt had worked its way out of his wine-colored breeches. "What I give up in speed, I'll make up in firepower and tactics." As he crossed-tucked his shirt into his breeches, he noticed a small blue crab sidestepping toward the tips of his brown leather bucket-top boots. "From high on her aftercastle, I'll have a bird's-eye view unlike what I had on the sloop's flat deck." He looked down on the blue crab, raising his right boot. "I'll be able to look down on the enemy and smash him." He brought his boot down, crushing the little crab. "Like that."

The quartermaster looked at the thunderhead. A flash of lightning silently exploded through the heart of the angry storm cloud rising.

The scratchy-voiced cox'n walked up to the quartermaster. "I feel duh devil's in dem clouds, Mr. Brown. Duh men are done loading duh boats. We'd best be getting on back to duh ship."

"Thank you, Jacobo." Mr. Brown turned to the captain. "After you, Captain Morgan."

The old mahogany bar and back cabinet at the Paradise Lounge heralded from the prohibition era in the United States. Don Macario bought the intricately detailed relic of the days of gangsters and speakeasies at an estate sale in New Orleans. It once belonged to an old bootlegger who used to smuggle liquor into New Orleans from Mexico, hidden in shipments of henequen and sugarcane. His lawyer took possession of it after the bootlegger met an early end at the hands of a rival, and it had been in the shyster's family ever since.

Pablo, the barman, spent as much time extricating dust from every corner of the ornately handcrafted bar and polishing the long brass foot rest and all its joints as he did managing the lounge. He had an intense dislike for dust and tarnish, and he saw to it that none should find the slightest repose on the bar he regarded as his own.

The clientele at that hour of the day varied between local businessmen stopping by after work to wind down under the slow turning antique ceiling fans and a few hotel guests looking for a drink before taking dinner at the hotel restaurant. Some came to listen to the soothing mixture of mellow jazz and samba that played softly throughout the tropical-style lounge while others came to enjoy pleasant and at times lively conversation.

The adult members of the crew of the Siete Mares also came to the lounge at the end of the workday normally to enjoy lively conversation with their landlord and share his love of jazz and samba, but on occasion, they came to talk business. Although Augie's dive shop served as the official business office for Seven Seas Adventure Cruises, Donovan and Augie preferred to discuss business with their clients at the Paradise Lounge. That afternoon, they had a meeting with their best client, Dr. Conrado Aurelio Ventura of the National Institute of Anthropology and History.

Dr. Ventura had the distinction of holding a coveted position as a professor emeritus with the institute. Before retiring, he held a tenured professorship at the Autonomous University of Yucatán in Mérida where he earned a reputation as a world-renowned expert on Mesoamerican civilization. Since taking the position at the institute, the professor also developed a reputation for his sometimes Quixotic pursuit of myths and legends.

He did not conform to the traditional image most people had of academics. He did not wear his hair in a tangled shock or a worn-out tweed jacket, nor did he smoke a pipe. He barely spent any time in the musty halls of the national archives and rarely gave long, tiresome lectures at university auditoriums. He preferred the outdoors and had competed in the Olympics as an archer in his youth. His skills also included marksmanship, mountaineering, scuba diving, sky diving, spelunking, and sailing.

The professor looked more like an aging war correspondent than a university scholar. He maintained a trim physique, relatively speaking, and had twenty-twenty vision thanks to laser surgery. He did, however, require the use of reading glasses. Never in his life had he sported a mustache, goatee, or Vandyke, although he did always seem to have a case of five o'clock shadow. He had a full head of mostly dark hair, which he swore he did not dye, with some graying on the sides. He kept it stylishly trimmed.

He had a fondness for gadgets, cameras, and understandably, pockets. He always wore cargo pants and photographer's vests no matter what the occasion. The loose-fitting clothes and hiking boots he liked to wear made him look more like a man on a quest to photograph a condor nest high up a mountain than some intellectual on his way to the library.

Dr. Ventura specialized in marine archeology and had made several groundbreaking discoveries relating to Mayan religious and cultural practices in the many underground rivers that flowed under the limestone of the Yucatán Peninsula. He also had an uncanny ability to sniff out significant shipwrecks from among the countless wrecks in the Bay of Campeche. However, the good professor also pursued legends, running down what most in his field considered nothing more than folk tales. One that he especially pursued involved a lost Lockheed Electra laden with priceless Mayan artifacts stolen by a Nazi archeologist in 1936.

If not for the good professor and the National Institute of Anthropology and History, Seven Seas Adventure Cruises would have surely gone out of business.

"Good afternoon, everyone," the professor greeted them as he took his seat across from Don Macario.

"When are you gonna cut us in on what we're going to do at the Sabancuy Channel?" Augie asked.

"I'm sorry about the secrecy, but you know how it is if it gets out that I'm working on a project."

"We're not the ones who like getting our pictures in the paper," Augie retorted.

"I'm afraid courting the media is a necessary evil," the professor said. "For me to do my work, I need funding. To get it, I have to generate publicity for the institute." He hunched his shoulders, "The more I generate, the more willing the institute is to fund my projects."

Augie scoffed. "You mean the more reporters come snooping around the ship."

"You don't seem to mind when the reporter is a woman," Don Macario teased.

"What about that?" Donovan chuckled. "I don't see you threatening to kick any of their butts."

"You have to treat a lady different than you do a man," he said humbly. "It ain't polite."

"I do my best to be discreet," the professor added, "but somehow, it gets leaked out to the press."

"I thought courting the press was how you raised money?" Donovan commented.

"It is, but the timing has to be right," he explained. "An inaccurate story or a misleading report could blunt the effect of any success I hope to achieve."

"That sounds like a whole lot of bilge to me," Augie muttered.

"So, Conrad," Donovan cleared his throat, "tell us about the Sabancuy Channel."

The professor brought his chair closer. He set his hands flat on the table and leaned closer. "About a month ago, a man dragging a net behind his fishing boat snagged it on something in the mouth of the channel. When the man dove to free the net, he saw what he thought might be the outline of an old shipwreck."

"It's probably just an old fishing boat," Augie remarked. "Who knows how many are strung out all along the coast?"

"It most likely is. However, from the man's description, there's a good chance it could be a colonial-era coastal vessel that was used to ferry supplies from Campeche City to the fort on Isla del Carmen." He looked into the eyes of everyone sitting at the table. "Who knows? It could even be a commerce raider."

"That's a fancy way of calling it a pirate ship," Donovan said. "What makes you think that?"

The professor held up his index finger. "I said it could be. More likely, it's a Spanish supply ship."

"All right." Donovan put an elbow on the table. "What makes you think it's an old supply ship?"

"The size of the wreck. Its proximity to Isla del Carmen." He looked at everyone sitting at the table. "I'm confident it's a ship supplying the fort at Isla del Carmen."

Augie sat back with a trace of skepticism in his eyes. "I'm more interested in why you think it might be a pirate ship?"

The professor looked over his shoulder before he continued, "Long before the fort on the isle was founded, Isla del Carmen was an uncontested pirate haven for over a hundred and fifty years."

"Like Port Royal or Tortuga?" Donovan commented.

"Not exactly. There was no established settlement on the island until hundreds of years later. The pirates lived in makeshift camps they could move or abandon on a moment's notice."

The professor drew a breath. "Fresh water was abundant, there were plenty of fish and game to live on, and the channels and shallow bays around the island were ideal for repairing and refitting their ships. Above all," he emphasized, "Isla del Carmen was strategically situated between Campeche City and Veracruz. It made an excellent base to attack the treasure ships sailing for Spain."

Augie frowned. "I didn't think you could get a ship that big up the channels around Isla del Carmen."

"That's because you're thinking Hollywood." The professor looked at Augie. "The pirates preferred smaller, faster vessels with shallow drafts so they could ambush the bigger, slower Spanish ships and make a quick getaway into waters the deeper-drafted ships couldn't go into."

"Like modern-day pirates," Don Macario added.

Augie lowered his brow. "Modern-day pirates?"

"He's referring to the Horn of Africa," the professor explained. "The pirates use skiffs to go out into the sea lanes to hijack container ships and cruise liners."

"You mean like those guys in Somalia?"

"Among other places," the professor added, "like the Caribbean."

"The Caribbean?" Augie scoffed.

"I saw it when I was in Panama," Donovan interjected. "They were always hijacking cabin cruisers off the Darién gap to run drugs. They'd come out of the Urabá in Colombia, jump the ship, and put the crew and passengers on a dingy if they didn't kill them."

"There was an incident just recently off Holbox Island," the professor added. "Pirates in two skiffs boarded a yacht belonging to a Canadian man, robbed him, and ravaged his daughter."

"Did they catch the bastards?" Augie asked.

"Unfortunately, no."

"There was another attack that occurred in Isla Aguada not too long ago by men in two skiffs like you described," Don Macario added. "They came ashore and robbed a group of campers at the RV park and made off with a substantial amount of money and other valuables just like the pirates during the colonial period."

"I heard about that." Donovan sat up. "It was reported as a robbery, not a pirate attack."

"Therein lies the problem," the professor remarked. "The crime of piracy has faded from our common perception. When we hear the word pirate, we picture someone wearing a scarf on their head with a large earring dangling from an ear and an eye patch over one eye."

"Don't forget the knife between his teeth," Donovan added.

"And a knife between his teeth," the professor added. "The point is, the crime of piracy is not being accurately reported. It's being reported by the specific crime committed, most generally robbery or hijacking."

"Come to think of it, the papers in Panama referred to the thefts of the cabin cruisers off the Darién Gap as maritime robberies."

"See what I mean?" the professor replied.

Augie put his elbow on the back of his chair. "Do you think the pirates who robbed those geezers on Isla Aguada and raped that girl near Holbox Island are the same guys?"

The professor drew down his cheeks and nodded slowly. "It could be."

"I'll bet that if you were to take all the incidents reported in the paper regarding thefts and robberies and other crimes by men in boats, you'd get a better idea if it's the same guys."

"I'm sure the Armada has already thought about that," Don Macario surmised.

Pablo, the barman, came to the table to deliver the drinks he anticipated they'd order. A good bartender knows his customer's tastes, and he knew exactly what each man preferred. He set a Bohemia and a pint glass in front of Donovan, a Negra Modelo with no pint glass in front of Augie, and a Cuba Libre in front of the professor. He knew that Don Macario customarily drank a single snifter of cognac in the afternoon and would not require another.

After Pablo returned to the mahogany bar, Donovan poured his beer into the pint glass and continued the conversation, "Did any of the big-name pirates operate in these waters, Professor?"

"They all did," the professor responded. "Among the more notorious were El Lorencillo, Mansfield, Morgan—"

"Morgan?" Augie set down his bottle of beer. "Harry Morgan?"

"Henry," Donovan corrected him. "Harry's the actor."

"The man known as Bloody Morgan, the future governor of Jamaica himself." The professor nodded. "He used the beach at Siho Playa down the road as an anchorage during the siege in 1663." He stirred the swizzle stick in his drink. "As nasty as Morgan may have been, he was by far not the bloodiest to pay unwanted visits to Campeche."

"You mean Laurent de Graff," Don Macario interjected. "El Lorencillo."

"Of all the notable pirates who paid an unwanted visit to Campeche City, Morgan included, he left the most lasting impression."

Donovan sipped from his pint glass. "Sounds like a pretty nasty guy."

"The Spanish thought him to be the devil incarnate," the professor added.

"We got a guy like that hanging around here today," Augie said under his breath.

"On his last raid, the townspeople had been forewarned of his approach and hid all their valuables," the professor continued. "De Graff knew that Spanish troops were not far away and didn't have time to force them into telling where they hid their valuables so he took a number of hostages and held them for ransom." He inhaled sharply. "To teach the townspeople a lesson, El Lorencillo murdered the hostages after the ransom was paid."

"Isn't there a restaurant in Campeche City called El Lorencillo?" Donovan raised the corner of his mouth. "In one of those old forts around the old town?"

"The forts you're referring to are called baluartes, and the restaurant isn't located in one of them. The government would never condone that," the professor explained to Donovan. "The building's only about ten years old. The owner had a team of architects from Spain build an authentic replica for his restaurant."

"That must have cost a chunk of change," Augie mused. "Who has that kind of money?"

"Arturo Farías," Don Macario interposed.

"The Campechano?" Donovan raised his brows and scoffed. "He certainly could afford it."

"He has enough money to rebuild the wall that once encircled old Campeche," Don Macario added. "Not just the bastions."

"What ever happened to the old wall?" Augie asked.

"Have you ever taken a stroll down the streets of old Campeche City?" Dr. Ventura asked Augie. "That's where the wall went. After the pirate raids stopped, much of the wall was disassembled and the stones were used to pave the streets."

"What about the cannons, anchor chains, and the binnacle they have at the restaurant?" Donovan took another sip of beer. "Are those replicas too?"

"They're the real thing," the professor replied. "They were dug up along with numerous other artifacts when the building's foundation was excavated. The institute awarded a few insignificant pieces on permanent loan to the restaurant with the condition that they be made available for public viewing."

"How about that?" Donovan remarked. "I thought it was impossible for anyone to have artifacts in their personal possession."

The professor hunched his shoulders. "It would depend on the significance of the artifact, I suppose."

"What about treasure?" Donovan pushed his empty pint glass aside and put both elbows on the table. "Any chance that wreck in the Sabancuy Channel's got treasure on it?"

The professor raised his brow and dropped the corners of his mouth. "In terms of gold, silver, or precious stones?" He shook his head subtly. "Probably not."

"The real treasure is the artifacts the pirates left behind," Don Macario commented. "Not just in shipwrecks but buried in the sand all around Campeche."

The old gentleman's comment piqued Augie's interest. "Like what exactly?"

"Shot, buttons, knives, dinner plates—just about anything," the professor replied.

"But no real treasure?" Augie concluded.

"If you're lucky, you might come across a semiprecious stone or perhaps a broken piece of jewelry." The professor took up the conversation. "If you're real lucky, you might find a Spanish doubloon."

Augie scoffed. "What good is a single doubloon?"

"To begin with, the gold content alone at today's prices could get you around three hundred dollars." The professor drew a long breath through his nostrils and then released it slowly. "Depending on the design elements, the condition of the coin, a single doubloon could fetch anywhere from a few hundred dollars to tens of thousands of dollars."

Augie fell back in his chair and looked at Donovan. "I've got to get me a metal detector."

Out of the corner of his eye, Donovan noticed someone coming toward him. He turned his head as a middle-aged man wearing a white golf shirt and green slacks and holding a captain's hat in his hands stopped next to their table. The Pemex logo on his shirt caught his eye as did the word capitán embroidered beneath it.

"May I have a word with you, Capitán Dónovan?"

Donovan looked at the man's rugged face and deep lines on his cheeks. "Do I know you?"

He glanced at the others sitting around the table. "Disculpame, Capitán," he excused himself. "My name is Capitán Santos. I'd like to discuss something with you."

"Go ahead."

"In private?"

Donovan looked at the others and then stood. "I'll be back in a minute."

The Pemex captain looked at each of the men at the table. "I apologize for the interruption."

Captain Santos led Donovan past a small gathering of businessmen huddled around a table like a group of conspirators plotting a crime, paying no mind to them. Santos led him to a corner away from the prying eyes and sharp ears of the curious.

"You may not know me, Capitán Dónovan, but I am very familiar with who you are or at least who you used to be." He held his captain's hat in front of him in both hands. "I used to run cargo between Coatzacoalcos and Colón." He pointed his hat at him. "You had quite a reputation around the canal as a man who could get difficult things done."

"Well," Donovan scoffed, "it's like you said. That's who I used to be. I run Seven Seas Adventure Cruises now, so whatever it is you want, I'm not in that line of work anymore."

"Do you know who Fausto López is?" he asked abruptly. "You may know him as El Demonio."

Donovan clenched his jaw. "What's this all about?"

"Are you aware that he's determined to have you work for him?"

"I've already turned him down."

"That's too bad." He hung his head and brushed back a loose thread on the logo on his hat. "I was hoping you would be interested."

"What makes you think I'd work for a drug trafficker?"

Santos raised his head. "Your reputation in Panama." He again lowered his eyes to fuss with the logo on his hat. "I thought it would be something you'd at least consider."

"No way in hell would I work for a drug trafficker."

"That's what I used to say too." He glared at him seriously. "But El Demonio is like a serpent. He lurks in the shadows, waiting for the right moment. He looks for a weakness and uses it to draw you in. Then he strikes." He snapped his fingers. "Like that."

Donovan scoffed as he grinned smugly. "I haven't got a weakness."

"He'll find one." He drew back his hat and held it in his hands. "He's determined to use your ship. It might be better to do what he wants and get it over with. That way, you have a chance to be free of him. If he gets something on you, he'll never let you go."

"I appreciate your concern, but I can watch out for myself." Donovan started to walk away.

"I wouldn't be so sure of that, if I were you," Santos said ominously.

Donovan's curiosity got the better of him, and he decided to hear what the Pemex captain had to say. "Oh, yeah?"

"Like you, I turned him down … twice." He inhaled deeply. "He made it impossible for me to turn him down a third time." The lines around Santos's mouth deepened. "The first time he asked me, he was very polite. He promised me money, beautiful women, and my own yacht." He looked to the side. "He knew exactly what to tempt me with."

Donovan exhaled, emphasizing his disinterest and looked at his watch.

"The next time, he left ten thousand American dollars in a paper bag on my desk."

"What did you do with the money?"

Santos gripped the sides of his hat. "His men had been following me since he made his first offer. I went to their car, threw the package on the driver's lap, and demanded that they stop bothering me." He dropped his head. "Of course, all that did was to stop them from being obvious."

"How'd they finally get to you?"

Santos wrinkled the corners of his mouth, drew another deep breath, and turned his head away. "Let's just say, I would have been better off accepting the first offer."

"And that's what you're advising me to do?"

"I wouldn't presume to give you any kind of advice." The supply boat captain looked at him. "All I'm saying's that if you were to change your mind, you can usually find me at the Tiburón."

Donovan glared at him for a moment before he started back to his table. "I won't be changing my mind."

The sun barely hung over the water as Lázaro strolled down the malecon toward the meat market to buy a kilo of pork ribs. He had just finished mending his net with the help of his cousin Benício and planned to celebrate with his wife of many years. He enjoyed spending the end of the day at home with his wife, something he never used to do.

In another time, he used to go to the cantina after a long day at work. In those days, he worked as a garbage collector while his wife worked as a live-in maid for six days out of the week. He didn't like going home to an empty house, so after a day of mindlessly collecting garbage, he went home to get cleaned up and go out on the town. He enjoyed drinking and seemingly had no limit to the number of beers he could ingest. He also had an eye for the ladies and pursued that interest with unbridled fervor.

He had the misfortune of believing while under the influence that he possessed the good looks and singing attributes of the famous Mexican movie icon Pedro Infante. In reality, he had more in common with his cousin Benício; he was short in stature and broad in girth. He did, however, have a full head of hair, which he dyed an unnatural shade of black, and could carry a tune. With the help of candlelight and a little alcohol, he had no trouble wooing many a dark-haired, doe-eyed lovely into sleeping with him. Sobriety and the coming of daylight removed the veil over his eyes that inevitably led to his utter disappointment.

Ten years had passed since last he partook of the demon drink. He had the love of his wife and his cousin's intervention to thank. His cousin reintroduced him to the fisherman's life he had all but abandoned. He appreciated what Benício had done for him and recognized that without his strength, he would still be seeing the world from the bottom of a bottle of tequila.

As he walked along the sea wall, he came upon a young woman standing on the curve by a compact car. The sea breeze flowed through her low-neck, sleeveless dress, outlining where her long, shapely thighs met under her sumptuously soft tummy, rounded hips, and narrow waist. She had her arms folded across the middle of her body, pushing up on her already ample bosom. She turned to look him as he came closer, immediately captivating him with the helplessness in her eyes.

"Aydame, señor," she appealed to him. "I locked myself out of my car."

The distress in the woman's voice and eyes enthralled Lázaro like a sailor entranced by the song of a sea nymph. He found himself stepping off the sidewalk and walking to her side, forgetting all about the pork ribs he intended to buy.

She put her slender finger through a slight opening on the driver's side window and pointed at the key in the ignition. "Do you think you can open it, señor?"

"It'll be easy." He looked at the street around him. "All I need is something to hook the door lock or pull back on the handle, like a stiff wire or a clothes hanger."

It seemed unlikely to Lázaro that they would find anything along the seawall. Having worked for the city, he knew that the maintenance crews were especially diligent about keeping the walk along the seawall clear of rubbish. As Lázaro went to search the ground behind the car, the woman shook her head softly, rolled her eyes up, and sighed in disgust. She walked to the front of the car and picked up an old clothes hanger.

She held the hanger out for Lázaro to see. "Will this do?"

He rose from his stooped position and grinned at their good fortune. He held his hand out and walked toward her, realizing for the first time that she stood at least a head taller than he.

"It's a good thing you smoke," he told her as he disassembled the hanger and reshaped it into a long hook.

"Smoke?" She glowered at him with distaste. "I don't—"

"Why else would you have your window cracked open a little like this?"

She looked at him in disbelief. "You're such a clever man." She continued to play him as he concentrated on unlocking the latch. "Are you a detective?"

He gave her a clever smile. "We'll have you on your way in no time."

She brushed back the hair and smiled coyly at him. "Gracias, señor."

After a while, her patience had worn thin with Lázaro's incompetence and she started to take the hanger from him, stopping herself on a couple of occasions to allow him to rescue her. Beto and Felipe amused themselves, watching Lázaro's inept attempt to unlock the car from a small mom-and-pop restaurant across the street.

"These locks are designed to prevent car thieves from doing what I'm trying to do," Lázaro explained to the young lady. The lock made a resounding pop when at last he succeeded in unlocking it. "There you go."

She wrapped her arms around him and pressed his face against the softness of her cleavage. "Muchas gracias, señor. How will I ever repay you?"

Lázaro felt himself swoon after she finally released him, intoxicated as much by her perfume as by the experience. She opened her purse and began to rummage through it.

"Oh, no!" He held a hand up. "I'm glad I could help."

"Nonsense." She closed her purse. "At least let me buy you dinner." She pointed at the small sidewalk restaurant across the street. "Do you like arroz con pollo?"

Although he loved chicken and rice, he declined. "No es necessario, señorita."

"A cerveza then."

He glanced at the empty table Felipe and Beto had abandoned and then looked at her ten-peso-sized brown eyes and pouting lips as she caressed the side of his face. He looked at his watch and then held a finger up to her. "Una Coca."

"A Coke would be nice." She giggled.

The Cocina Maya did not serve an evening meal. The restaurant depended wholly on the port and did not have a sufficient clientele to justify staying open after the close of the workday. Like most families, la cena represented the only meal that Benício, Itzél, and Poli shared as a family. Itzél would prepare a scrumptious meal, generally light in nature to stave off the further expansion of Benício's waistline. They would talk about the kind of day they had and laugh at the funny stories Benício would tell. Now that Poli had left home, la cena seemed hollow to Itzél. That evening, she prepared chicken and lime soup and made lemonade, Poli's favorites, which made her feel worse.

Benício watched Itzél through his brow as he sipped the soup from his spoon. She sat quietly balancing her spoon between her fingers, looking absentmindedly out the plate glass window.

"What are you thinking about?"

Itzél inhaled deeply as she snapped out of it and dipped her spoon into her soup. "Just thinking." She stirred the spoon in her bowl for a moment and then looked back out the window.

He craned his neck to look out the window and saw a freighter steaming toward the horizon. "Are you thinking about that ship?"

"Mm-hmm." She nodded subtly.

After a moment, Benício dropped his head to finish eating his soup. Itzél set her spoon aside and started playing with her ring. She looked down at the wedding band Poli's father had put on her finger and then across the table at the wedding band on Benício's finger. Although it appeared to match her ring, it did not. She looked back out the window as she continued to play with her ring.

Benício pushed his bowl away after he finished his soup and looked at Itzél, who continued to daydream. He glanced at her bowl. "You hardly touched your soup."

"I'm not hungry."

Watching ships heading toward the horizon is like watching grass grow. The harder you watch them, the harder it is to see them move. It's only when you look away and then look back at them that they seem to make any progress.

"Do you miss Poli?" Benício asked her.

She nodded her head subtly as she continued to watch the freighter, lost in her thoughts.

He lifted his glass of lemonade as he looked at her curiously. "He's been away from home before." He took a sip. "He'll be fine."

"Why do some men want to go to sea?" She looked at him. "And go so far away from their homes?"

"I don't know." Benício inhaled deeply and looked out the plate glass window. The freighter had moved to the brink of the horizon. "Maybe to look for adventure." He emptied his lungs and turned to Itzél. "Maybe to run away from something."

She looked back out at the freighter. "It has to be a lonely life," she mused. "Out there in the middle of the ocean, all by yourself."

"I suppose they get used to it," he said as he turned to look at the freighter.

"How do you get used to being separated from the ones you love?"

"Some men don't have the sense of family other men do," Benício suggested. He looked across the table at her. "They're selfish and inconsiderate, interested only in themselves."

She stopped playing with her ring and looked at his unsympathetic eyes. He gazed at her with stern, unflinching eyes, as if demanding an explanation. Her eyes, soft and melancholic, looked to him for understanding. They considered the question from two different perspectives: hers from a metaphysical point of view, his from a distinctly earthly one. She sighed and turned to look back out the window. The freighter had slipped below the horizon.

"I think it takes a special type of man," she continued musing, "a man of action, a man who's not afraid to lose sight of the shore, a man who doesn't look for trouble but isn't afraid to face it when it comes."

The normally passive minister, who did not anger easily, bit down on his lip and put his hand softly on the table. He drew a long breath. "A man like Capitán Dónovan?"

"Sí." She nodded softy. "A man like Capitán Dónovan."

Benício looked away and took a couple of long, calming breaths. When he faced her again, his wounded heart showed in his eyes.

"Are you happy?" Benício asked her.

She looked at him curiously. "You know I am."

"I mean, are you happy here with me?"

She wrinkled her brow. "Why are you asking me this?"

"What has it been?" He scoffed. "Eleven years since we came to Seyba Playa?"

"Eleven wonderful years," she added.

"Wonderful?" Benício sat back in his chair. "If only that were true."

"It is true," Itzél insisted. "You've made a loving home for us."

Benício sighed. "I knew when I asked you to marry me that I could never replace your husband."

"You're my husband now." She put her hands on her lap and began playing with her ring.

"Am I? Am I really your husband?"

"Of course you are." Itzél let go of her ring. "You've been a good husband and a great father to Poli."

He grinned sadly as he turned away. "In hindsight, I was wrong to ask you to marry me. I knew that you could never love me."

"But I do love you." She reached across the table and took his hand with both of hers. "I know it might not have seemed that way at first, but you were right. I have learned to love you. It's been a good marriage."

Benício scoffed. "You mean arrangement."

"I mean marriage," she said firmly. "I love you, Benício."

He looked at the wedding band on her finger and then at the one he wore. He withdrew his hand. "You're still a young woman. There's still time for you to find somebody you can … love."

"I don't want anybody else."

He drew a breath and lowered his eyes for a moment and then looked away. "That's not what I mean."

Itzél pulled her hands back and put them on her lap. She turned her head to the side. "I've already known that kind of love." She sighed and then looked at him. "The love I have for you is a deeper, more sincere love."

"Sincere love?" Benício again scoffed and pushed himself back into his chair. "You won't even sleep in the same room with me."

"I already told you." She looked into his eyes. "I sleep better alone."

"You don't think I hear you crying at night," he said frankly. "I can tell you're lonely."

She turned away. "I was probably having a bad dream."

"It's natural to be lonely." Benício hung his head and scoffed. "I know loneliness all too well." He raised his eyes.

They both looked out the window for the freighter that no longer graced the horizon. It had slipped into the beyond bound for a port unknown. In the eleven years they had lived together, they had never spoken of their lack of intimacy. Each thought they had a happy life together even though she brooded for a dead husband and he longed for a normal marriage.

"I've noticed the way you look at Capitán Dónovan."

Her face flushed. "You're imagining things."

There is no denying human nature. Even happily married women appreciate when a handsome man looks their way. They may not act on it, but they do enjoy the attention, just like happily married men appreciate an attractive woman, except that a married man is more likely to act on it. Neither married men nor married women can deny how they react to the opposite sex, as long as the conversation is with themselves.

"You don't think he's handsome?"

The question made her uncomfortable. "Handsome men seldom have substance."

"It took substance to defy El Demonio."

"You defied El Demonio when you refused to work for him."

"All I did was refuse, but Capitán Dónovan stood up to him." He inhaled deeply. "That took courage."

"I don't see the difference," she argued. "It took just as much courage to tell him no."

"There's a difference." He raised his brows. "It's like you said. He's a man of action. He's not afraid to lose sight of the shore."

"Neither are you," she insisted. "You go to the reef every day. It takes courage to do something like that after what happened to you and your uncle."

What happened to his father and uncle occurred long before the state built the artificial reef fifteen miles west of Seyba Playa. In those days, before the creation of fiberglass pangas, the fishermen of Seyba Playa went out in small rowboats with handmade sails to look for the schools of fish that meandered up and down the coast in search of plankton, shrimp, and algae. Back then, fishing depended on luck that often eluded the pescadores of Seyba Playa. Everyone knew that the reefs around the Arcas cays abounded with fish, but the cays lay eighty miles from Seyba Playa. Only the daring or the foolish chanced the arduous and dangerous journey to the Arcas. Storms in the Sonda of Campeche rise unexpectedly, and those unfortunates who get caught in the sound when a storm rises are seldom seen again. Benício's father and uncle realized that misfortune.

"The kind of courage Capitán Dónovan has is rare," Benício insisted. "He's special."

"He's nothing special." She looked at him firmly. "He's just a man, just like you."

Benício smiled affectionately. "You don't think he's dashing?" he teased. "Adventurous?" He leaned closer. "Maybe even a little mysterious?"

Itzél stopped playing with her ring. "A woman needs security, not adventure and mystery."

After Donovan finished his conversation with Captain Santos and started back to his table, he had two sets of eyes watching him. He had seen Pablo hovering around both sides of the bar like the proverbial fly on the wall. He had come to the lounge far too often not to have recognized that Pablo enjoyed eavesdropping and kept that in mind whenever they discussed the charter business at the lounge. Don Macario tolerated his eavesdropping since he never heard him gossiping, nor had he ever heard him spreading what he learned around town.

The other set of eyes watching him belonged to his partner. Unlike the barman, who had mastered the art of invisibility, Augie lacked the subtle nuances Pablo had developed over his many years of watching people.

"What?" Donovan blared at his partner as he took his seat.

"What was that all about?" Augie demanded.

"Nothing important."

"You know what they're saying about that guy?"

"What guy?"

Augie huffed in frustration. "The guy you were talking to."

"How well do you know Captain Santos?" Don Macario asked him.

"You know him?"

"He comes to the restaurant from time to time." The old gentleman took a sip from his cognac. "He runs supplies between the port and the Los Arcas platforms for Pemex."

"I've heard he runs drugs for El Demonio." Augie looked at his partner intently. "You'd better stay clear of him."

"I don't see how?" Doctor Ventura interjected. "The preventive police search every ship putting into the port."

Donovan thought about the run-in he had with El Demonio and his men at the Cocina Maya. "He's probably transferring the drugs to a panga long before he gets near Seyba Playa."

"The Armada just detained a panguero on the other side of the Seyba Reef." Augie cocked his head in the direction where the Pemex captain had stood. "Probably after meeting the good captain."

The professor chuckled. "You're just speculating. Where's he getting the drugs?"

"Probably from another ship he meets on the high seas," Augie countered.

"Pemex keeps track of their boats." The professor shook his head. "I don't see him deviating very far from his course to meet another ship."

"I know the man is a shameless philanderer," Don Macario commented. "Every time he comes to the restaurant, he's with a different girl."

"So the guy has an eye for the ladies." Donovan grinned playfully. "That doesn't make him a bad person."

"I've never seen him bring his wife here," Don Macario added.

Augie drew closer to the professor. "He's been seen talking to El Demonio's men at the Tiburón."

The professor scrunched his brows. "The Tiburón?"

"It's a hangout for the people working at the port," Donovan explained.

"I hear he's there all the time," Augie commented. "I'll bet that's where they set up their deals."

The conversation he had with the Pemex boat captain confirmed the rumor in Donovan's mind. He dared not mention it to his partner, who he knew would be consumed with worry.

CHAPTER

7

The putrid scent of urine, rotting food, and stale vomit hung over the trash cans and discarded cardboard boxes in the dank alley like a ground fog. The dawn light cast a subtle shadow across the scratches on Lázaro's face as he lay on his back, drenched in sweat and his own vomit. A pair of meaty hands belonging to a heavyset municipal police officer lifted him by his shirt into a sitting position.

"¡Despierta, cabrón!" The policeman shook the drunk violently, ordering him to awaken.

Lázaro opened his eyes slowly and put his hand on the bloody scratches on the left side of his face. He turned his head from side to side, obviously confused by his surroundings. A sudden flash from a camera blinded him, and he threw his hand up over his face.

Felipe stood over him while Beto, who had his hair slicked down and pulled back behind his head in a ponytail took pictures of the woman in the alley.

"I am Licensiado De la Peña Eguía with the Procuduría Estatal." He briefly flashed a state attorney general's badge at him. "Why did you do it?"

Lázaro tried to get up. "De que hablas?"

"You know what I'm talking about." He raised his voice. "Why did you kill the girl?"

The heavyset policeman pulled him to his feet, spun him around, and then forced him to look at the body of a woman lying on the ground with her dress pulled up over her face and her panties around her ankles. Lázaro's eyes widened in horror.

Felipe knelt by the body and lifted the woman's right hand to show Lázaro. He shined a flashlight on her fingers, pointing out the blood under her nails. "She scratched you before you strangled her." He turned to Beto standing behind him. "Did you get a picture of the scratches?"

"Sí, ministerio publico." Beto nodded.

Felipe moved the light down to Lázaro's pants. "What about his clothes? Did you get a picture of the way he was found before the officer pulled his pants up?"

"Sí, ministerio publico." Beto tapped the side of his camera. "It's all here. The scratches on his face, the marks on her throat, and the scrapes on his knuckles. Everything."

The first customers to come into the Cocina Maya for breakfast got there around seven in the morning. They came in groups of two or three, finishing their meals or coffee generally within the hour before rushing off to their jobs at the port. Then came the bricklayers, carpenters, and city workers who darted in for Itzél's taquitos or a quick breakfast plate. The businessmen were the last to come in and stayed the longest, drinking cup after cup of coffee as they chatted among themselves.

After the last group of businessmen had left, only an old man sitting by the door remained at the Cocina Maya, finishing his taquito. Itzél went to fill his cup with coffee when she heard the bell over the door jingle. She glanced at the door to greet the new arrival but didn't when she recognized him.

Donovan tipped an imaginary hat at her before going to sit at a small table by the counter. He picked up the laminated breakfast menu from the table, pushing the coffee cup aside as he sat.

He glanced at Itzél, who wore a silk, button-down blouse and loose-fitting slacks and not the traditional Mayan garb she normally wore at work. He turned his attention to the menu.

"Will you be having breakfast?" she asked him, taking him by surprise. He had not expected her to get to his table so quickly.

"Just coffee, please." He set the menu aside. As he watched her pour coffee into his cup, he felt his heart stir at the daintiness of her hand and the smoothness of her skin. Her hand seemed unsteady to him, and he raised his eyes to look at her face. She turned her head abruptly to look at the door after hearing the bell chime.

"Gracias," she called in a singsong voice to the old man as he walked out the door.

Donovan looked down at his cup as the coffee began to spill into the saucer. He put his hand on her wrist, startling her. She gasped when she realized that she had overfilled his cup.

"I'm so sorry." She put the pot on the table and used several napkins from the holder to soak up the spill.

"That's quite all right."

He took a couple of napkins and soaked up the coffee that fell into the saucer. He looked up and lost himself in the green pools of her eyes when her eyes met his. Itzél also seemed transfixed by the moment, but was the first to break the connection. She gathered the coffee-soaked napkins in her hand and went to discard them behind the counter.

"What are you doing in town?" Itzél dried her hands with a counter towel, ignoring his steady gaze.

Donovan took his cup and went to sit at the counter across from her. "I had a few errands to run before we head out this afternoon."

"Is my son going with you?" She pulled a plastic container from under the counter and went to bus the old man's table.

"Of course." Donovan spun around on the bar stool to watch her. Her slacks flowed gracefully with her gait, clinging to her legs and outlining her perfectly shaped derriere. "He's part of the crew."

"Will it be dangerous?" She gathered the old man's dirty dishes and put them on the tray. She raised her head to look at him as she wiped the table. "He's not a very good swimmer."

Donovan chuckled to himself. "If you're worried that the ship will sink, there's little chance of that happening."

She went back behind the counter and put the tray of dirty dishes under it. "What if he falls in the water and nobody sees him?"

Donovan spun the stool around. "We're very careful about watching out for each other."

Itzél sighed, the concern visible in her eyes. "I worry he'll drown."

"He'll be fine. I've seen him swim," Donovan reassured her. "Besides, he's got his swimming things."

She looked at him, the concern in her face slowly turning into a faint smile. She wrinkled her nose. "Do you think I worry too much?"

Donovan resisted the urge to round the counter and put his arms around her. He put his elbows on the counter. "That's what good mothers do."

She cocked her head to the side, causing a lock of hair to fall over her right eye and sending a chill through him.

"Are you a father?" Itzél asked him.

"No." He hesitated, turning his eyes to the side. "I've never had the privilege."

"Have you ever been married?"

He exhaled slowly. "I never got the chance."

"What about that Indian girl you're in love with?"

The question stunned Donovan. He didn't know how to respond. "What Indian girl?"

"The one who taught you about Indian culture."

"I never said I was in love with her."

"You didn't have to." Itzél brushed the hair back over her ear. "It was all over your face."

Her uncanny insight struck him senseless, like a boom swinging wildly across the stern of the ship. He sat, dumbfounded and disoriented, not knowing how to respond. He stood, pulled several peso coins from his pocket, and laid them on the counter. "That didn't work out." He turned to leave.

"Why don't you finish your coffee?" Itzél said, stopping him in his tracks.

He didn't want to talk about Xochitl anymore than he wanted to talk about her dead husband. He wanted to talk to her but feared that the conversation would not follow the course he set out to follow. His interest lay on the horizon before him and not in his wake.

"Can we talk about something else?"

Itzél smiled at him with her eyes. "Of course."

José Luis stood on the veranda next to a patio table behind the plantation house, waiting for Fausto to return from his morning run. He looked across the lawn to the path that cut through the coconut grove and to the beach, expecting to see him emerge at any moment. It had been almost an hour, the usual time El Demonio set aside for his morning run. He took his eyes off the path when he heard the housekeeper coming through the patio door holding a tray of bottled water.

"¿Agua, señor?" San Juana offered José Luis a bottle.

"Leave the water and get back in the house, San Juana," Fausto said to her as he stepped up on the veranda, startling José Luis. He took a plastic bottle of water off the old woman's tray and collapsed into a rattan chair by the patio table.

The old housekeeper averted her eyes to avoid staring at the Satanic tattoos on his chest. She set the rest of the water bottles on the table and then went back into the house.

"I didn't see you come up the path." José Luis sat across the table from Fausto.

"Your mind must have gotten lost in the coconut grove." Fausto removed his T-shirt and dried his face with it. "It does that to people."

"I spoke with Flavio in Tegucigalpa." José Luis looked over his shoulder to make sure they were alone. "He heard about Chacho getting picked up by the Armada. He's afraid Don Arturo's going to find out he's selling us cocaine behind his back." He hesitated. "He's cutting us off."

El Demonio threw the shirt into the chair next to him and exhaled sharply. "Did you offer him more money?" He screwed off the top of his water bottle.

"He wasn't interested."

An iguana walked lazily across the lawn. Fausto flung the bottle top at it, missing it by a foot. "Can you find another supplier?"

"I'll have to go to Tegucigalpa to talk to some people after I get back from Houston with your money. By the way"—José Luis waited for Fausto to finish taking a long swallow of water—"the broker at the port of Houston knows that Don Arturo blackballed Billy Chávez. Like Flavio, he's afraid to jeopardize his relationship with the Campechanos."

Fausto set the bottle down and emptied his lungs. "Will a bribe make him look the other way?"

"It will have to be a good one." He looked at Fausto. "He's pretty nervous."

"I just need this one more load."

"Speaking of the load"—José Luis sat back in his chair—"the next container is going out at the end of the week. If you're going to put your stuff in it, I need to get it to Ciudad del Carmen in the next couple of days." He leaned toward Fausto. "How soon can you get it to me?"

The housekeeper slid the patio door open. "Pasale, señores," she said, inviting Felipe and Beto to the veranda.

"Here's Felipe with your answer." Fausto grinned.

The old woman slid the door closed behind them, pulled the curtain, and returned to the kitchen where she quietly resumed washing dishes with an ear to conversation outside through the kitchen window.

"How did it go?" El Demonio asked Felipe.

Felipe sat between El Demonio and José Luis while Beto remained standing. "He was a little nervous about taking a panga so far past the artificial reef, but he's sure he can persuade his cousin to go with him, just like you said he would."

"Excellente." Fausto grinned. "How soon can you set it up?"

"I'll have to talk to Santos." Felipe shrugged his shoulders. "Tomorrow, in the late afternoon."

"See that it happens."

"Are you sure you still want to use Santos?" José Luis commented. "You can't be sure that Chacho didn't talk."

"He wouldn't dare say anything. He knows what to expect if he does."

"It's an unnecessary risk. You have to assume he's compromised." José Luis eased back into his chair. "You should find someone else to get the stuff off the island."

"You said it yourself." Fausto expelled his breath forcefully. "There isn't time."

"He's no fool." José Luis scratched his brow. "He knows the Armada picked up the panguero. He might refuse to get the load."

135

"He can't refuse," Fausto barked. "We own him."

"Are you prepared to lose fifty kilos of cocaine?" José Luis retorted. "We have to assume the Armada will be watching Santos."

New to the business, Fausto had to rely on José Luis's experience, and up to that point, he had taken his advice without question. However, the loss of the guns at Punta Morro had put him in a precarious situation. "It's a chance I'm going to have to take."

José Luis glared at Fausto in disbelief. He turned to Felipe and Beto for support. Neither gave any sign that they disagreed with his decision.

"I'm asking you to reconsider."

Fausto's odd-colored eyes narrowed. "I need those fifty kilos."

"What about using the captain of the velero? Dónovan?" Felipe suggested. "He's been going to see the preacher's wife like you said he would. We can use her to get to him."

"Have you seen them together?"

"I don't have to." Felipe squirmed uncomfortably. "He's been going to the restaurant when her husband's away. It doesn't take a genius to figure what's going on."

"That's not good enough." Fausto shook his head.

"I don't understand," Felipe objected. "What are we waiting for?"

"It's one thing to long for a taste." Fausto stared into the coconut grove. "But until he takes a bite"—he looked at the sicario—"we have nothing on him."

The housekeeper wiped her hands with the dish towel and quietly left the kitchen. She stood momentarily in the hallway and stared at the patio door to make sure the men would not come into the house. After a moment, she sneaked out the front door and hurried across the lawn to the servants' quarters across the plantation grounds.

She went into her kitchen and opened the cutlery drawer where she had taped a cell phone to the bottom. She took the phone and looked out the kitchen window at the plantation house as she punched in the number she wanted to call.

"¿Bueno?" a man answered.

"Soy yo. San Juana," the elderly housekeeper whispered. "They're sending another panga to get the fifty kilos."

"Did you find out the name of the ship he's meeting?"

"No, but I think I heard them say something about Pemex." San Juana jumped when she heard a car engine start. "I can't talk now."

"Gracias, Doña Juanita," Casimiro said. "Call me when you can."

As Itzél refilled Donovan's coffee cup, he never took his eyes off her. He turned his eyes away when she caught him staring. She turned around to put the pot back on the warmer and smiled to herself. She took the container of dirty dishes from under the counter and set them next to the sink.

"Have you always been a sailboat captain?" Itzél asked, making conversation as she turned on the water.

"Not always." He rested his elbows on the counter. "I worked for a maritime shipping company out of Houston."

"Doing what?" she asked over the sound of the water splashing in the double aluminum sink.

"I started out as a shipping agent, making sure cargo got to where it was going." He took a sip of coffee. "After a while, the company made me a troubleshooter."

"Troubleshooter?"

"I fixed problems for the company," he explained. "If a ship or cargo got jammed up, the company would send me to fix it."

She glanced over her shoulder. "That must have been exciting work."

"You have no idea," he commented, not wanting to go into detail. He set the cup down. "Eventually, I was put in charge of their subsidiary in Panama City."

She stared at the suds rising in the sink. "The company must have had a lot faith in you."

"The company just wanted me closer to the problem. Much of their business went through the canal."

"A promotion is a promotion."

As Itzél turned her attention to washing the dirty dishes, Donovan sat quietly, watching her work. She moved quickly and gracefully, starting with the plates. After scrubbing them vigorously, she rinsed them in the next sink and then stacked them on the opposite side of the back counter. He admired the grace of her movements and the way her clothes conformed to her body with her every turn.

"What about you?" He cleared his throat. "Have you always been in the restaurant business?"

"My mother had a small kitchen in Mérida," she explained as she dried a plate with a dish towel. "That's where I learned to cook. We moved to Ciudad del Carmen after my husband got hired by Pemex. We were saving money to start a small restaurant." She set the plate gently on the stack. "Then he got killed in an accident."

For some reason, she insisted on bringing up her dead husband. Then he remembered what Poli told him about his mother's obsession with her love for him. He wanted to explore the uncharted waters that lay beyond those moments when their eyes met, but he had to get her past the memory of her late husband first.

"How did you meet Benício?" Donovan asked.

Itzél stopped washing the plate in her hand and stared at the wall. After a moment, she resumed washing.

"I took a job working at a restaurant," she began. "He was studying to be a minister at the church nearby." She began to rinse the plate. "He'd come by every day to have supper."

Donovan didn't have the slightest interest in how she met Benício. What he really wanted to know concerned her relationship with him. What he'd gathered from his conversation with her son made him believe she'd married out of convenience and not love. He wanted to get her to admit that so that he could make his move.

"When did you fall in love with him?"

She stopped rinsing the plate and began to dry it without answering his question for what seemed to Donovan like an eternity. He feared that he might have gone too fast and a little too far. She finished drying the plate, set it on the stack, and then dried her hands with the towel.

She turned to face him. "I was working double shifts to make ends meet. Poli was always getting sick. I couldn't find anyone to take care of him." Her eyes saddened at the memory. She lowered her head and sniffled. "Benício promised to take care of Poli and me if I agreed to marry him." She looked at Donovan. "So I did."

Her response did not satisfy his need to know how she felt about her current husband. He had the wind and decided to push his luck.

"Do you love him?"

She drew back, astonished by the boldness of the question. He could see in her eyes that he had disconcerted her. She seemed unable or unwilling to answer. She turned around abruptly and put her hands on the edge of the sink, gazing vacantly into the dishwater.

"He's been good to me and a good father to Poli," she finally responded.

He could hear the water moving past the hull and the wind whistling in the rigging, but he didn't hear what he wanted to hear. "You didn't answer the question."

She lowered her head and started pushing the suds in the sink to the sides. The silence made him anxious. A landlubber might say that his persistence had put him in deep water. However, to a sailor, deep water meant room to navigate, a good thing. Shallow water meant trouble to a mariner, and he had strayed into the dangerous shallows of Itzél's wrath.

"It's none of your business how I feel about my husband," she said firmly. She turned around slowly to face him, her eyes glaring at him like a pair of burning emeralds. Even in anger, her eyes bewitched him, and he had to come about lest he run himself aground.

"I didn't mean to upset you."

"Why do you want to know if I love my husband?"

"I, uh—" Her words had hit him like a rogue wave.

"Is it because he's so much older than me?"

"Well, uh—"

"Or is it because he's not a handsome man?"

"It just seemed strange—"

"What seemed strange?" She took a step toward him. "That a woman like me could be married to an old man like him?" She scoffed. "You don't think I've heard that before?" She emptied her lungs. "The stares, the whispers, mothers bringing their unmarried sons to the restaurant hoping that they would sweep me off my feet." She took another step toward him. "Is that what you came here to do? To sweep me off my feet?"

He realized his decision to come about had come too late. Her words had swamped his deck and washed his feet out from under him. He had to resume the course he had chosen and defy the current as he pushed through the rough waters into which he had strayed.

"Yes, I did," he heard himself say. His response seemed to drive the anger from her eyes. They widened as she stepped slowly away from him. "I could see it in your eyes the first time we met." He had regained his footing. "You don't look at a man like that and not expect him to respond." He watched her continue to back slowly away from him. She gasped when she felt herself back against the sink. "You're living like a church mouse, afraid to come out during the daylight."

She began rubbing her right thumb on her wedding ring, a nervous habit she had. "What if I told you I liked living like a church mouse?"

"You deserve more," Donovan said boldly. "You deserve being wined and dined and having the nicer things in life." He looked at the way she played with her ring, assuming incorrectly that Benício had given it to her and not realizing the attachment she had to it. "That ring, for example."

Itzél stopped playing with the simple wedding band. "What's wrong with my ring?"

"It's so … ordinary." He looked firmly into her eyes. "A woman like you deserves something better."

The fear left her eyes, and the embers began to glow.

"Better?"

"Yes, better." Donovan pointed at her ring. "The ring you're wearing doesn't even have a diamond." He sat up. "You deserve to have a diamond the size of your eyes."

She glared at him angrily. "And you can give me a ring with a diamond like that?"

"I'd give you a ring with a hundred diamonds like that if I thought that's what you wanted."

Itzél held out her left hand and looked at her ring. Donovan ached for her as he watched her chest rise and fall with every breath she took. She raised her head, a strand of her hair falling over one eye.

"A woman needs more than just diamonds." She looked at Donovan through the thick strand of raven-black hair over her eye. "A diamond is just a rock," she said softly.

A cold bit into him, and he felt his heart sink. He could see the commitment to her marriage in her eyes. He had misread her, taken a chance, and failed. He pushed his cup away and turned his head to the side as he thought about what she had said. He rose to his feet and reached into his pocket. He gently set several coins on the counter and took one last look at her.

"You're right," he said softly. "It's just a rock." He turned around and left.

OLD TOWN VERACRUZ
THREE YEARS AGO

The balcony at the restaurant where Donovan took Xochitl for a romantic candlelight dinner overlooked the old plaza in Veracruz. It had a spectacular view of the old cathedral and the cobblestone-covered town square below. A trio serenaded the guests sitting at the tables outside of the restaurant enjoying the cool night air. Donovan adjusted his tie and started to remove his suit jacket but decided against it. Since he worked primarily in the tropics, Donovan had all his suits made by a tailor in Panama specializing in tropical-weight formal wear.

"You can take your coat off, if you want," Xochitl said to him.

He smiled and shook his head. He thought that she looked especially radiant dressed in the sheath she wore that night and didn't want to cheapen it by removing his coat. He liked the way the tiny white silk dress looked against her velvet mocha-colored skin and the way the deep V-neck made her long, sleek neck look. He didn't own a white suit, so he decided to wear his black suit to contrast with rather than match her dress.

The headwaiter, an older man in a tuxedo with a napkin draped over his left forearm, stepped through the french doors holding an expensive bottle of red wine. Xochitl subtly rocked her head, impressed by the waiter's elegant movements as he uncorked the bottle and showed the label to Donovan before pouring a small amount into his wineglass. He made no less an exhibition of handing him the cork. Xochitl giggled playfully as she watched Donovan imitate the motions of a connoisseur of fine wines.

After filling their glasses, the waiter set the bottle on a small table by the wrought iron balustrade and turned to Donovan. "¿Algo más, caballero?"

"Gracias, Señor," Donovan said. "That'll be all."

"Muy elegante," Xochitl teased.

Donovan reached across the table and took Xochitl by the hand. "Only the best for you, mí amor."

Xochitl giggled impishly. "And gallant too."

Without letting go of her hand, Donovan reached into his coat pocket, slid off his chair, and got on one knee.

Xochitl's eyes widened. "What are you doing?"

Donovan held an engagement ring up to her. Her eyes teared up, and she covered her mouth with her free hand.

"I love you, Doctora Tonatzin." Donovan waited until she turned her charcoal eyes at him before he continued, "Will you do me the honor of being my Mrs. Donovan?"

She removed her hand from her mouth. "The diamond is so beautiful."

"Next to your beauty, it's just a rock."

The bow of the panga rose out of the water after Benício turned off the outboard motor as he approached the narrow beach across the street from La Cocina Maya. Lázaro waded out to grab the bowline and helped him pull the launch to the beach. Benício frowned when he saw the large bandage pad on Lázaro's left cheek.

"What happened to you this morning? I waited for you as long as I could."

"I'm in trouble, primo." Lázaro's hands shook so badly that he couldn't tie the bowline to the concrete ball on the malecon.

Benício took the line from him and grimaced. "Have you been drinking?"

"You have to help me, Benício," he said, his voice trembling. His breaths came in pants as he spoke. "I helped this woman who locked her keys in her car. We went to get a soft drink. The next thing I knew, I was in an alley." He covered his face with his hands and slid them down over his mouth. He dropped his hands. "They're saying I–I ..." He began to whimper.

"Shush, shush, shush." Benício took Lázaro by the shoulders. "You're not making any sense." He led him to the seawall and sat him down where he spotted Donovan's convertible parked in front of the Cocina Maya. He dropped the corners of his mouth, and his face hardened.

"They're saying I killed her."

"Killed who?" Benício asked, his attention still focused on Donovan's convertible.

"The woman I helped to unlock her car, primo." He looked up at him. "Haven't you been listening?" He noticed his cousin staring across the street. "What are you looking at?"

"Nothing." Benício turned to his troubled cousin. "Tell me what happened."

"Yesterday, I was walking home when this woman asked me to help her because she locked her keys in her car. After I opened it, she invited me to have a drink, and I told her I would drink a Coke with her."

Benício looked at him suspiciously. "Are you sure that's all you had to drink?"

"I swear, primo. That's all." He ran his hand through the hair on top of his head and started to sob. "Why don't I remember what happened after that?"

Benício had one eye on the Cocina Maya and Donovan's car as he listened. He put his hand on Lázaro's shoulder. "Tell me what you do remember."

Lázaro sniffled. "The next thing I knew, I was in an alley. The police were there. They showed me the body of the woman in the alley close to me. They told me I did it."

"What do you remember about being with the woman?"

Lázaro began to pant. He shook his head and turned his swollen eyes to Benício. "Nothing." He dropped his head into his hands and began to whimper.

"Stand up." Benício pulled him to his feet. He looked at his clothes and then leaned over and sniffed his shirt. Like a hound, he worked his way up toward his cousin's face. "Let me smell your breath."

"What?"

"Your breath, primo." Benício put his nose next to his mouth. Lázaro looked at him for a moment and then exhaled. Benício inhaled deeply and then turned his head. "Your clothes are what smell of liquor." He nodded to himself and then turned to his cousin. "Somebody must have put something in your Coke."

"Do you think so?"

"It seems like that to me." Benício glanced briefly at the Donovan's car. "We have to go to the public ministry and talk to an agent."

"I already have," Lázaro insisted. "There was an agent there."

"What did he say?"

"He told me I was guilty of murder."

Benício glared at him doubtfully. "If he thought you were guilty of murder, why are you not in jail?"

"He was very nice, this agente." Lázaro stopped sobbing, changing his demeanor. "We started talking, and the fact that I was a panguero came up." He looked at Benício. "He told me he could help me if I would do a favor for a friend of his."

"Go on," Benício said warily.

"He wants me to meet a boat on the other side of the Seyba Reef."

"To do what?"

"To bring a package to him."

"Did he say what kind of package?"

Lázaro hesitated for a moment and then shook his head.

"I see." Benício clicked his tongue and then sighed. "How far on the other side of the reef do you have to go?"

"The boat won't come closer than a couple of hours west of the Seyba Reef." He rubbed the tears from his eyes with the back of his hand. "They told me to make sure I had plenty of fuel in case I had to go farther out to meet the ship."

"You can't meet the ship that far out." Benício glared at him. "You have trouble finding the Seyba Reef. You'll never find your way back."

"I told them that."

"What did they say?"

Lázaro hesitated and then dropped his eyes. "They told me to make sure you came with me."

Benício scowled at him. "You told them about me?"

"I didn't have to." Lázaro may have stopped sobbing, but the fear in his eyes remained. "They knew about you."

Benício took a step back. "Was this agent tall? Thin? With long hair?"

"No." Lázaro shook his head. "He was average size with nice clothes, but there was somebody like that wearing a ponytail, taking pictures for him."

"Hmm." Benício scratched his brow. "It all makes sense now," he muttered.

The sound of a door slamming caught Benício's attention. He looked back toward the restaurant and saw Donovan sitting in his convertible with his head down and his arms draped around the steering wheel. After a short while, Donovan started the car and drove away toward the port. Scarcely a moment later, he saw Itzél come to the window and look down the street toward the port.

"Primo," Lázaro interrupted Benício's focus. "You don't have to go with me. Just show me. Go over how to find my way with a compass again." Lázaro looked at him. "I can do it by myself. I won't get lost."

"You're not going to get lost." Benício glanced briefly at Itzél, still staring out the window. "I'm going with you."

CHAPTER

8

The hour for the serving of la comida had arrived, and Benício had yet to return from the reef. Itzél hurried to prepare for the midday rush with one eye on the clock and an ear tuned to the chime of the bell over the door. He had always come in from the reef in time to help her with la comida, and although he had come in late before, he had never come in this late. She took a dishrag and began to wipe down the counter, periodically glancing out the plate glass window, hoping to see her husband crossing the street with his net over his shoulder.

The malecon seemed sadly quiet. The fishermen had all come in from the reef and beached their pangas on the other side of the seawall. The few who stayed to peddle their catches or drink beer and talk about their day at the reef had gone. Only a solitary seagull hovered over the malecon, looking for a scrap to eat.

As Itzél wiped the long countertop, she stopped to look at the cup Donovan had used earlier that day. She purposely left it where he had set it down. She drew a long breath and stared at it. "It's my fault," she muttered to herself.

For the moment, guilt replaced the worry on Itzél's face as she stared at the cup, although she had done nothing wrong other than to bask in the attention of a handsome man. Sexual attraction is biological and ingrained in human nature. Marriage does not turn it off. Most happily married people enjoy the attention but never act on the attraction. They simply take it as an affirmation of their desirability, as she had. Although she had done nothing wrong, she had not considered the danger inherently involved when it came to attracting the opposite sex.

It was understandable for any woman to be drawn to someone like Donovan, who, like a gallant knight or avenging angel, came onto the scene in time to rescue her family from the clutches of an evil man and his minions. It was only natural that his dashing good looks and bravado would catch her eye. However, like so many other women in her position, she made the mistake of having looked for too long. His advances had put a kink in his armor and taken the glow from his halo. She turned abruptly when she heard the doorbell chime and gasped when she saw Benício walk through the door with his cousin Lázaro one step behind him.

"Where have you been?" She put down the dishrag. "I was worried something bad had happened."

Benício ignored her and glared at her bitterly as he walked toward the hallway. He glanced back at his cousin. "I'll be back with the gas cans in a minute."

Lázaro stood a few feet from the counter, his face tortured with worry. He dropped his eyes when Itzél went around the counter to talk to him.

"What's going on?" she asked him.

The little man, who stood no taller than Benício and had the same girth but with a full head of hair, drew away from her like a child cowering before a scolding.

"Why does he need gas cans?" Itzél stepped into his space. "Where are you going?"

Like a cornered animal, Lázaro tried to find a way out with nowhere to run. He turned away from her.

"Tell me," she demanded.

Lázaro slowly turned to face her, on the verge of crying. "I'm in trouble with some very bad people." He shuddered. "Benício's going to help me."

"Lázaro!" Benício called. He stood in the hallway, glaring angrily at him. He walked up to him and gave him the plastic gas cans. "Go wait for me in the truck."

"Sí, primo." Lázaro took the containers and left.

"¿Que esta pasando?" Itzél asked Benício. "What's happening?"

Benício walked around the counter and poured himself a cup of coffee. "I'm going with Lázaro to meet a ship on the other side of the Seyba Reef."

She looked at him apprehensively. "I thought that was all over."

He took a sip of coffee. "So did I." He walked back around the counter and sat on a bar stool facing her. "El Demonio's people killed a girl and made it look like Lázaro did it." He drew a sharp breath and exhaled slowly. "If we don't meet that ship like they want, they'll turn Lázaro in."

"Why doesn't he go to the ministerio publico and explain what happened?"

"Because a public ministry agent is the one who set him up."

Her apprehension turned into fear. "Why do you have to go?" Itzél panted to catch her breath. "Can't Lázaro go by himself?"

"Lázaro's never been beyond the reef." He took another sip of coffee, his eyes reflecting resolve with no hint of fear betraying him. "He'll get lost."

"How far do you have to go?"

"I don't know." He turned around to put the cup on the counter but hesitated when he saw Donovan's empty cup. He glared at it for a moment before continuing, "All I was told is to head due west for the Arcas and look for a ship flying a Pemex flag."

She shook her head nervously. "Didn't you tell me once that the Arcas cays are a hundred kilometers from Seyba Playa?"

"Closer to a hundred and thirty." He tucked his shirt into his pants. "From what they told me, we shouldn't have to go more than an hour or so west of the reef."

"What if you're caught?"

"We won't get caught," Benício said confidently. He looked at the clock. "I have to go."

"I don't want you to go." Itzél stood in his way. "It's too dangerous."

He glanced briefly at Donovan's cup. "I thought you admired men who weren't afraid of danger?"

"I said I admired men who weren't afraid to face danger they didn't go looking for." She glared at him. "You're looking for it."

"You think I went looking for this?" He retorted sternly. When she didn't respond, he started to leave. "I wasn't given a choice."

"You always said we have a choice to choose right from wrong." She again blocked his way. "You know what you're doing is wrong."

"Sometimes doing something wrong is the right choice." He gently moved her to the side. "I'll be back."

"I still don't understand why you have to go with him," she said, stopping him.

"I already told you." He turned to face her. "He'll get lost without me."

"You're using that as an excuse to go with him," she blurted to him. "You're just trying to prove something."

Her remark upset Benício, and he stared into her eyes resentfully as the undulating drone of a heavy truck passing outside rolled through the restaurant. He waited for the sound to fade. "Nothing you say can stop me from helping my cousin."

"We'll see." Itzél turned abruptly and hurried to the cash register.

Benício followed her behind the counter and watched her open the drawer, lift the tray, and begin sorting through the various receipts and business cards she kept in the drawer. "What are you looking for?"

"Capitán Dónovan's number."

"What for?"

"We need his help," she said over the sound of paper shuffling. "He'll know what to do."

Itzél withdrew her hands as Benício pushed down on the tray. "You don't think I know what I'm doing?"

"He has more experience with these kinds of things." She pushed his hand aside and resumed looking for Donovan's business card.

"How do you know that?" He glared at her with the cold eyes of a Spanish inquisitor. "Did he tell you during one of his little visits?" He took her hand out of the register. "I wonder what other things you two talked about." He slammed the drawer shut, startling her. He glared at her as he started to leave. "At least allow me my dignity."

The story about the panguero's detention by the Armada took but a small corner of the police section of the local newspaper. Most would have overlooked the story of little consequence. However, it attracted the keen interest of Don Arturo, who sat behind the polished oak desk in his study, carefully analyzing the article. Casimiro sat across from him in one of the two winged-back leather chairs, waiting for his commentary.

The article related how the Armada's patrol boat intercepted a panguero, wandering well beyond the Seyba Playa Reef, away from the usual fishing grounds. "Fearing that he may be lost, the patrol boat captain offered to help the wayward fisherman, only to find him with a restricted firearm. When questioned, the panguero made contradictory statements and otherwise failed to suitably explain the reason for his presence so far from the Seyba Playa Reef, resulting in his detention not only for the unlawful possession of a firearm but for suspicion of piracy as well." The article went on to mention the pirate attack near Holbox Island and the rash of offshore robberies and thefts being perpetrated by armed men in high-speed launches.

The photographs accompanying the article showed the hapless panguero standing on the dock between two marineros, holding an obviously unloaded revolver, his hair in wild disarray and dressed only in red swimming trunks. A second photo showed the inside of the panga, empty but for an array of gasoline containers arranged in the aft section of the launch. The caption under the second photograph explained how the panga did not have the items normally associated with fishing, suggesting that the panguero might be working as a high seas hijacker.

The head of the Campechanos closed the newspaper, folded it in half, and handed it across his desk to Casimiro. "From the article, it looks like the Armada believes he's part of that band of seagoing bandidos that's been terrorizing the coast the last couple of weeks."

"My go-between tells me that it's not unusual for the Armada to make misleading remarks to the press to keep from scaring off the people they're after."

"So you believe this is the panguero your informer told you about?"

Casimiro nodded. "The Armada must have jumped him before he met the ship," he speculated.

"If he was meeting a ship," Don Arturo emphasized. "He could have been out there waiting for a plane to drop the drugs into the water near him. That's a common technique."

"He went to meet a ship," Casimiro retorted confidently. "My informer confirmed it later."

"Too bad your informer didn't confirm it before the Armada jumped the panguero."

"You can only expect so much from the old woman." Casimiro laid the newspaper on the small cherrywood table between the high-back chairs. "If she was young and beautiful, she might have been able to use her charms to get better details." He chuckled. "I'm afraid all she has left of her natural attributes are her ears."

"I appreciate what she's doing for us." Arturo reclined his head on the back of his chair, gazing aimlessly. He lowered his eyes. "How fortunate she used to work for you."

"Um-hmm." Casimiro chuckled. "I hated to lose her when she left me to work for the Mireles family in Lorenzo, but as it turns out, it worked out for the best."

"Has she heard anything about what her employer plans to do next?"

"As a matter of fact, she has. He's sending another panguero to get fifty kilos this afternoon. This time, she's sure he'll be meeting a service boat."

"Did she get the ship's name?"

Casimiro shook his head. "No, but she did hear them mention Pemex." He leaned toward him. "It has to be Capitán Santos."

Arturo sighed. "I don't know."

"Who else could it be?" Casimiro sat up. "The only service boat I know operating between Seyba Playa and the Arcas is captained by Santos. It has to be him."

"I don't see how." Arturo shook his head. "Pemex checks their boat for drugs and alcohol before it leaves the port, and the PFP checks him when he comes back in. The Federal Preventive Police use drug dogs. They've never found so much as a trace of contraband."

"All that means is that he's careful." Casimiro took his cell phone out of his pocket. "If we can get the Armada to watch his boat, he should lead them to the where he's making the exchange with the panguero." He put his reading glasses on to check the contact list on his phone. "My go-between with the Armada should be able to sell it."

"Why not just follow the panguero like they did the last time?" Arturo recommended. "Only this time, tell them there's another boat involved and to wait until they make the exchange. If you're wrong about Santos, it could ruin your go-between's credibility with the Armada."

Casimiro set his phone on his lap and looked at him pensively.

"You don't know who the panguero is," Arturo surmised.

"Unfortunately, she was unable to get his name."

"Can you call her to see if she can find out who they're sending?"

"Because of her situation, I have to wait for her to call me." He clicked his teeth like an old typewriter as he thought about it. "She's a resourceful old woman." Casimiro scoffed. "Superstitious but very sneaky. If she's able to learn anything more about the service boat or the panguero, she'll call me."

"Hmm." Arturo dropped the corners of his mouth. "Let's hope she doesn't get caught in the process."

There were other matters of concern for the association besides the apparent breach of their territorial exclusivity by the sudden appearance of another drug trafficker. La Comisión continued to grow in influence not only threatening the Campechanos' long-standing dominance in the Yucatán Peninsula but potentially pitting the Norteño cartel against them.

The Norteño cartel had its sights set on settling accounts with La Comisión for hijacking their narcotics shipments while they fought the Frontera cartel. Anastasio Noches Treviño, the head of the Norteños, accepted Don Arturo's reluctance to ally the Campechanos with his cartel to forcefully end Comandante Sánchez and his task force's arrangement with La Comisión, opting to negotiate with and pay off the corrupt Campeche comandantes instead. When Don Rodrigo persuaded a faction within the association to hire the Campeche gangs to form a security force, Don Arturo worried that such an action might give the Norteños the wrong impression. He worried that if Rodrigo was able to persuade the Campechanos to arm the Campeche gangs and convert the security force into a paramilitary army, then Anastasio would have no choice but to head-off an alliance between La Comisión and Los Campechanos.

To exacerbate the situation, Casimiro recently learned that Comandante Sánchez planned to attend a conference in Tuxtla Gutiérrez, disguising his true purpose: to meet with a personal representative of Alejandro Pelayo Diaz, the leader of La Comisión. Suddenly, it appeared that Anastasio Noches Treviño might have been right all along.

"What have you found out about Comandante Sánchez's trip to Chiapas?"

"Not much, I'm afraid." He crossed his legs. "I checked with the municipal president's office in Tuxtla Gutiérrez. The law enforcement conference he told his office he was attending isn't for another week."

The head of the growers association sat quietly, his eyes shifting to one side and then the other as if looking for a misplaced item. He then focused them on his friend. "I wonder what he's up to."

The terminal at Campeche City's Alberto Acuña Ongay International Airport is not very big. It only has two gates and a single runway that can accommodate only the smaller range of passenger jets. Most of the modest shops wrapped around the outer walls of the terminal seldom seem to be open, especially the tiny restaurant that appears to offer little more than chips and cold cuts sandwiches. Comandante Sánchez, dressed typically in his short-sleeved leisure suit and golfing hat, sat next to Comandante Prieto, waiting for his flight to Tuxtla Gutiérrez. Not far from where they were sitting stood two Federal Preventive Police officers assigned to the airport.

"So you're not meeting with Alejandro," Prieto said.

Sánchez scoffed. "Pinche carcelero, bueno para nada," he cussed barely under his breath. "Who does that good-for-nothing jailer think he is?"

Alejandro Pelayo Díaz did start his criminal career in jail—not as an inmate but as a lowly jailer in the state prison at Tuxtla Gutiérrez. Through the inmates, he learned the mechanics of the drug trade and made important connections with several highly placed members of the Frontera cartel in Tamaulipas. Using his contacts working in the Chiapas state prison system, he learned the names of several corrupt police commanders across the state who accepted bribes to allow narcotics destined to the Norteño cartel to traverse their jurisdictions. Pelayo Díaz contacted them, and through his powers of persuasion, he convinced them that he could get them infinitely more money selling the drugs to the Frontera cartel than just taking a percentage from the Norteño mules they detained. His success emboldened other police commanders to enter into a partnership with the lowly jailer, and in time, these partnerships evolved into what is now known as La Comisión with Alejandro Pelayo Díaz as the head.

Despite the lack of respect he had for him, Sánchez hoped to emulate the lowly jailer's success and organize the Campeche gangs under his task force's control into his own narcotics-trafficking organization.

"Who are they sending to talk to you?" Prieto asked Sánchez.

Sánchez glanced over his shoulder at the federal preventive policemen before responding, "Tercero. I'm meeting him at the Soldadera."

"I know that place." He chuckled. "They have good-looking meseras."

"I'm not going there to flirt with the waitresses."

The smile left his face. "Of course not, Heriberto." Comandante Prieto turned his head to the side. "I've been talking with some of the others." He inhaled deeply. "You might have a problem getting them to renew the arrangement." He turned to his colleague. "El Chino and Tápia are trying to convince the others that López is their best bet, should the Norteños decide to send Colonel Barca to Campeche."

Sánchez grinned smugly at Prieto. "When I start bringing in the guns, they'll see who's their best bet."

"El Chino and Tápia insist that Fausto can get us better guns than you can."

He looked at Prieto with the leering eyes of an Arab trader. "What are they saying?"

"They pointed out the guns you got from the La Comisión the last time were pieces of junk." Prieto cocked his brows. "You have to admit they have a point. Some of the guns didn't have stocks. Only a few of them worked properly. We had to strip parts out of half of them to get the others to work."

Sánchez exhaled sharply. "I'll take care of that. I'll take an armorer to inspect the guns and certify each one before they ship them to us."

"I don't know." Prieto wavered. "The others like the idea of getting new American guns."

"At least I've proved that I can get guns. Umm?" He glared angrily at him. "Fausto has yet to show that he can." Sánchez glanced over his shoulder and lowered his voice. "Have they forgotten about the guns he lost at Punta Morro?"

"It's more than just the guns."

"What is it then?"

Prieto hesitated. "They trust El Demonio. He showed them how to use the gangs to make money." He cocked a brow. "They're making more money now than what you were giving them selling the drugs we seized to Alejandro."

Comandante Sánchez looked behind him. The federal policemen had gone. "This time, I'll make it worth their while. I'll give each of them a substantial cut of the profits."

"That might not be enough." Prieto sighed. "Chino and Tápia have convinced the others that only El Demonio can stop Colonel Barca because of his combat experience."

"Did you remind them that he was chased out of Michoacán and Tamaulipas by the colonel with his tail between his legs?"

Prieto retreated. "I'm just saying, you're going to have to convince them that they have a better chance sticking with you."

"I expect they'll see that for themselves when they're holding my fully functioning automatic rifles in their hands."

Taking inventory never bothered Pablo. He rather enjoyed measuring the contents of every bottle on his back cabinet, recording the measurements, and checking it against sales with the sharp eye of a Prohibition-era Chicago bean counter. He found the activity relaxing, but more important, it enabled him to exercise his favorite pastime of eavesdropping during the cocktail hour. He went about recording his measurements as he drifted toward the end of the bar where the only two patrons in the lounge talked over their beers.

Don Macario shook his head as he watched Pablo drift closer and closer to the two patrons sitting near the end of the bar closest to him. He guessed what interested his nosy barman; both men were known for their womanizing ways. He had often admonished his bar manager in private against pursuing this shameless pleasure he so enjoyed. However, the proprietor of the Paradise Lounge could not deny that there were instances when his barman's desire to know what he was not meant to know produced some interesting results.

Others appreciated his guilty pleasures as well, like Casimiro Mendiola of the Campeche Growers Association, who recognized the valuable services he could provide, especially in terms of collecting and passing on information. The dandy barman, who bordered on the effeminate, did not use his penchant for nosiness as fodder for gossip. He collected it and filed it away until a need for it presented itself. That need generally came in the form of a payoff.

Pablo laid down his clipboard to answer his cell phone.

"¿Bueno?"

"Buenas tardes, Pablito. Do you know who this is?" Don Casimiro said softly.

"Of course." The dapper barman scurried to the other end of the bar to take the call, leaving the two patrons to discuss their wives and lovers without his attentive ear. "Is there something I can do for you?"

"First, thank you for passing that tidbit I gave you to our friends in Lerma." Casimiro twitched his nose to the side, "Did they show you the proper appreciation for the information about that scandalous fisherman?"

"They were disappointed that the escandoloso only had the one thing and not what I told them they might find."

"I hope that it hasn't ruined your friendship with them?"

"No, no." Pablo looked over his shoulder at Don Macario, who had stopped working his crossword puzzle to look at him. "They believed he was out there to do what I told them he was doing. They asked me to keep in touch."

"Good." Casimiro stretched the word. "Because they're sending another escandoloso to the Seyba Reef to get fifty big ones later this afternoon."

"Have they no shame?" Pablo clicked his tongue twice. "Do you have a name?"

"No, not this time," Don Casimiro replied. "But I think I know who he's meeting."

"¿Quien?"

"Do you know who Capitán Santos is?"

Pablo raised his head to nod a greeting to another pair of men entering the lounge. He shielded his mouth and lowered his voice even further. "So then it's true what they say about him?"

Recognizing that the Armada would likely dismiss the tip based on the scant information the housekeeper provided, Casimiro decided to pass on his supposition regarding the Pemex supply boat captain. "Can you see that our friends in Lerma get the information?"

"Of course." He held an index finger up, signaling the new arrivals he would be with them in a moment. "I'll leave right away."

"Somebody will be by later to compensate you for your trouble."

"Gracias, Don Casimiro."

Pablo put the phone into his pocket and hurried around the bar to the restaurant. After a moment, he came back into the lounge and walked at a quick pace to talk with Don Macario at the back of the lounge.

"If it's all right with you, I have to go out for about an hour, Don Macario," Pablo said humbly. "Micaela has agreed to watch the bar until I get back."

Don Macario lowered his head to look at Pablo through his reading glasses and then went back to work on the crossword puzzle in his hand. "Hurry back."

The gears on the foresail winch clattered noisily as Poli cranked it as fast as he could. Sandy stood over him, holding a stopwatch with an eye on him and one on the sail rising up the mast. Augie, who just finished greasing the gears on the davits, cringed at the obnoxious sound coming from the winch.

"Belay that racket!" he yelled to his nephew. He finished greasing the davits and walked toward the foremast. "Let me grease that sucker."

Below deck, Donovan sat on the edge of his bunk, staring at Xochitl's picture. He rubbed the image of her face gently with his thumb and sighed deeply. He looked at the metal box next to him on the bunk and opened it, running his fingertips along the bottom until he found what he wanted. He raised the diamond-studded engagement ring and looked at the stone.

"Just a rock," he muttered to himself.

Old Town Veracruz
Three years ago

Xochitl spread her fingers, admiring the diamond ring on her hand. She raised her eyes and looked at Donovan sitting across the table from her. She laughed softly as she took her dinner napkin and reached for his lips.

"You have lipstick on your lips, Mr. Donovan," she said playfully as she dabbed them with the napkin. "How careless of your wife to let you leave the house that way."

Donovan smiled. "I'm going to have to talk to her about that."

She clicked her tongue disapprovingly. "Shame on Mrs. Donovan."

A strand of hair fell over her right eye. Donovan reached over and brushed it behind her ear. The trio playing below the balcony began a romantic song as the two lovers became lost in each other's eyes. The soft glow from the streetlamp below made Xochitl's olive skin seem like velvet against the brightness of the white sheath she wore. She smiled at him with her eyes as she gazed deeply into his.

"Let's get married tonight," he declared. "There's a company ship in port. I'll wake up the captain."

"You'll do no such thing, Mr. Donovan," she protested. "I want a big wedding with all my family present."

"When then?"

The question seemed to catch her by surprise. She looked to her right and dropped her head slightly, draping the side of her face with her silky black hair. Donovan felt his throat tighten and an anxious pang in his stomach.

"You're not changing your mind?" he asked cautiously.

"Of course not." She looked up at him, her face showing signs of distress. "I've been meaning to tell you something." She inhaled deeply. "I've signed up for a tour with Médecins Sans Frontières."

"Doctors without Borders?" Donovan fell into his chair and put his elbow on the back. He laid the other hand flat on the table. "For how long?"

She released her breath. "A year." Xochitl sat uneasily, waiting for him to say something. She grabbed his hand and massaged it with her fingertips. "We can get married when I get back."

Donovan looked down on the tables below the balcony as Xochitl dug her fingertips deep into his hand. Up to that moment, they had never had a serious argument, and he didn't want to start. He didn't like the idea but knew that standing in her way would make her unhappy and he didn't want that either.

"Where are they sending you?"

"There's a tribe in the Chocó with a high mortality rate." She lifted his hand and kissed it. "I'll be providing expectant mothers with prenatal care."

He looked down on the diners below the balcony, searching for something that he could say to change her mind. "I don't suppose I have to tell you that it's going to be dangerous." He reached across the table to brush the strand of hair over her right eye behind her ear. "The FARC have a big operation in the Chocó."

"The guerrillas haven't bothered the mission yet."

He tried another approach, "You'll probably be living in a tent."

"You know I like camping."

Donovan smiled dolefully. "You'll be among strangers."

"Doctor Aguirre will be going also."

"Doctor Aguirre?" Donovan withdrew his hand. "The guy you work with?"

"Um-hmm." She laughed. "You're not jealous, are you?"

"Why shouldn't I be?" Donovan feigned jealousy. "He's a good-looking guy."

She reached back across the table and pulled him by the hand toward her. "He's cute, but nowhere as good-looking as my fiancé." She pulled herself close to him and kissed his lips. She giggled playfully as she wiped the lipstick from his lips with her thumb.

CHAPTER

9

Getting the ship ready to sail involves as much attention to detail as a preflight inspection. Like an airplane, a sailing vessel relies on various systems to make the ship go. The sails harness the power of the wind, the hydrodynamic keel keeps the ship steady, and the rudder directs the ship through the current. The wind can take you to faraway and exotic places no matter the current. Happiness is a good ship and a favorable wind. However, beyond the romantic exists the reality that the sun, sea, and wind visit on any ship good or otherwise. Rust, rot, and harbors are a sailor's worse enemy. A sailor may look for a harbor in a storm, but harbors play hell on canvas, wood, and iron.

The predeparture inspection gave Poli an opportunity to demonstrate what he had learned. He single-handedly hoisted the sails for Donovan to check for rot and tears and then lowered and secured them. With Donovan's guidance, he tested the connections on all the halyards, sheets, and stays as well as the associated blocks and tackle to make sure they ran freely. They also checked the cleats and clutches to see that they would hold fast when called upon. Poli threw out the anchor, checked the chain, and weighed and stored it in its locker. They checked the pivots and winches and the ship's tenders for seaworthiness.

While Donovan and Poli checked everything on the deck and hull from stem to stern, Augie and Sandy took charge of everything below deck. They checked the ship's supply of potable water. They checked the engine's fuel, oil, coolant, and transmission-fluid levels. They inspected the belts and the spark plug wires for fray and tears. They checked the equipment locker for extra oil, coolant, fuses, spare belts, hoses, and gaskets. They inspected the toolbox to make sure they had all the tools and adhesives necessary to handle any contingency. They tested both the electric and manual bilge pumps and the emergency generator to see that they functioned properly.

Each crewman had specific responsibilities entrusted to him. As the skipper and navigator, Donovan took charge of communications and the chart table. He maintained the radio and satellite phone, signal lights, flares, and navigational instruments. He kept the charts current and in order, noting hazards to navigation and other dangers, such as epidemics, crime rates, or unfriendly natives. He also kept the ship's log.

As the first mate, Augie ran the ship. He assigned responsibilities and oversaw the execution. He also served as the ship's cook, surgeon, and engineer. He personally stocked the galley, planned all meals, and, of course, prepared them. He maintained the first-aid kit and boasted that he could expertly treat all wounds and injuries from soothing insect bites to setting broken limbs to extracting foreign objects, like fish hooks and the captain's boot from an errant crewman's posterior. Augie had worked as a mechanic, a machinist, a carpenter, a plumber, and an electrician. He had all the skills necessary to handle emergency repairs at sea.

The responsibilities of the safety officer fell upon Sandy. He maintained the fire extinguisher, personal flotation devices, and smoke and carbon monoxide detectors. He also had the unsavory task of using his nose to detect strange odors, like coolant and fuel leaks, burning oil, and any other malodorous scents that could affect the safety of the crew. With that in mind, his uncle also awarded him the dubious responsibility of ensuring that the head and the sea cocks functioned properly with the added responsibility of clearing any problems that might occur with them during the voyage.

To Poli fell the unenviable responsibility of being, as the first mate put it, the ship's "gopher, extra hand, and all-purpose flunky." The responsibility had not been given to him in a mean-spirited way but as an opportunity to familiarize himself with the many tasks expected of an able seaman. From Donovan, he learned the basics of navigation; from Augie, he learned how to maneuver the ship; and from Sandy, he learned how to work the sails, swab the deck, and yes, clear a toilet.

Finally, they checked the helm. Donovan and Augie conducted the inspection together. As Donovan stood by the ship's wheel, Augie squatted down by the steering box and opened the hatch to look at the steering mechanism.

"Turn the wheel hard to starboard and then hard to port," Augie called to Donovan.

Donovan spun the wheel all the way to the right. "Hard to starboard." He then spun it back to his left as far as he could. "Hard to port."

Augie slammed the door shut and stood. "Everything looks and sounds good." He walked behind the boom crutch and looked over the stern into the water. "Turn the wheel hard to starboard."

"Hard to starboard!" Donovan called.

Augie watched the rudder move smoothly to the right. "Now hard to port."

"Hard to port," Donovan repeated the order.

"Rudder's good." Augie leaned over the transom as far as he dared to look at the exhaust pipe. "Start the engine." A stream of water blasted out of the exhaust pipe as Donovan started the engine. He watched the flow and listened over the low hum of the engine. "Exhaust's good."

Donovan switched off the engine when he thought he heard his name called from the dock below. He walked to the port side of the ship and looked down on the dock. A young Mexican man dressed in a hotel uniform looked up at him.

"Buenas tardes, Capitán Dónovan."

"Buenas tardes, Quino," Donovan returned the greeting.

Quino not only worked as the hotel's principal portero and concierge but also served as Don Macario's valet, driver, and all-around get-it-done man.

"Good afternoon, Capitán. Don Macario would like to see you."

Donovan turned to Augie, who shrugged his shoulders and shook his head. He called down to Quino, "Do you know what about?"

"I think it has something to do with la Señora Itzél," he replied. "She came to talk with Don Macario. She looked upset."

The color left Donovan's face, which did not go unnoticed by his partner. Augie leaned on the rail to look into his face. "Are you all right, Skipper?"

Since coming back to his ancestral home, Don Macario had assumed the unofficial distinction of village elder in Seyba Playa to many of its citizens, Benício and Itzél among them. Donovan had no doubt that Itzél confided in him what had transpired between them. He had asked the girl to dance; now the fiddler would need his pay.

"Tell him I'll be right over." Donovan pushed himself off the rail, ignoring his partner's unflinching gaze.

"Capitán." Quino took a step closer. "Don Macario told me not to come back without you."

"What's this all about, Skipper?" Augie asked him.

Donovan ignored the question. "Can you get by without me for a bit?"

"All that's left is to get the professor's gear on board and a final check of the weather."

"Have you heard from Conrad?"

"No, but there's still a couple of hours before the tide comes in."

The summoning had clearly disconcerted Donovan. When Quino mentioned Itzél's name, it threw him off an even keel. He lost his rudder and appeared confused, his movements awkward like a man who'd lost his sea legs. He turned his head from side-to-side as if looking for a way out of a narrow channel.

"I'll be right back," he told Augie as he walked unsteadily toward the gangplank.

"Skipper." Augie stopped him. He looked for Quino, who had gone to wait for Donovan at the foot of the gangplank. He stepped up to him and looked into his eyes. "Is there something going on between you and Poli's mother?"

Donovan looked away. "I don't know what you're talking about."

"When you first brought Poli aboard, I thought it might have something to do with the fact that his mother is a beautiful woman."

"That had nothing to do with it."

"I tried telling myself that." Augie hesitated before continuing. He expelled his breath. "Then I saw the picture you dropped when you were showing me the ship's papers." He glared at his partner. "Who's the girl in the picture?"

Donovan's face hardened. "That's none of your business."

"Don't you think she looks a lot like Poli's mother?"

"No, she doesn't."

"Like hell she doesn't." Augie turned his head to the side. "I don't want to sound like a prude." He scoffed. "Hell, I've been married three times. Two of my wives I met when I was still married, so I know a little something about what you're going through."

"What's your point?"

He looked at him sternly. "I just want to make sure you know what you're doing before you break up a marriage. I don't know what that woman in the picture means to you." He paused to take a breath and then sighed. "Just be sure what you're feeling is for Itzél and not somebody else."

The two men glared at each other like a pair of dogs sizing each other up on the street, each standing his ground, neither knowing what to do next. Augie had no way of knowing that he had dragged out into the open what Donovan so desperately tried to bury deep within himself. Already shaken by the reckoning he expected for having made a run at a man's wife, Donovan now had to contend with the reopening of a wound that refused to heal.

"Capitán." Quino had walked up the gangplank. "Don Macario's waiting."

Augie took a work rag from his back pocket and started to wipe his hands. "You'd better go see what he wants," he said calmly as he headed for the main cabin. "I'll check on the weather."

Quino waited for Donovan to come down the gangplank before leading him up the pier to the hotel. As Donovan prepared himself for at the very least an unpleasant conversation, his mind wandered, seeking refuge in his surroundings.

His thoughts turned to the lagoon and how time and tide had made what man blasted from the limestone into a veritable paradise. Nothing that man creates can escape the hand of the master builder. Like the rib extracted from Adam, the lagoon matured into something finer that gave man respite from the toils of everyday life. Like a beautiful woman who teases with her charms and seduces with her beauty, the lagoon used the tide to tease and seduce the weary eye.

Like a well-endowed woman wearing a bikini, concealing her charms under a thin blouse with the buttons fastened to the top and her shapely hips beneath a wrap, the lagoon concealed the true wonder of the sun-bleached limestone boulders that lined her waters under a translucent aquamarine blouse and the pearly sands of her beach under a wrap of gently lapping blue-green water.

As the tide receded, the lagoon gradually undid the buttons of her blouse, slowly revealing the true size of the wonders she concealed. The water lapping against the massive boulders she kept hidden rose and fell like a woman's chest anticipating a lover's kiss. The receding waters also unveiled the virgin sands of her beach like a woman dropping the wrap from her voluptuous, rounded hips. In another two hours or so, the tide would remind the lagoon of her modesty and subtly button her blouse and throw her wrap around her sunbaked hips.

When Donovan topped the stairway above the marina, he saw Itzél walking down the stairs of the Paradise Inn. She turned to look at him for a moment. Her eyes seemed to say something to him that he could not make out from where he stood, dumbfounded by her beauty. The wind blowing through her loose-fitting clothes outlined her figure like a backlight silhouetting a woman's shape through a light-colored dress. She continued down the steps to her car as Don Macario stepped out on the veranda to wave off his portero.

"Buena suerte, Capitán," Quino said, wishing Donovan luck as he parted company with him. He hurried along the concrete rail to the outdoor patio.

Donovan took a hard swallow as he looked at Don Macario watching him from the veranda. His face had the look of someone about to deliver a death message. Like a man facing a long march, he took a deep breath and forced himself to take the first step. He heard a car door slam and an engine start as he made his way to the veranda. His eyes followed Itzél's two-door sedan driving away from the parking lot, passing Pablo's Camaro as it rounded down the hill toward the hotel.

As Don Macario waited for Donovan to step up to the veranda, he watched Pablo walking toward the hotel.

"Itzél's very upset," he said softly to Donovan with an eye on Pablo.

"I know. I don't know what made me do it," Donovan blurted unexpectedly. "We were talking about our jobs, and the next thing I know, I'm making a pass at her."

His outburst surprised the old gentleman. He looked beyond Donovan and motioned for him to lower his voice with his hand. Donovan turned his head to look behind him. He saw Pablo walking casually toward them, pretending not to have heard the outburst.

"She said something about regretting that she gave you the wrong impression," Don Macario continued in a low voice, "but she didn't say anything about you making a pass at her."

"She didn't?" Donovan turned his head briefly to watch for Pablo. "By the way she reacted, I was sure she was upset with me."

"She might be, but she has a bigger problem to think about." He folded his arms and turned his attention to Pablo. "Tell Micaela to go back to the restaurant."

"Sí, Don Macario," Pablo said as he stepped up to the veranda. "I'm sorry I took so long."

"That's all right." Don Macario waited for Pablo to get out of earshot before he continued. He took a deep breath. "Benício is making a run for El Demonio."

"What?" Donovan blurted, causing Pablo to slow his step.

"He and Lázaro are meeting a ship on the other side of the Seyba Reef."

Donovan reached into his pocket for his car keys. "Maybe I can catch them before they head out."

"It's too late." Don Macario stopped him. "They've already left."

Pablo started to look back at them and then reluctantly took a step toward the entrance.

"How long ago?" Donovan asked.

"In the last hour. There's nothing anybody can do." Don Macario sighed. "All we can do is pray that he doesn't end up like the last panguero caught on the other side of the Seyba Reef."

"It's a big ocean," Donovan said, unconvinced by his own words. "Maybe he'll pull it off without a hitch."

Pablo put his hand on the door handle and then dropped his head as he continued to listen to his boss talking with Donovan.

"That's what I told Itzél." He sighed and then turned his head to the side. "That's what I've been telling myself."

Pablo stared at the door handle, his breathing long and deep. He wrapped his fingers around the handle and pulled down on it, opening the door slightly. He looked back at his employer, his face pallid and conflicted.

"I could head out to the Seyba Reef," Donovan suggested. "If he's not too far out, I might be able to find him before he meets the ship and talk some sense into him."

"Excuse me," Pablo said as he walked up to them. "I couldn't help but hear what's going on." He looked at Don Macario with torment in his eyes. "Do you know what ship they're meeting?"

"Not specifically." Don Macario shrugged. "Only that it'll be flying a Pemex flag."

Pablo shut his eyes. "I think I know who he's meeting."

"Hold on a moment," Donovan said as he recalled his conversation with Captain Santos at the lounge. "Is it Captain Santos?"

Pablo lowered his head and nodded. "The Armada knows about the rendezvous. They're going to be watching his ship when it leaves port this afternoon."

"How do you know this?" Don Macario demanded.

"I heard it from someone."

Donovan turned around abruptly and started for the stairs.

"Where are you going?" Don Macario called to him.

"To my cabaña to get my car," he said as he hurried down the stairs. "There might be something I can do help Benício."

The Tiburón sat just inside the gates of the port of Seyba Playa where the road running along the malecon turned sharply to the east, away from the ocean. It stood alone, across the parking lot from the dock, like a guard shack and indeed had served as one at one point of its storied life. It served as an office building for many years until the cinder block and stucco port administration building replaced it. It sat vacant for a while, used as a storeroom and a guard shack until someone realized it could be used as a lunchroom for the employees working at the port. The port administration sold off the office furniture and moved in several metal tables and chairs where the employees could eat their sack lunches. As the lunchroom grew in popularity, the administration added several more metal tables and a soft-drink machine.

For many years, the old weather-beaten clapboard building with the rust-stained corrugated metal roof had been the only place where the people working at the port could eat lunch until the small convenience store across the street from the gates set out several plastic tables and chairs on the sidewalk and began serving hot food. Other smaller mom-and-pop eateries sprang up all along the malecon, drawing the port employees away from the lunchroom. The port administration considered closing it, believing it too expensive to maintain and no longer serving its intended purpose. They considered tearing down the old building until an enterprising young manager suggested turning the building into a recreational hall managed by the employees. The suggestion included bringing in coin-operated pool tables, the proceeds of which were to be used to maintain the building.

That was how El Tiburón came into existence. The employees slapped a coat of sea-blue paint on the weather-beaten clapboard walls. An artistically skilled employee painted a mural of a menacing great white shark over the front door, inserting the jaw of a rather large shark into the shark's mouth, giving it a lifelike appearance. Using his best calligraphic skills, he added a stylized banner over the shark with the name of the hall on it.

The Tiburón became a social center for the dockworkers, workboat crews, shrimpers, and commercial fishermen operating out of the port. In recent years, the employees set up a food cart on the street just outside the gates to help defray the costs of maintaining the building. Although the port administration officially frowned on the consumption of alcohol on its grounds, it chose to look the other way when the employees brought in beer and rum bought at the convenience store across the street.

Captain Octavio Santos sat at the rear of the Tiburón with his back to the wall, holding a pool cue. He had his right elbow on the edge of the counter-high table next to him as he watched two roughnecks dressed in orange coveralls shoot pool. It had become his practice to mingle with the oilfield workers he ferried to and from the oil rigs south of the Arcas cays while he waited for the dockworkers to load his boat with supplies.

The attention he paid to his company uniform reflected the pride he took in his work. He refused to allow his wife to press his uniform trousers and white uniform golf shirt, insisting that he do it himself. He meticulously removed every wrinkle, errant strand of thread, and particle of lint from his uniform before he reported for duty. Only his captain's hat, the badge of his authority, did he exempt from his careful attention to detail. He refused to steam out the wrinkles, believing every line and crease to represent his years of experience and because he felt it made him look cool.

The chatter in the Tiburón came to a stop when a tall gringo walked into the room. The roughnecks, crane operators, and other dockworkers looked at the outsider, some with curiosity and others offended by his presence. The tall gringo dropped several peso coins into the soft-drink machine by the entrance. By the hat he wore, the men presumed that he might be the captain of a visiting ship since he wore it crumpled down on his head, much like Capitán Santos wore his. Unlike the good captain, the gringo wore his white cotton shirt with the collar open to the third button and the sleeves rolled sloppily up to the elbow. His khaki trousers, like his shirt, desperately needed pressing.

After the first ten-ounce bottle thumped out of the machine, the outsider dropped several more peso coins and waited for the second soft drink to thud into the tray. Ignoring the curious eyes fixed on him, the outsider walked toward the back of the Tiburón, holding both bottles by the neck with one hand. With his free hand, he took a pocket knife from his trousers and snapped the blade out with a sharp flip of his wrist.

The roughnecks shooting pool with Santos stopped their game to watch the gringo walk toward the Pemex supply-boat captain, holding a knife in his hand. Captain Santos turned his head when he heard Donovan open the first bottle with the blunt edge of his knife. He slid his hat to one side to make room for the bottle Donovan had just opened. The roughnecks resumed their game after Santos reassured them with a wave of his hand.

"You should consider getting a Swiss Army knife," he said to Donovan as he sat in the chair opposite him. "They come with a bottle opener." He watched Donovan pop off the cap on the second bottle. "Where'd you learn that little trick?"

"My grandfather."

"Was he a sailor too?"

"He was many things but never a sailor." Donovan set his bottle on the table. "He learned how to do that tending bar in a Chicago speakeasy during Prohibition."

"It sounds like you have an interesting family," Santos commented.

Donovan scoffed. "You have no idea."

The crack of a pool ball striking another drew their attention. The two roughnecks shooting pool began to laugh boisterously at the impossible shot one of them had made. Santos snickered and then took a sip of his soft drink.

"Have you changed your mind?" he asked Donovan.

Donovan leaned his back against the wall. The two roughnecks shooting pool obviously had their focus more on him than on their game. "I was thinking about our little talk the other day at the lounge."

Santos looked at Donovan and then turned to look at the roughnecks. "¿Me pueden dar un momento por favor?"

The men rested their cues on the table and went to join several other roughnecks at a nearby table. Donovan took a sip of his soft drink and ran his eyes across the various pictures hanging on the opposite wall, including one taken from the air at night of the oil rigs south of the Arcas cays.

"What's on your mind?"

Donovan set his soft drink on the table. "I didn't fully appreciate what it took for you to come to the lounge to warn me."

"Warn you?" The Pemex captain scoffed. "I went there hoping to persuade you to work for El Demonio so that he could let me off the hook."

"Regardless, I took it as a warning, and I appreciate that."

"Can you get to the point?" He took another sip. "If you didn't come here because you changed your mind, then why did you come?"

"Fair enough." Donovan cleared his throat. "I came here to return the favor."

Santos looked at him suspiciously. "Go on."

"I heard the Armada was setting a trap to catch a cocaine runner west of the Seyba Reef."

He looked away. "How do you know this?"

"Let's just say that I heard a rumor."

"You know what they say about rumors?" Captain Santos took another sip. "Only a fool listens to them."

"What if it's not a rumor?"

"Are you telling me you know this for a fact?"

"Are you willing to take a chance that it isn't?"

The Pemex supply boat's horn blurted two short bursts followed by a long one signaling the passengers and crew to board. The orange-clad roughnecks, including the two Captain Santos had been watching shoot pool collected their gear and shuffled toward the door.

Santos let the air out of his lungs. "If I accept what you're telling me and it turns out that it was just a rumor ..." Santos rested the pool cue in his hand against the wall. "Things will get very unpleasant for me."

"Hmm." Donovan nodded. "On the other hand, if you ignore what I'm telling you and there's a gunboat patrolling the Seyba Reef ..." He looked at him. "Things can get just as unpleasant."

"Given a choice," he finished his soft drink, "I'd rather take my chances with the Armada." He set the empty bottle on the table. "At least I'll be able to see them coming."

Santos grabbed his captain's hat from the table and started to leave. He put it on his head and pulled down on it by the sides as he started for the exit. Donovan had failed to persuade him not to make the rendezvous. He felt he had done all that he could. Then a thought flashed through his head. With Benício in jail, it would clear the way for him with Itzél. He closed his eyes, hating himself for even thinking it. He had to find a way to keep him from making the rendezvous.

"The Armada hid a tracker on board your ship," he lied.

Santos stopped and looked over his shoulder at him. "You're making that up."

Donovan poured the rest of the ten-ounce soft drink into his throat. "Maybe I am." The empty bottle made a resounding plop when he set it on the table. "Maybe I'm not." He slid the bottle away from him and looked directly into Santos's eyes. "Can you afford to take that chance?"

The supply boat's horn blared out another two short bursts followed by a long one. Captain Santos glared at Donovan suspiciously. "I'll have the boat swept."

"You can try, but you won't find it. It's probably hardwired to one of your systems." He looked for something else he could tell him to make him reconsider meeting Benício. "How well do you know the men you're ferrying to the platforms?"

"I know most of them."

"But not all of them," Donovan posed. "It could be one of the new guys is an AFI agent working undercover."

The Pemex captain's eyes shifted from side to side, indicating to Donovan that he had successfully planted the seeds of doubt in his mind, at least for the moment.

179

Santos straightened his shirt and pulled up on his trousers. "Nice try." He pulled down on his captain's hat and gave him one last look. "Thanks for the soft drink."

Donovan sighed and shrugged his shoulders. "I tried," he said to himself. He slapped his hands on his knees to hoist himself and nearly bumped into Santos.

"Why are you doing this?"

After overcoming his initial surprise, Donovan decided to tell him the truth. "The people you're meeting are friends of mine. They left before I could stop them. I figured the only way to keep them from going to jail was by stopping you from making the delivery."

They stared at each other like boxers at a weigh-in. Santos, his eyes hard and deliberate, stared coldly into Donovan's looking for signs of deception. After a moment, Santos let out a long, deep sigh and relaxed his posture. He turned his head to look toward the exit.

"I knew it was only a matter of time before the Armada or the AFI would catch up to me," he muttered to himself. He turned to Donovan and clicked his tongue. "I knew every time I diverted from my course, every time I was late getting back to port that someone would eventually notice. Well ..." He exhaled sharply. "I'm not going to jail for anyone."

"What are you going to do?"

The Pemex captain looked toward the door. "I'm going to make the supply run to the Ta'Kuntah platform like I normally would do." He turned to Donovan. "Then I'm coming straight back to port."

"What about El Demonio?"

"Hmm." He dropped his head and then looked at Donovan. "Remember how I told you that he'll find your weakness and use it against you?" He removed his hat. "I'm married to the most wonderful woman in the world. I'd die if I ever lost her." He scoffed. "Unfortunately, I have a weakness for beautiful women. I enjoy the chase, the wooing"—he took a sharp breath—"and ultimately, the conquest." He sneered. "El Demonio used it to blackmail me into making the runs for him."

As he listened to the penitent captain, Donovan thought about Itzél and the snide remark El Demonio had made that morning at the Cocina Maya. He obviously noticed his attraction to her when he said that he didn't seem like a man "afraid to take a bite of forbidden fruit." At that moment, he realized that El Demonio already knew his weakness. It didn't matter that the object of his affection had no interest in him.

Santos smiled dolefully at Donovan. "I'm going to confess to my wife and pray she doesn't leave me." His melancholic smile turned into a defiant one. "Then I'm going to tell El Demonio to go back to hell." He grinned triumphantly at him.

"Bravo, Capitán." Donovan nodded his head subtly. "Bravo."

As Santos started for the exit, he stopped suddenly as if he had forgotten something. "Speaking of rumors"—he turned around and pointed at Donovan with his hat—"I heard a rumor too." He hesitated before continuing, "I heard that there was fifty kilos of cocaine buried on the south side of a porch on the west side of Cayo del Centro beneath the range beacon." He waited for Donovan to bite. When he didn't, he fed him some more line. "You can't miss it. The porch is attached to the remains of a house destroyed by a storm surge. The slab is red, and the cocaine is buried about two feet deep on the inside of the house right next to the center of the old porch."

"What do you expect me to do with that?"

"The Captain Simon Donovan I heard about in Panama would know what to do with it."

The ship's horn blurted out the signal to come to the ship a third time. Captain Santos looked over his shoulder toward the door and then back at Donovan. "El Demonio won't stop trying to get his hands on that cocaine until he either gets it or it goes away. I don't know if he's going to let me off the hook, but what I do know is that he is determined to get you to work for him. If he loses confidence in me—and I will do everything I can to see that he does—I expect that he will find a way to force you to make a run for him to get his cocaine." Santos put his hat back on his head. "If I were you, I'd find a way to make it go away."

"I told you"—Donovan took a breath—"I'm not that guy anymore."

Captain Santos looked at him for a moment and then smiled. "I think you are." He adjusted his hat and pulled down on the sides. He bounced a casual salute at Donovan. "Buena suerte, Capitán Dónovan." He turned around and left the Tiburón.

CHAPTER
10

On the outside, the old boathouse where Augie set up his dive shop looked like any other dive shop might. He remodeled the old clapboard building with the rusted metal roof that once housed the longboats that carried henequen and sugarcane to the ships that came to Seyba Playa before the building of the harbor. As part of his agreement with Don Macario, the boathouse also served as the marina's headquarters, which he had to manage from his dive shop. On the opposite end from where he established his dive shop, he built a shower facility and a small lounge where he put vending machines for the boaters coming to the marina to use. He hung an elaborate hand-carved wooden sign with the words "Paradise Dive Shop" in large block letters over the entrance and a simple hand-painted sign with "Marina HQ" on the right side of the door.

On the inside, the dive shop seemed more like an antique shop or a museum, as Don Macario so adequately put it. The old scuba gear Augie started his dive shop with now adorned the walls and corners of the shop, as did a variety of old nets, Japanese glass fishing floats, and an old harpoon. On the shelves, he kept old chart books, sextants, compasses, beer steins, and other knickknacks one might find lying about an old ship, sail shop, or seaside tavern. He even had an old canvas dive suit and dive helmet propped up in a corner.

Like Augie maintained, everything in his shop worked, from the dive equipment he had lying around to the sixties-vintage percolator on the back cabinet behind the counter in the main room. He kept an antique desk in his bedroom from where he conducted his business. On it, he had an old-fashioned brass desk light and metal oscillating fan to cool him on especially hot days. He didn't fancy the so-called modern conveniences of the day, except perhaps for his cell phone and laptop computer.

Augie sat quietly, his eyes mesmerized by what he saw on the screen. A large green mass with yellow and red blotches loomed off the coast of Campeche. "That ain't good," he muttered to himself.

Squalls in the Bay of Campeche form quickly and suddenly, especially in the afternoon. What might have started out as a sunny day could suddenly and unexpectedly churn up into a ship-killing storm. The clouds seem to come out of nowhere as if conjured by the hand of some mean-spirited sea witch that lurks unseen in the wave tops. The wind begins to pick up, gradually at first, but soon the seas begin to churn, pushed by the gale. The skies turn black, and the crackling sound of thunder rattles through the air down into your bones. Then the swells begin to roll in, one after another, each climbing ever higher before crashing in a thunderous roar followed by deep troughs that drop so suddenly that it seems like the bottom of the sea is falling out.

Augie looked at the clock on the wall above the small desk in his bedroom as he sent the weather report to the printer sitting on the back counter in the next room. He walked into the front room and waited by the printer. He looked over his shoulder when he heard the screen door screeching.

"Oh, it's you," he said, surprised to see Don Macario.

"I'm sorry to disappoint," the old gentleman said over the whirring and thumping of the printer.

He looked down on the printer. "Is the skipper with you?"

"He had to go out." Don Macario went to sit on a stool across the work counter from where Augie waited for the weather report to print.

Augie gazed vacantly at the printer as it slowly whirred and thumped out the report. "Quino mentioned that Itzél was upset."

Don Macario raised his eyes and took a long, slow breath. "Benício and Lázaro are making a run for El Demonio."

Augie looked at him, and his expression went blank. The printer made a high-pitched hum as it spat out the printout. "Where?"

"They're meeting a ship. Somewhere west of the Seyba Reef."

"Is the skipper trying to stop them?"

"They already left."

"Where did he go then?"

"Pablo believes to the Tiburón."

"Why the Tiburón?"

"Pablo thinks to talk to Captain Santos."

"Captain Santos?" Augie frowned. "I thought that was only a rumor?"

"Evidently, there's some substance to the rumor." He looked warily at his friend. "Pablo hears things."

Augie pulled the printout from the tray and set it on the work counter. He looked at Don Macario. "So it was all for nothing. The skipper paying off the outboard for Benício, assuming his debt. El Demonio got his way."

"It would seem so."

"Only now, he's put us in the middle of it." Augie scoffed and shook his head. "If only I had been the one to go talk with Benício."

"Things would have been no different." Don Macario chuckled. "I know you too well, my friend."

He scoffed and then grinned demurely. "I suppose you're right." He looked out the window at the end of the counter at the boys following Dr. Ventura up the pier, helping him carry his equipment to the ship. He chuckled at Poli struggling with the load he carried. "We did end up with a pretty good crewman."

Don Macario turned to look out the window. "I see the professor's already here." Sandy and Poli each toted a heavy aluminum case, while the professor pulled a large black, hard plastic trunk on rollers behind him.

"Yeah," Augie said, "he's itching to get underway." He handed the printout to him. "Too bad it won't be till the morning."

Don Macario glanced at the weather report. "Looks serious."

"They're expecting it to stall before coming ashore." He took it back from him. "No sense going out in that. We'll be fighting the wind to keep off the shoals all the way to the Sabancuy Channel." He dropped the page on the counter and looked back out the window. "I'll let the professor know we're not shoving off till the next tide."

"He's going to be disappointed."

"Better disappointed than ending up like the ship he's looking for."

The two men sat quietly, gazing out the window at the sailboats and cabin cruisers anchored in their slips. None of them ever seemed to go out except on weekends or holidays and then only in good weather. Augie made no secret of his regard for fair-weather sailors. He considered them little better than boat-owning landlubbers and way down the food chain from blue-water sailors.

Poli stopped at the foot of the gangplank, sizing up the task before him. He lifted the professor's heavy case and ran up the gangplank.

"Whoa." Augie chuckled as he watched Poli nearly lose his balance.

"I don't know what's in the case." Don Macario grinned. "But judging by the professor's reaction, it must be important."

Both men grinned as they watched Poli wrestle with the case. Sandy set the case he carried on the deck and went down the plank to help him. They both laughed at something Poli said as they waited for the professor to pull his trunk up the gangplank.

"Do you think we ought to tell Poli about what's happening?" Augie asked Don Macario.

"Why don't we wait until we hear from Simon? No use in worrying him."

In the short time the two boys had worked together, they had taken to each other like brothers. Poli followed Sandy around like younger brothers do, mimicking his every move. He even copied the way he dressed, cutting off all the legs of his good pants. It seemed to serve him well, as he learned the ropes and proved himself a quick learner and a hard worker. Poli always had a smile on his face and never objected to performing even the most menial of tasks. Even Augie, who seldom expressed how he felt, had taken to him. It didn't seem to bother him when Poli started calling him "Uncle Augie."

"You know …" Augie turned to Don Macario. "At first, I was against hiring Poli, especially when the skipper told me how he came to hire him. I mean, giving your money away like that."

"I'm not concerned about the money," Don Macario said. "It was a noble thing Simon did to help his family."

Augie looked back out the window. "I don't know if his reasons were all that noble."

"What are you saying?"

"Oh …" Augie picked up the weather report. "Nothing, I guess." He tossed the page aside. "I'm just not so sure why he did it."

"You mean Itzél." Don Macario raised his brow. "She is a beautiful woman."

"Drop dead gorgeous, but that's not what I mean." He gazed at his old friend, his hesitance still showing on his face.

"Don't tell me you've never been attracted to a married woman?"

"Sure I have." Augie fidgeted uncomfortably. "But I wouldn't have acted on it. I mean, now that Poli's part of the crew …" He looked away unable to find the words. "He's like family."

"And you think it's inappropriate."

"Yeah." Augie looked at him. "That's it. It's inappropriate. She's the mother of a crewman, let alone a married woman." His eyes widened. "Damn. She's even married to a preacher. That's got to be a one-way ticket to hell."

Don Macario chuckled. "I wouldn't worry about his immortal soul."

"I don't know." Augie looked back out the window. "He's been going over there an awful lot. I'm afraid he might make a move on her or something."

"He already has."

Augie turned to him. "Really?"

"I'm afraid so. She refused his advances, of course." Don Macario sighed. "Itzél blames herself for not stopping him before it got that far."

"It's not her fault." Augie shook his head. "I should have seen it coming," he muttered to himself.

"I'm sure Simon realizes he made a mistake. In time, it will be forgotten."

Augie scoffed. "I don't think the skipper's the type to forget."

Donovan parked the convertible under the open-sided, thatch-roofed garage Augie built behind the cabañas. He sat in his car for a moment, thinking about Itzél and how good she looked as she left the hotel after talking with Don Macario. He had to get her out of his mind. She had made it more than plain she had no interest in him.

He started to go see her after leaving the Tiburón to tell her that he stopped the ship Benício went to meet but got cold feet when he saw her looking out to sea from her bedroom window, her eyes lost somewhere over the horizon. He realized that nothing he would say could fix what he had done. He felt his heart grow heavy at the thought he had lost her forever too.

He put his hand on top of the steering wheel and imagined what it would be like to hold her in his arms and feel her arms around him. He imagined taking her to the best restaurant in Campeche City, the Lorenzillo, where he would reserve the best table, order their most expensive wine, and dine like royalty. Afterward, he imagined her sitting snugly by his side as they drove in his convertible along the coast road on a cloudless moonlit night, listening to a romantic tune on his player.

ALVARADO, VERACRUZ
THREE YEARS AGO

It took some doing, but Donovan finally persuaded Xochitl to go on a drive to Alvarado to have dinner at a restaurant he found on his way to surprise her with the much-needed medical supplies he had pilfered from a cargo ship he attended. He put his arm around her shoulder and she rested her head on his as they drove along the coast to Alvarado. He started to tell her about the Camaronero restaurant and the old shrimp boats moored along the seawall across the street when he noticed that she had fallen asleep. He turned down the soft jazz mix he burned and settled into the drive.

It didn't bother him that she slept during most of the drive from Pajapan to Alvarado. He knew that she had learned to exist on catnaps since working as an intern, and continued to do so after becoming a doctor. He considered waking Xochitl as they drove over the Alvarado lagoon. The sun had started to set, its fading rays casting long shadows of the shrimpers moored along the seawall that meandered lazily along the harbor. He decided to let her sleep.

After getting off the bridge, he turned left to drive to the restaurant, slowing to take a speed bump by the mercado, waking Xochitl. She lifted her head off Donovan's shoulder and sat up to look at the market.

"Stop, stop, stop!" she demanded.

"What's wrong?"

"They're selling Día de Muertos stuff," she said. "Let's go take a look."

No sooner had he parked the car than Xochitl jumped out and went to a stall selling pastries. Donovan smiled as he watched her hover over the hard plastic display case with childlike enthusiasm. He locked the Suburban and went to join her.

The colorful assortment of pastries contained in the display case included sweet rolls shaped like human skulls topped with sugar and gingerbread skeletons. The case also contained traditional Mexican pastries, like churros, a tubelike fritter, and molletes, a sugarcoated muffin. The old woman running the stall had her face painted a dull white with the skin around her eyes and mouth painted black, making her look like a gaping calavera, a death's head.

"You're going to ruin your appetite," he said to her, knowing that she ate like a bird.

"I'm just looking," she said half-heartedly. "I love eating pan de muerto."

"It's just a sugarcoated sweet roll shaped like a skull."

"It's more than that," she corrected him. "It's a celebration of the dead."

"I get that," Donovan responded. "I'm just saying you can get sweetbread every day at your local market. The taste's the same."

"They're not fun to eat like pan de muerto," she said out of the side of her face as she pointed at a gingerbread skeleton and a large skull-shaped cookie. The old woman picked up the pastries with a pair of tongs and gently put them in a small paper bag. "Pay her," Xochitl said to him as she darted to the next stall.

Donovan shook his head and grinned at the old woman as he paid her, taking the paper bag from her before following Xochitl to the next stall. The attendant behind the table was dressed like the Grim Reaper, his face also painted like a death's head, only with a more ominous sneer. He had a varied assortment of masks laid out on his table, some simple half masks, some Mardi Gras–like, others just ghoulish.

"Aren't these fun?" Xochitl said to him as he joined her.

He glanced at the attendant, whose makeup made him look menacing. He picked up a feathered half mask. "This would look good on you."

She picked up a red-faced mask with horns. "This one suits you."

"Are you saying that I'm some kind of demonio?"

"If the mask fits …"

"I thought that only applied to shoes." He scanned the macabre array of masks, looking for one he could use to tease her. "Theater masks," he said as he pointed at two plain white masks, one wearing a smile, the other a sad look.

"That's tragedy," she said, pointing at the sad mask, and then picked up the happy mask, "and comedy." She held it up to her face. "This one would be a good one for Tony."

"Who's Tony?"

"That's Doctor Aguirre's first name," she said nonchalantly.

"So you're on a first-name basis now?"

"Why shouldn't we be? We work together. Don't you call the people you work with by their first names?"

Donovan felt his face getting warm. "Isn't he the guy going to Colombia with you?"

"That's right." She leaned closer to the table to look over the other masks. "We just found out they're keeping us together."

"That makes me feel so much better," he said half under his breath.

She chuckled as she continued poring over the masks. "You're not jealous, are you?"

"Me? Jealous?" He glanced briefly at the Grim Reaper waiting on them, who hadn't moved since they got to his stall. He stood silently, holding a long sickle over his shoulder with his bony hand, his unflinching eyes gazing emptily at him. "Of course not," he lied. "Do you know where they're sending you?"

"Not specifically." She picked up a skull mask with a lifeless expression on it. "The Llanos, most likely. Maybe the Choco." She put the mask over her face and looked at Donovan.

The attendant set the heel of the sickle on the ground and stepped closer to the table. The image of Xochitl holding the lifeless mask on her face with the attendant standing ghoulishly behind her unnerved him. He gently put his hand on hers and pulled the mask from her face.

"I don't like that mask."

She turned around and put the sad theatrical mask on her face instead. "What about this one?"

He looked at the happy mask and immediately thought about her leaving for Colombia with Dr. Aguirre. "I don't really care for the whole Day of the Dead thing."

"Día de Muertos is how we celebrate death. It's a part of life. It's the final act in our personal story."

Donovan gently took the mask from her hand and laid it back on the table. "Let's go."

After they got to his suburban, Donovan opened the door for Xochitl and glanced back at the stall for the attendant dressed as the personification of death. He had vanished from sight.

"Tell me more about this woman in the picture," Don Macario said to Augie.

"I really don't know anything else other than she could be Itzél's sister."

"And Simon didn't say who she was?"

"Not a word. He just gave me a sort of go-to-hell look and went about what he was doing."

"Hmm," Don Macario muttered in silent thought. "Could it be that Simon's just attracted to beautiful Mesoamerican women?"

"It's gotta be more than that." Augie tightened the right side of his face. "If you saw the picture, you'd agree."

"Didn't you say you only saw it for a second or so?"

"Long enough for me to see that the woman's a spittin' image of Poli's mother."

The two men sat quietly, Augie staring out the window while Don Macario looked at the image on the weather report.

"Could it be his ex-wife?" Don Macario suggested.

"I don't think the skipper was ever married." Augie exhaled. "By the way he was acting, she must've been special to him."

"We all have someone like that," the old gentleman commented.

"Tell me about it," Augie mused. "I've got three of them."

Don Macario chuckled softly. "I know about the last Mrs. Fagan."

The aptly named Angela differed greatly from his previous loves. She did not possess the calendar-girl class charms the other two did; their bodacious physical qualities could make a World War II pinup girl green with envy. That notwithstanding, Angela definitely could turn a head and inflict serious whiplash on a man, especially when she dressed for the evening. To be sure, she was in every sense a beautiful woman, though not as tantalizing as Tanya, his first wife, nor as comely as Camille, Angel's immediate predecessor. She possessed the kind of good looks found in the proverbial girl next door but with a face that could have rivaled even the one that launched a thousand ships.

"Wasn't Angela a classical pianist?"

"That's right," Augie replied. "She put herself through school playing the piano at some hotel in downtown Houston."

"Where did you meet her?"

"Port Aransas. During spring break. She came down with a group of friends from Rice. I was playing at an icehouse by the channel. There was this old upright piano, I thought was there just for looks. I was doing my usual set of beach tunes, folk ballads, and love songs when she went to that old piano and started accompanying me." Augie smiled and let out a slow, melancholic sigh. "She was wearing beige slacks and a black oversized sweatshirt that almost swallowed her."

"I liked her hair," Don Macario commented. "Auburn, wasn't it?"

"Um-hmm."

He smiled. "I used to like talking with her at your tavern," he added, referring to the bar he ran with his wife in South Padre Island. "She was so soft-spoken."

Augie shook his head slowly. "I never could understand how she could have anything to do with an old channel rat like me."

"She once told me that you had a young soul and that hers was much, much older."

"She liked to talk about deep, metaphysical stuff like that." He grinned. "All I had to offer was my waterfront savvy."

"Opposites do attract."

"We had a force-eight whirlwind romance, and then we got married. I put some money together working offshore as a welder and then as a shrimper for a season in Port O'Connor and as a dockworker in the port of Houston. After she graduated, we moved to South Padre Island and bought that run-down bar you used to come by."

Opposites might attract, but it seldom lasts. It could be the mystery that draws opposites together as it had with Angela and Augie, whose love of music formed the basis of that attraction. Though they both loved music, they kept beat with decidedly different drummers. The tavern also reflected the difference in their personalities. By day, the bar had the atmosphere of a seafarer's tavern, serving cold beer and English fare. By night, it transformed into a wine and piano bar, serving a quaint selection of gourmet dishes. As the beat of their drummers drifted further and further apart, so did they. He left her the tavern and went to Campeche to work for Don Macario.

"How did you meet your first wife?"

"Tanya?" He chuckled. "She was my high school sweetheart. Her eyes were as blue as a Robin's egg, and her hair reminded me of copper wire. Her skin was like an eggshell, except with a bunch of freckles, especially around her nose. She was a little thing, like a miniature Venus de Milo except with arms."

"She sounds adorable."

"She was." Augie sighed. "Of all my wives, she was the one I had the most in common with. She was a shrimper's daughter and didn't mind the smell of the sea on me. It was the pilot light that kept our love burning." He chuckled. "We opened a bait shop in Bayside, Texas, and were as happy as anyone could possibly be." He raised his head as he reminisced. "We used to sit on the porch behind the bait shop, watching the sunset, me playing my guitar and singing to her."

"Sounds like heaven."

"It was good while it lasted." His mood turned. "Then business got slow, and we started having money problems. I started working nights at a couple of honky tonks in Corpus Christi and Port Aransas to help make ends meet." He inhaled deeply. "Soon, I forgot all about the bait shop. One thing led to another, and me and Tanya drifted apart like flotsam in a crosscurrent."

After the pilot light went out in the marriage, Augie signed the bait shop over to Tanya and moved to Port Aransas where he supported himself working on an offshore fishing boat by day and playing at a local bar at night. Tanya went on to marry a car dealer in Aransas Pass and moved into a big house at the country club.

"Then I met Camille," Augie said, continuing the saga of his failed marriages. "I had just come in from a day fishing for marlin. She was working on an old cabin cruiser her father left her called the Sea Nymph." He smiled. "She was a good lookin' boat. Worn out, but great lines."

Don Macario chuckled at his friend's meanderings. "Did she have red hair too?"

"Oh no." He shook his head. "Camille was different from Tanya. She was a towhead with eyes like India ink and a killer tan." He held his hand horizontally across his forehead. "She was near as tall as I am, and I swear she had the longest legs." He sighed dreamily. "No one could fill a pair of cutoff jeans like Camille." He smiled as he recalled fondly, "I invited her to come to the Channel Bar, where I was playing. She showed up wearing a chambray shirt and a khaki skirt. She had her hair tied behind her head with a red bandana and wore a pair of brown leather boots that came up almost to her knees."

"She sounds absolutely gorgeous, but could she cook?" Don Macario asked facetiously.

"Cook, cut her own bait, and handle the Sea Nymph," he counted out using his hands.

"Together, we refitted the Sea Nymph. We updated all the instruments, rebuilt both engines, and redid all the teak from stem to stern." He stuck out his chest proudly. "After we were done, we started up a pretty respectable deep-sea charter business of our own. Everything was perfect."

"Then you married her."

"How could I not? We bought a bungalow not far from the beach and settled into married life like a pair of bottle-nosed dolphins." He let out a long, dolorous sigh. "She was a sea goddess and the perfect woman."

What Duncan Augustus Fagan would not relate to his friend showed plainly on his face. His sea goddess began to spend less time on the Sea Nymph and more time redecorating the bungalow as she approached that dreaded milestone women use to mark the end of their youth. She wanted children, and the mere suggestion so distressed Augie that he used a lull in business as an excuse to return to his old gig at the Channel Bar.

Camille, disillusioned with his lack of enthusiasm, continued to watch the minutes tick off her biological clock while Augie returned to the Buffetesque lifestyle. One night, as she sat at home listening to the surf outside her window alone with her thoughts, she decided to ask Augie for a divorce. Their love had risen on the crest of a wave, and like every wave, it crashed back into the sea. Camille went to work for a doctor in Rockport, eventually marrying him and finally getting what she wanted—three sets of twins, all boys.

"Why's everybody so glum?" Donovan asked as he let the screen door to the dive shop slam behind him.

"How did it go with Captain Santos?" Augie came to the point, taking Donovan by surprise.

"How'd you know I went to talk to him?" He looked at Don Macario.

The old gentleman sat up. "Pablo guessed that's where you went."

"Pablo hears things," Augie echoed his old friend's explanation.

Not entirely satisfied with the explanation, Donovan glanced warily at each of them as he went to stand at the end of the counter. "Santos won't be going to the Seyba Reef."

Don Macario looked at Donovan. "Have you told Itzél?"

The image of her looking out to sea from her bedroom window flashed through his mind, "Uh …" He looked away. "I thought it might be better if you told her Benício was out of danger."

"I wouldn't say that he was completely out of danger." Augie slid the weather report to him.

Donovan glanced at it. The look on his face reflected his concern. "How old is this report?"

"Just printed it out." Augie looked out the window at the professor, sitting on the main cabin, chatting with the boys. "I haven't told the professor we're not heading out till the next tide."

His decision not to leave until the next tide thwarted what Donovan had in mind. He had hoped to divert the ship to the Arcas and take Santos's advice. He wanted to use the cover of night to slip ashore, find the cocaine, and dispose of it before El Demonio made another attempt to get it. With the Armada on to Captain Santos, he would undoubtedly try to force him to make the run to get his cocaine. He only had an hour before the tide went out, and he had to find a reason to shove off before it did.

He looked at Don Macario and then at his partner. "Benício might get caught in the squall."

"Not if he's smart," Augie disagreed. "I'm sure he'll come in after he sees the weather start to turn."

"Certainly after he realizes that Captain Santos is not coming," Don Macario added.

"You can't be sure of that," Donovan argued.

Augie scrunched his brow. "You're not suggesting we go looking for him?" He leaned toward him. "Are you?"

"Of course not." Donovan knew as well as anybody that finding a small boat at sea is next to impossible, even from the air in good weather.

Augie emptied his lungs. "For a minute there, I thought you were gonna suggest going out in that beast."

"I wouldn't worry about Benício," Don Macario added. "Both he and Lázaro have a healthy respect for storms." He glanced at each of them. "Their fathers were lost in one when they were both young boys."

"I didn't know that," Augie said.

As the old gentleman explained to him how Benício and Lázaro lost their fathers to a storm when they went to fish the reefs around the Arcas cays, Donovan had a different kind of storm in mind—his partner's reaction when he learned of El Demonio's determination to get his clutches on their ship. He had to find a way to persuade him to agree to go the Arcas before they would be forced to make the run against their will. Then, as Don Macario concluded his story, his partner handed it to him on a silver platter.

"I wonder how El Demonio's going to react when he finds out that he's not getting his cocaine?" Augie mused.

"He's not going to quit until he gets what he wants," Donovan commented, paraphrasing Captain Santos. "The Armada's watching Santos. There's no way he can use him again," he concluded. "He'll have to find someone else."

"Someone else, like who?" Augie retorted.

Donovan just looked at him.

"You don't mean us?"

He dropped his head, grabbed the edges of the counter, and then looked at him. "Do you remember when Santos came to see me at the lounge?"

"Yeah," Augie responded apprehensively. "You said he didn't have anything important to say."

"He came there to tell me that El Demonio wanted to use the Siete Mares to run drugs for him." Donovan straightened his back. "I told him I wasn't interested."

"Why didn't you tell me that?"

"I didn't want to worry you." Donovan looked at Don Macario. "That's how I knew where to find Captain Santos. He told me he'd be at the Tiburón if I changed my mind."

"That's great. That's just frickin' great," Augie began to rant. "That's all we needed. Teniente Baeza already has his eye on us, and now you're telling me that the devil wants us to run drugs for him."

Donovan waited for him to settle down. "Santos told me there was a way to keep 'that devil' from bothering us."

Augie glared at him warily. "How?"

"You're not going to like it."

"I don't like it already," Augie snapped.

"We'll have to go to the Arcas."

"When?"

"Before the tide goes out."

"In the storm?"

"In the storm."

Augie dropped his head and then raised his eyes. "What's in the Arcas?"

Donovan drew a breath and released it slowly. "The means to stop El Demonio from bothering us."

Augie's gaze hardened. "I'm afraid to ask what that involves."

"Then don't." Donovan turned his head. "It's better that you don't know the details." He drew another breath and looked at him. "As far as you're concerned, we went to the Arcas to get out of the storm."

CHAPTER

11

A lot goes through a man's mind when he's alone at the helm, besides minding the heading and the trim of the sails and keeping his senses sharp for the unexpected. Still, the mind wanders, at times dredging a man's most intimate thoughts to the surface.

He didn't want to think about Itzél, but the memory of her face wouldn't let him forget. He tried thinking of other things, including the skies overhead, which hardly hinted at what lay ahead. In an hour, maybe less, the skies would change and the seas would start to undulate. Soon afterward, troughs would start to form, growing deeper and deeper, turning into rolling swells that would crest into white caps, becoming luminescent after dark. The wind, whistling gently through the guide wires, would turn into a steady, mournful drone, spitting a stinging sea spray against his face. How he wished he had taken things slower with Itzél. In his haste to win her love, he had run what hope he had aground.

The thump of the slider coming to a stop and the hatch opening snapped Donovan out of his daydream. Dr. Ventura paused when he saw Donovan dressed in a rain suit. "Are you expecting heavy weather?"

"You mean the rain suit?"

The professor chuckled as he came on deck. "Your main is reefed." He pointed at the reduced size of the mainsail. He looked forward at the other sails. "So are your mizzen and headsail."

He had forgotten that the professor counted seamanship among his many skills. "There's a squall forming between us and the Sabancuy Channel," Donovan admitted. "I rolled up the sails in case we get hit by a stiff wind."

"I know." He coughed into his hand. "I just checked the weather on my computer." He looked at the heavy clouds rising ominously ahead of them. "It looks like we're heading right into it."

"If I calculate it right, we should be able to skirt around it and follow it into the Sabancuy Channel without any problems." Donovan turned the ship closer to the wind. "We'll get in there with plenty of time to get a good night's sleep and an early start diving on your wreck."

Augie popped his head out of the hatchway and rested his arms on the top of the main cabin. He glanced briefly at the professor, who had obviously taken notice of the oilskins he wore. "Is everything okay up here, Skipper?" he asked before coming on deck.

"I was just telling the professor about going around the storm."

Augie looked at the horizon and whistled. "Looks like a doozy."

"That it does," Doctor Ventura agreed. He stood on the right side of the steering box and looked causally into the binnacle at the compass. "You're heading is just north of west." He turned to Donovan. "If I didn't know any better, I'd say you were headed for the Arcas?"

"The Arcas?" Augie chuckled nervously as he went to stand across the steering box from the professor. "We'll be around the squall long before we reach the cays."

"You're not going around the storm. Not on this heading," the professor said unequivocally. "You're headed right into it. If you wanted to skirt the storm, you'd be running more to the northeast under full sail. Instead, your sails are reefed and both of you are wearing rain gear." He glared at Donovan suspiciously. "You're taking us to the Arcas."

As the professor waited for an explanation, Augie put his right hand on the steering box and looked dead ahead. "I knew we couldn't keep it from him," he muttered under his breath.

Donovan shushed him. He turned to the professor. "All right. Something important came up, and we need to make a quick trip to the Arcas to handle it."

"What's so important that you would deliberately sail into a storm?"

"It's better that you don't know."

The professor sighed. "I see." He turned his eyes forward. "You don't think I can be trusted."

"It's not that, Professor." The ship began to heel to starboard. Donovan turned the wheel to let out some of the wind. "What I have to do is tricky." He brought the ship back to an even keel. "We talked about postponing the charter until after we got back, but we know how important it is for you to get started on that wreck. So we decided to bring you along."

The professor kept his eyes dead ahead. "Can you at least give me a hint what it is you have to do?"

"It's better that you don't know," Donovan reiterated.

"Is it illegal?"

A flock of seagulls squawked overhead as they headed away from the approaching storm. Donovan looked up at them, thinking of a way to answer the question. He glanced at his partner, who looked at him also, anticipating an answer.

"I tell you what I told my first mate," Donovan began. "As far as anyone is concerned, we went to the Arcas to get out of the storm."

"That didn't answer my question." The professor looked at him sternly. "Is what you're doing illegal?"

A flash of lightning illuminated the professor's and his partner's faces as they waited for an answer. Shortly afterward, the sound of thunder rolled lethargically across the horizon. The wind began to whistle through the guide wires.

Donovan let the air out of his lungs slowly. "Only if I get caught."

The professor nodded sullenly and then started for the main cabin. "I'd better go below and check on my equipment."

Augie followed him to the hatchway, slid the top closed, and shut the hatch doors. He returned to the steering box and looked at Donovan. "I knew you couldn't keep what you're doing from the professor."

"I didn't think so either," Donovan responded calmly.

"Did you see the look on his face?"

He scoffed. "He did look hurt."

"Is that all you've got to say?" Augie looked at him apprehensively. "What if we're spotted and boarded? What if he doesn't play along?"

"Conrad didn't get where he is by playing by the rules." Donovan looked at the mainsail. "He'll play along."

Augie stared out to sea in thought. The seas had started to rise slowly and fall gently with the wind. He turned to Donovan. "I hope for our sake, he does."

More than an hour had passed since the Pemex supply ship left the Ta'Kuntah oil platform. For reasons unknown to Captain Mendiola and Lieutenant Baeza, who watched the Pemex supply ship struggle through the heavy seas back to the port of Seyba Playa, Captain Santos took more time unloading his cargo than they expected. The fact that he decided to leave when he did also seemed strange to them. He had to know about the fast-approaching storm, and yet he dallied as if he deliberately waited for it before he shoved off for Seyba Playa.

As the helmsman struggled to keep the patrol boat on course, Lieutenant Baeza stood on the bridge, watching the Pemex ship rise and fall in and out of view through his binoculars. He lowered his binoculars and covered his mouth. The young naval infantry lieutenant's discomfort amused Captain Mendiola, who sat in the captain's chair in the center of the enclosed room overlooking the bridge.

"It's a lot different looking through a pair of those at sea than it is on land," he said to the woozy lieutenant.

Lieutenant Baeza quietly released the gas that had swelled up in his throat through his fist. "I thought looking through binoculars from the air was bad."

The captain chuckled. "You'll get used to it."

The bridge of the patrol boat had all the conveniences of a modern warship, including consoles that controlled all the systems on the ship from the engine room to weapons. From where he sat, the captain had a clear view through the five square portholes wrapped around the front of the bridge. The executive officer oversaw the overall operation of the ship, and the helmsman, of course, steered the ship from his console on the starboard side of the bridge. Lieutenant Baeza stood on the port side of the bridge, struggling to keep not only his balance but his supper in place.

The executive officer, a frigate lieutenant named Paniagua, turned to the helmsman on his right. "Stay on him, but don't get too close."

"Entendido, mí teniente," the helmsman acknowledged.

From where Lieutenant Baeza stood, he watched the Pemex supply ship disappear into a deep trough and then reemerge, riding the crest of an enormous swell. A crewman came through the hatch into the bridge from the radio room and handed the executive officer a clipboard with a dispatch on it.

"It looks like he's headed back to Seyba Playa, teniente," Captain Mendiola commented. "He hasn't given any sign that he intends to divert to the Seyba Reef."

Lieutenant Baeza lowered his binoculars and caught his breath. "It could be he aborted the rendezvous because of the storm." He put his hand holding the binoculars on the console to support himself. "They probably didn't know about the storm when they made their plan."

"He had plenty of time to unload his cargo and divert for the Seyba Reef," Captain Mendiola argued. "He was waiting for the storm."

After Teniente de Frigata Paniagua read the communiqué, he scribbled his signature on it and then turned to the captain. "The communications center reports two overdue pangueros from the Seyba Reef."

The captain sighed and shook his head slowly. "When will they ever learn?"

"What are your orders, mí capitán?" Teniente de Frigata Paniagua waited for his response.

The captain motioned for him to stand by. He turned to Baeza. "How long do you want to keep following Santos, teniente?"

All eyes turned to the naval infantry lieutenant. Baeza took another look across the swells at the pitching and rolling Pemex supply ship.

"There's no sense in following him," he told the captain.

Captain Mendiola turned to his executive officer. "Notify Lerma that we're going to the Seyba Reef."

"Sí, mí capitán." He turned to the helmsman. "Set course for the Seyba Reef."

"A la orden, Señor Paniagua." The helmsman worked the console with his left hand before easing the wheel slowly to port. The crewman tucked the clipboard under his arm and walked through the hatch to the radio room.

The captain looked at Lieutenant Baeza and smiled sympathetically. "It's all right, Ramiro. We've all been led astray by an informer at one time or another." He chuckled. "I seriously doubt that the fifty kilos he told you about even exist."

"I was sure he had something this time."

The captain hunched his shoulders. "He's been wrong before."

"If you mean the panguero we detained for piracy, the informer told me we jumped him too soon."

"What else could we do? He came about abruptly and was headed back to Seyba Playa. He obviously spotted us," Captain Mendiola explained. "For all we know, he's one of the pirates who's been giving us trouble."

"With all due respect, mí capitán, he was alone and that panga he was in can barely do fifteen knots. The pirates you're talking about conduct their raids in two high-speed skiffs and carry AK-47 rifles, not some worthless antique revolver like he had."

"Perhaps," the captain conceded, "but I'm just not convinced that your informer is as good as you think he is." He braced himself as the bow of the ship topped a swell. "I think he hears a rumor and fills in the blanks, hoping to make a few pesos." The bow crashed into a trough. "He's an embellisher. You need to reel him in."

Donovan braced himself as a large swell swept across the deck of the Siete Mares. The gale had worsened, agitating the seas into a maelstrom of whirling terror. Between the sound of the wind howling and the roar of the sea crashing into itself, Donovan managed to hear the words Itzél spoke to him in anger when he made his ill-considered advance. A mixture of fear and despair filled the hollow he felt in his heart. He tried to focus on keeping the ship steady as he guided it through the swells. He tried remembering the words of a song his grandfather used to sing to his grandmother on their ranch in Central Texas, hoping to take his mind off the sound of Itzél's voice. It didn't help.

Then he thought he heard someone calling, and he turned an ear to see if he could hear it again. He heard it again. The wind seemed to carry it away from him, so he cupped a hand in front of his right ear to divert the whoosh of the wind.

"Skipper!" Sandy called through a gap in the hatch. "Skipper!"

He looked down from the helm at where Sandy stood on the companionway with his head barely peering out of the hatch. He cupped a hand on the side of his mouth, daring not to release the ship's wheel. "What is it?"

"Don Macario called." He put a hand on the deck to steady himself as the ship rolled to starboard. "Benício and Lázaro are home!" he yelled over the wind.

Donovan nodded and cupped his hand by the side of his mouth, "Has he told the navy?"

"No!" Sandy yelled, shaking his hand and head as he did. "Not yet."

"Tell him to wait awhile before he does."

Sandy nodded, acknowledging his instructions, and then cupped his hands around his mouth. "He also said that Poli's mother is worried about him." The wind blasted spray on his face.

Donovan gave him a thumbs-up and nodded his head. He then forcefully pointed his index finger a couple of times at Sandy, signaling him to go back below. Sandy nodded and closed the hatch.

The sea spray bit into Donovan's eyes, and he rubbed them with the back of his hand. He chuckled to himself when he thought about Itzél's concern for Poli. Mothers and lovers are the worst about reminding a man he's not immortal, he thought to himself.

VERACRUZ
THREE YEARS AGO

The mercado near Old Town Veracruz, like any market of its kind around Mexico, offered much more than just fresh produce or meat. The cotton candy and shaved ice machines, the piñatas and kites hanging from the ceiling, and the colorful vendors gave the market a carnival-like ambience. Unlike most typical farmers markets, it occupied an expansive space in an open-walled building encompassing a city block. It had an open-air atmosphere where the vendors displayed their goods on tables, stands, or booths. The fishmongers demonstrated the freshness of the catch by taking a fish from their ice-packed stands and thumping their fingers off the poor beastie's lifeless eyes. The mom-and-pop eateries offered a scrumptious selection of typical Mexican fare, including tacos with any type of filling imaginable, some even defying the imagination. The stands offering liquid refreshment also offered a varied menu of drinks primarily made of fruit and horchata, a sweet rice drink dashed with cinnamon.

Xochitl liked going to the market, and she went there often. She bought everything she cooked as she needed it. She went through a ritualistic process when buying produce, employing all of her senses. She studied each piece for coloration, shape, and flaws. She squeezed, prodded, or rubbed the fruit or vegetables, checking for firmness and freshness. When necessary, she sampled to check if a fruit was too sour or a vegetable too bitter.

She liked to haggle over the price. At times, it seemed she did it just to keep in practice, with no intention of buying. None of the vendors had any idea that the petite brunette with her hair in a ponytail, wearing oversized sunglasses, cutoff jeans, and a sweatshirt worked as a doctor. The sunglasses did little to hide the delicate features of her face. The vendors, most of them men, didn't seem to mind haggling with the pretty little girl. They smiled as she made her counteroffers and chuckled when she acted disgusted with the price, sharing their amusement with the tall Americano standing next to her.

"Why don't you give the guy a break?" Donovan said to Xochitl. He pulled some coins from his pocket and handed them to the appreciative vendor, upsetting her.

"What are you doing?"

"That's a fair price for a papaya."

"I don't want to buy a papaya." She handed the fruit back to the vendor. "No lo necesito." The vendor looked at Donovan, shrugged his shoulders, and chuckled.

"Then why were you giving him such a hard time?" Donovan waved off the vendor when he tried to hand him back the coins.

"I buy fruit from him all the time. I couldn't come to the mercado and not stop to see him." She turned to the vendor. "Hasta luego, Don Proforio."

"Que le vaya bíen, señorita," the vendor responded with a dip of his head, wishing her well.

Xochitl bolted off toward the nearest exit, leaving Donovan behind. He grinned as he shook his head at the vendor, who laughed softly in agreement. He picked up the plastic bags containing the groceries Xochitl had bought and hurried to catch her.

"Hold up," Donovan called to her as she crossed the street headed for her apartment.

The building where Xochitl lived had no elevator, having been built over a century and half ago, and they had to walk up three flights of stairs to get to her apartment. For the money she paid, she could have afforded something more modern and closer to the hospital where she worked, but she chose that particular apartment because of its proximity to the market and Old Town Veracruz. Xochitl also liked the way the old-time apartment looked and the antique furnishings it contained. The refrigerator, which she hardly used, and the stove predated the Second World War.

For that matter, the wiring in the one-bedroom apartment also predated the war. The hard plaster walls had antique metal tubing running along the floor above the antique molding with electrical sockets spaced uniformly around the apartment. The living room took up most of the space. The dining area, situated next to the small kitchen, could barely seat four people. Like her favorite restaurant in Old Town Veracruz, it had a small, French-style wrought iron balcony too small, however, to accommodate even a small table.

"So." Donovan laid the grocery bags on the table. "What are we having tonight?"

She pushed Donovan aside and began emptying the grocery bags. "I thought I'd try out a new recipe." She took the chicken she had just bought and put it in the refrigerator. "How does chicken cordon bleu sound."

"Sounds great." He lifted the bottle of wine he had put on the counter earlier that day. "I brought red wine."

"Is it pinot noir?"

"Merlot."

"I think I have some whites in the wine rack." She went back to the refrigerator to put away a block of Swiss cheese and a slab of ham. "Can you go check for me?"

"Sure." He looked at the six-bottle wire wine rack on the counter and pulled out a bottle. He didn't care for white wines. "Chablis?"

"Pick another one."

He pulled out another bottle. "Chardonnay?"

"That's good."

As Donovan watched her rummage through the cabinets over her head for the pots and pans she needed to prepare the meal, he lowered his eyes and began pulling on the corner of the label. "I, uh …" He cleared his throat. "I have to leave Veracruz."

She closed the cutlery drawer and looked at him. "When?"

He gulped. "Tomorrow."

"Tomorrow?" She exhaled sharply and dropped her shoulders. The strand of hair she had trouble controlling fell across her eye. She wrinkled her forehead. "I thought you had the whole month off?"

"Something came up." He brushed the strand of hair behind her ear. "The boss wants me to do a quick job for him in Limón."

"Costa Rica?" She huffed. "Isn't that place dangerous?" The look in her eyes went from disappointment to concern. "Isn't there a gang war going on there?"

"You mean like the one here?"

She gave her back to him and folded her arms. "You know what I mean."

He cupped his hands around her shoulders and kissed her behind the ear. Donovan snapped his head back when she slapped the side of his head and turned around.

"What will you be doing?"

Donovan liked it when she looked angry. "The boss wants me to go down there and bring back a yacht for a boat dealer friend of his in Seabrook. I'll be in and out." He snapped his finger. "Like that."

He didn't tell her that the yacht belonged to a violent Jamaican drug trafficker living in Limón who decided that he had paid enough for the yacht. Somehow, whether by instinct or intuition, she knew he had left out important details about his trip.

She didn't try to hide the worry on her face. "I know you're not telling me everything and I don't want to know." She put her head against his chest and wrapped her arms around him. "Just remember"—she inhaled deeply and sighed—"you're not bulletproof."

The gale finally began to mellow as the squall moved past the Siete Mares on its way to the coast. The grieving moan of the wind through the shrouds faded gradually until it hummed through the guide wires like a bow across the strings of a finely tuned violin. The swells no longer broke into rolling masses of bioluminescence, having lost the corrupting influence of the gale. Overhead, the storm no longer dominated the skies as the stars began to glimmer between the breaks in the clouds like broken chips of diamonds scattered on a black cloth. The ship and the wind resumed their love affair, and the breeze filled her sails, slipping her hull gently through the water on her way to the Arcas cays.

The cool breeze that caressed the rain from Donovan's face deepened the longing he felt for Xochitl. It made him feel good when he thought about her, but her memory came with a price. It made him brood over her, and he didn't like that, especially when he knew where he could get his hands on a bottle of rum. Sometimes, he would go for days hurting deep within his heart, feeling an unfathomable abyss within his soul. He knew that rum couldn't extinguish the ache he felt, but it at least it brought him some semblance of repose.

Augie threw the slider back until it thumped to a stop. He swung open the hatch and looked up at the gaps in the sky. "Looks like the worst is over."

"Yeah," Donovan said with his breath as he raised his eyes. He saw the moon for the first time as it broke through the clouds. "The moon's nearly full."

"We're gonna need that light to navigate the shoals around the cays," Augie commented. He stepped through the hatch and joined Donovan by the steering box. He looked to port at the lights shining from the Ta'Kuntah oil platform far off to the west of their position. "We're not far now." He turned to Donovan. "Do you want me to take the wheel?"

"Can you shake out the sails first?" Donovan replied. "My back's killing me."

"Sure, Skipper." Augie went forward to untie the reefs and increase the sail area to better catch the wind.

The professor peered out from the hatch in the main cabin. He took another step up the companionway and rested his elbows on the slider rails. "Is it all right to come topside?"

"Come on up."

The professor looked over his shoulder at Augie, who had just finished letting out the mainsail. He watched him move to the mizzen mast to undo the ties on the sail. "That was fun," he commented ironically as he went to stand by the steering box.

"I'm sorry about not letting you in on what we were doing—"

"That's all right," the professor headed off the apology. "You did what you believed you had to do to take care of your emergency and not delay us from getting to the Sabancuy Channel. I understand that." He drew a deep, pensive breath. "I only wish there was a way I could have been given a choice beforehand."

"I regret there wasn't."

The professor turned to watch Augie unfurl the mizzen sail and secure it. "I understand," he said softly. He stood silently moving his eyes from the moon to Augie as he moved to the foresail. Donovan felt the ship respond to the sails as the wind popped against the canvas.

After securing the fore, Augie came back to the afterdeck and stood on the other side of the steering box from the professor.

He put his left hand on the top peg and took the wheel from Donovan, who stepped back and put his hand on the boom crutch at the stern of the afterdeck. Augie glanced at the binnacle to check the course and adjusted the wheel accordingly. He gazed upon the moonlit horizon, as did Donovan and the professor, each deep in thought.

"Which of the islets are we headed to?" Dr. Ventura asked, breaking the silence.

"Cayo del Centro," Donovan replied.

"How much do you know about the Arcas?"

"About as much as I need to know, I guess," he responded as he undid the snaps on his rain jacket. "There's a reef running from it to the east and tidal islands all around it." He shook the water from the jacket before dropping it to the deck.

"Do you know anything about their history?"

He pulled down on the suspenders holding up his oilskins and started to remove them. "Never thought about it," he replied.

"The Arcas were used as a base of operations by the Republic of Texas Navy."

Donovan and Augie smiled at each other, pleased that the professor seemed to have gotten over the slight.

Augie turned to the professor. "I didn't know Texas even had a navy."

"Oh, yes." The professor raised his brows as he bobbed his head. "The Texas navy and the armada of the Republic of Yucatán used to work together to keep the Mexican armada from attacking their fledging republics."

Donovan shook the water from his oilskins and started to fold them. "I had no idea."

"After the battle of San Jacinto, Texas struggled to defend its shipping lanes against marauding Mexican ships and the threat of a Mexican seaborne invasion."

"I thought all that was settled after the Battle of San Jacinto," Augie interjected.

"Not really." The professor shook his head. "Mexico refused to recognize Texas independence, and Santa Ana vowed to reclaim the renegade state. Within a couple of years, most of the Texas navy's ships had been sunk, captured, or sold off to pay debts. By late 1837 into early 1839, the Texas navy was virtually without any ships."

Donovan dropped his oilskins and picked up his rain jacket to fold it. "Why didn't Santa Ana make his move then?"

"Mexico had problems of its own," the professor responded. "An economic crisis in 1837, an insurrection in the three states that bordered Texas, the establishment of the Republic of Yucatán, and the French blockade of Veracruz. If not for that, Texas would have felt the full brunt of Mexico's military might."

The professor paused to take a breath. "However, the Mexicans settled their differences with France and the insurrection in the north fell apart. The Texans realized that Mexico was free to send its armada against Texas, so they commissioned a half dozen ships to blockade Mexico's gulf coast and issued letters of mark to privateers to attack Mexican shipping to compel Mexico to defend its coastline, hoping it would head off any attempt by Mexico to attack Texas."

"A good defense starts with a good offense," Augie added.

"Precisely," the professor agreed. "The Republic of Yucatán, which in those days included Campeche and Quintana Roo, pursued a similar strategy to defend against a seaborne invasion. The president of Texas …" The professor paused. "Lamar, I believe was his name—ordered the commodore of the Texas navy to establish a friendly relationship with the Yucatecan armada. For the next year or so, the Texas and Yucatecan navies coordinated their efforts to keep the Mexican armada in check."

"What about the base on the Arcas cays?" Donovan picked up his neatly folded rain gear and put it on the steering box. "Did anything historical happen there?"

"Not much, really. The Texans used the largest islet, Cayo del Centro as an anchorage to repair damages to their ships and to keep casks of water, ammunition, and other stores on it." The professor took a moment to gather his thoughts. "They did lose a schooner on the shoals."

The wreck piqued Augie's interest. "What happened?"

"It obviously broke up and sank," Donovan commented sarcastically. He yawned and stretched his back by extending his arms. "I'm going below to catch a few winks." He picked up his rain gear and headed for the main cabin. "Wake me up when we get to Cayo del Centro."

CHAPTER

12

CAYO DEL CENTRO
OCTOBER 14, 1840

From the deck of the schooner San Jacinto, Mr. Gray watched the landing party run their longboat on the beach through the eyepiece of his spyglass. Except for several clusters of coconut palms and a smattering of sand shrubs, the sandy mound that barely qualified as an island did not offer much in the way of shelter. A gale had blown in from the north, angering the waters around the Arcas cays, and he cautioned his captain to wait until it passed before attempting to fetch the casks of fresh water the flotilla had stored on the islet. Not only did he ignore his advice; he insisted on accompanying the landing party despite his protests.

"I don't like it, Mr. Gibbs." Lieutenant Gray collapsed his spyglass and tucked it into the inside pocket of his faded blue, double-breasted tailcoat. Like his coat, the sun had weathered the rest of his uniform, yellowing the white of his shirt, vest, and pantaloons and taking the life from the gold piping on his standing collar and braiding on his shoulder tabs. The salt air had tarnished the brass on his insignia, buckle, and buttons. "If the winds get any stronger, that anchor will never hold."

"I can already feel it slipping," said Lieutenant Gibbs, who also wore the uniform of an officer in the Republic of Texas Navy. He put his hands on the rail on the port beam and looked down into the water. "There's nothing for the anchor to grab but sand."

Lieutenant Gray cast his tired eyes upon the islet and sighed. "He knows about the sandbars. We've all seen them during low tide." He turned to Gibbs. "And still he insisted on going ashore." He inhaled deeply and forced the air out through his nostrils. "Why couldn't he wait for the storm to pass?"

The first officer had good reason to question his captain's judgment. In the two weeks since he had assumed command of the San Jacinto, Captain O'Shaunessy had done little to win the respect of the officers and crew. Besides an arrogant disposition, he also demonstrated a total disregard for the opinions of his subordinates. His decision to go ashore and risk the ship added poor judgment to the faults in his character.

"He said the commodore wanted the dispatches delivered to Galveston posthaste."

Mr. Gray scoffed. "I doubt that the commodore's dispatches have anything to do with it." Gray again turned his eyes toward the island. "I'd venture to guess the ladies attending the weekend gala at the Tremont Hotel have more to do with it."

The wind bellowed a deep, mournful groan, bringing with it an angry torrent of rain. The ship jerked suddenly, causing both men to momentarily lose their balance. Gibbs looked at Mr. Gray. "The wind is pushing us toward the surf!" The ship jerked yet again. "We need to hoist the sails and take her out!"

"It's too late to get underway!" Mr. Gray yelled over the howling wind. His face reflected the intensity of his thoughts as he ran his eyes about the ship. He fixed his gaze on a twelve-pound cannon sitting in its cradle amidships. He turned to the gunner standing at his post. "Get your gun crew!" he yelled over the wind. "Tie a cable to that cannon and throw it over the starboard side!"

"Aye, sir!" The gunner mustered his crew and turned to the job at hand.

A large swell lifted the ship and carried it ever closer to the breaking waters of the surf. Lieutenant Gibbs, his face ashen and grim, stared in awe at the rows of massive swells gathering off the starboard side.

"God help us."

The knock on the cabin door woke Donovan from a restless sleep. He opened his eyes and propped himself up on his elbows. "Yeah?" he said through a yawn.

"We're here, Skipper," Sandy called through the door.

Donovan swung his legs off the bed and wiped the sleep from his face. He breathed in deeply, emptied his lungs, and then cleared his throat. "I'm coming."

"Uncle Augie—I mean Mr. Fagan said to tell you that there are two go-fast boats on the island."

Donovan opened the door. "Did they see us?"

"Uncle Augie doesn't think so."

Sandy followed Donovan through the main cabin and up the companionway to the deck. The sky had cleared, and the ring around the gibbous moon hanging low in the predawn sky glowed like a white halo around a fat cherub's face. The pale moonlight reflecting off the white sands around the island illuminated the shallow waters in a surrealistic display of varying shades of blues and greens. Augie and Dr. Ventura stood on the starboard side, looking up the beach through a single pair of binoculars. Sandy propped himself up on the steering box next to Poli, almost knocking him off as Donovan headed for the starboard side.

"Where are the go-fast boats?" Donovan inquired.

Augie put the binoculars down. "On the other side of the island camped below the lighthouse."

"Are you sure they didn't see us?"

"No way to tell for sure. I had the boys drop the sails as soon as we rounded the point."

"You have any idea who they are?"

"Whoever they are, they're hombres malos," the professor interjected. "They had a man holding a machine gun guarding the speedboats."

"How many?"

"About six of them," Augie replied. "I think they're drug runners."

"They could be the pirates that robbed that Canadian boater," the professor suggested.

"Whoever they are, we don't want anything to do with them." Donovan looked up the beach. "What were you looking at?"

Augie handed Donovan the binoculars and pointed up the beach. "There's a house by a clump of palms about halfway up the beach." Augie waited for Donovan to look through the binoculars. "It looks abandoned."

The white facade of the house glowed softly in the moonlight. The porch covering attached to the front of the house had partly collapsed, sloping down along with the porch to the water's edge. Other than that, the house looked well maintained and suitable for habitation. It did not fit Captain Santos's description of where to find the buried cocaine.

"I wonder why they didn't use the house?" Donovan commented.

"They looked plenty comfortable where they are," Augie remarked.

"Somebody's living there." Donovan lowered the binoculars. "There are clothes hanging from a line behind the house."

"Probably the lighthouse keepers," the professor suggested.

"I wonder if they know about the campers on the other side of the island." Donovan thought out loud.

"They're probably in cahoots with them," Augie assumed. "Best we stay clear of that house."

Donovan trained the binoculars beyond the house at the ruins up the beach. The structure lay completely in ruin but for a low rectangular block on the north side of the fallen building that could be a porch. Just beyond the ruins stood the range beacon Captain Santos had told him about. He lowered the binoculars and looked at the flashing white light perched on top of the pyramid-shaped, steel skeletal tower. The light flashed for a second every two seconds, consistent with Santos's description.

He moved the binoculars to the east of the steel tower where he spotted the lighthouse standing near the center of the island. Its white stone tower also glowed softly in the light of the gibbous moon. The light on it flashed twice as long as and brighter than the light on the range beacon, every twenty seconds or so.

He took another look through the binoculars at the ruins of the collapsed building. He focused on the low rectangular structure and saw the porch Captain Santos spoke about.

Donovan handed the binoculars to Augie. "I'm going ashore."

Sandy stepped off the steering box. "Do you want us to lower the Mona, Skipper?"

"No. The night's pretty still." Donovan removed his shirt and kicked off his boat shoes. "The cranks'll make too much noise."

The crew and the professor gathered around where Donovan swung his legs over the side and lowered himself into the water.

"You still gonna keep us in the dark about what you're doing?" Augie asked.

Donovan looked at the boys and then at the professor and finally at Augie. "Be ready to get underway as soon as I get back."

He pushed himself off the side and quietly swam away from the ship, using a modified breaststroke. Augie had anchored the Siete Mares off the southwest tip of the islet at the end of a long spit. As he swam toward the range beacon in the shallow semilagoon between the beach and the reef flat to his left, he came close enough to the first house to get a good look at it.

The main part of the house rose above the rest of the building and had a flat roof that served as an observation deck. The rest of the structure to the sides of the main part had red shedlike roofs with a gable roofed porch attached to the front. The porch had apparently collapsed as a result of a storm surge that swept the sand away from its foundation.

The silhouettes of the palms that encircled the back of the house against the deep blue of the moonlit night and the lighter blues and greens reflecting off the pale sands and concrete rubble below the clear water in front of the house would have made a good postcard, he thought.

As he swam past the house, he could easily see the bottom and the shadows of the fish swimming beneath him. He thought about his partner and his struggling dive shop. The reefs around the Arcas would make good spots to bring divers, he thought. That part of the business had yet to turn a profit, despite his partner's efforts to drum up divers at the hotels in Campeche City and Ciudad del Carmen. Campeche did not have the nightlife or beaches that Cancun and Playa del Carmen enjoyed. The only tourists who came to Campeche came there for the ruins at Edzna, the Spanish colonial fortifications, or the Calakmul biosphere.

After he made his way past the house, he decided to go ashore. Although he found the swim refreshing, he decided that he could cover the distance faster on land. Over countless storms, the surge had pushed the sands up against the wild grasses on the islet, forming a ridge that he could use to conceal his movement should the guard on the east side of the island happen to look his way.

He smiled when he came to the rectangular structure beneath the range beacon abutting the ruins of the collapsed building, realizing he had found the porch Captain Santos had described to him. He didn't know how long it would take to find and dig up the packages of cocaine or how he would go about destroying them. The flashing light of the range beacon lit the ground around him, and it would undoubtedly expose him should someone walk to his side of the islet.

He looked to his right at the lighthouse tower and wondered about the men camped on the other side of the narrow islet. He crouched low as he went to the sandy ridge to see if he could spot the campers. He looked over the ridge, keeping his head as low and still as possible. As far as he could tell, the men had not posted a guard to cover their backs. However, he couldn't assume that the guard watching their boats didn't occasionally check the back of the lighthouse.

The same conditions that created the sand ridge existed on the opposite beach, making it impossible for him to get a clear view. The scrub brush and tall grass that made it impossible to see across the island would also give him enough cover to get to the back of the lighthouse. The moonlight that made it easy for him to find his objective now menaced his safety.

Disregarding the slow, strobing flashes from the range beacon, he ran to the nearest clump of scrub brush where he spooked a covey of brown boobies that awkwardly thrashed their wings in a clumsy effort to take flight. He dropped to the ground, barely raising his eyes to see if the birds attracted any unwanted attention. Satisfied that they had not, Donovan lifted himself on the heels of his hands and surveyed the building behind the lighthouse.

The long, single-story, multifaceted building made of concrete and plaster had a flat roof and a concrete patio that ran the length of the building. It had fallen into disrepair, the white finish spotted with gray and black and the glass on the windows all broken. He could see the other side through an open hall on the far right side of the building. He rose to his feet and dashed to the back of the building, working his way to the hall where he peered around the corner. The hall blocked the moonlight, and he decided to take advantage of the darkness to get a good look at the other side.

After he entered the hallway, he stumbled on something soft and uneven. He waited for his eyes to adjust to see what had caused him to stumble. As they did, the dark mass began to take shape. It didn't take long for him to realize that he had found a body, and he presumed it belonged to the lighthouse keeper. He put his fingers on the side of the dead man's throat to check for a pulse. He recoiled when his fingers slid into a gaping wound. He tried lifting an arm, but the stiffness kept him from succeeding. He stepped over the body and worked his way as far as he dared to the end of the hallway to look for the men camped on the beach.

The ground dropped gradually toward the beach where he saw the two single outboard launches tied to a piece of driftwood. He watched as the guard sat down on the old log that somehow found its way to the island and buried itself firmly in the sand. The guard propped the stock of his AK-47 on the sand and used the barrel to hold himself up as he hung his head to rest his eyes. After a while, he shook the sleep from his head and stood up to keep himself from falling asleep. A moment later, he again lowered himself to sit on the log, this time laying the assault rifle across his lap before hanging his head.

Donovan backed his way into the hall, feeling for the dead lighthouse keeper with the heel of his foot. He stepped over the unfortunate man and hurried back the short distance to the other side of the island, making sure no one followed him. He jumped over the ridge of sand and went directly to the south side of the lopsided porch where he stepped over the broken cinder-block foundation into the room that once stood there. He dropped to his knees and began pushing sand away from the center of the concrete block. The sand in his hands felt like white powder as he pushed it to the sides in search of the packages of cocaine. He looked around him for something he could use to dig. He saw a broken piece of siding lying amid the rubble and crawled over to get it.

He resumed digging until he felt the edge of the plank hit something. He set it aside and went back to using his hands to push away the sand. He ran his fingers around the edges and pulled the first kilo bundle out of the sand. He rested his back against the concrete slab and looked at the rectangular package wrapped in a beige-colored tape. He set it aside to catch his breath, scooping a handful of sand as he did. He looked at the fine granules glowing in the moonlight. He closed his hand and turned it sideways, letting the grains slip slowly through the heel of his hand.

"Baby food," he muttered to himself.

Supermarket in Veracruz
Three years ago

The young woman dressed in a blue jogging suit tried to keep pace with the grocery clerk walking briskly toward a locked cabinet in the middle of the grocery aisle. As he fumbled with the key ring, the clerk looked anxiously over his shoulder at his register where a long line of frustrated customers waited for his return. Donovan and Xochitl entered the aisle from the opposite end as the nervous clerk dropped the cylindrical box he tried to hand to the young woman, spilling its white powdery contents on the floor.

"Uh-oh," Xochitl said to Donovan. "That was an expensive mistake."

Donovan switched the hand basket to the other hand. "What did he drop?"

"Infant formula."

"Why do they lock the stuff up?" Donovan looked down at the white powder as they walked by the mess. He looked through the glass at the price on one of the containers. "Whew, look at the price!"

Xochitl tugged on his shirt to move him along. "It's one of the most shoplifted items there is."

"Who would've thought baby food would be so expensive."

"It's not just baby food. It's infant formula." She took his free hand. "It simulates human milk. It contains nutrients essential for an infant's healthy development."

"I can see why a mother would shoplift it." He looked back over his shoulder at the locked cabinet. "How can the average mother afford to buy that stuff?"

"Mothers are not the problem."

"Who then?"

"Petty thieves and drug addicts. Organized crime."

Donovan let go of Xochitl's hand and stopped. "You can't be serious."

"But I am." Xochitl turned around to look at him. "There's a tremendous black market for it."

"I don't see mothers buying it on street corners like some coke fiend," he remarked facetiously.

"It's not sold on the streets."

"Who buys it then?"

"Traffickers." She held her hand out for him to take. "They spread the word that they're interested in infant formula, offering as much as ten dollars a can. When they have enough cans, they sell them to a buyer who repackages it and sells it."

Donovan took her hand. "Who does the buyer sell it to?"

"To a wholesaler or they ship it overseas. It's a billion-dollar industry." Xochitl sighed deeply. "I wish I had a ton of it to take with me when I go to Colombia."

"There might be something I can do about that," Donovan muttered to himself.

"Dr. Aguirre believes in it."

Donovan felt his face getting hot. It happened every time she mentioned his name. He waited for the feeling to subside before he said something that might upset her.

"You really like that guy, don't you?"

"He's a gifted doctor." She smiled.

Her response didn't satisfy the reason behind his question. He looked at her. "Is he married?"

Xochitl stopped suddenly, releasing his hand. She grinned at him. "You're jealous."

"I am not." Donovan felt his face turning red. "Okay. Maybe a little."

Xochitl laughed softly, putting an arm around his waist and tucking her head against his side. "You have nothing to worry about."

Digging in the light of a pale moon with an eye on the ridge and fighting the sand collapsing back into the hole, Donovan worked feverishly to remove the brick-shaped packages from their hiding place. The wider he made the hole, the more the walls of sand wanted to reclaim their prize. Using his left arm as a cradle, he stacked several bricks against the front of his body and walked to the water's edge where he set them down to get his pocket knife. He took one of the bundles and waded out a few feet into the water where he plunged the tip of his large pocket knife into it. The tape gave easily to the sharpness of the blade as he ran it down the center of the package, exposing its white powdery contents.

He put the knife between his teeth and split the bundle open with his thumbs. He looked over his shoulder as he emptied the contents, hoping that he could finish dumping the rest of the packages without being discovered. The beacon from the lighthouse caught his eye. It glowed on for two seconds before fading off for another twenty seconds. He thought about the poor lighthouse keeper lying in a lifeless mass on the cold concrete floor.

Living alone on a desolate island with only the brown boobies for company takes a special kind of man, one who doesn't mind the loneliness and who can spend countless hours alone. He probably went to greet the men on the other side of the island, excited about having someone he could chat with and perhaps even share a meal with. Instead, the guests he had gone to welcome ran a sharp blade across his throat and left him in a heap for the crabs to eat without a Christian burial and nobody to mourn him.

He took the knife from his mouth and walked back to the beach, throwing the empty package to the side as he put a knee down to get the next bundle by the water's edge. He gazed at the beige-colored bricks and then looked back at the lighthouse.

What kind of men would do something like that? he thought. Could they be the pirates who robbed that Canadian boater off Holbox Island?

He turned his head to look at the Siete Mares anchored off the southern tip of the islet. Even with her sails down, her white hull glowed like a neon light in the moonlight. The longer he took to dispose of the cocaine, the higher the risk the ship would be spotted. He looked back at the lighthouse and then back at the ship. He gazed at it for a moment and then dropped the brick from his hand and closed his knife.

The guard sitting on the log struggled to keep his eyes open as he watched the glowing embers on the campfire slowly die. He heard a sharp crack coming from the lighthouse and craned his neck to look that way. He heard a second sound of something rolling on the concrete slab and rose to his feet to get a better look. He looked at the others, snuggled in their sleeping bags around the campfire. He looked back at the lighthouse and then again at the sleeping men before following the barrel of his AK-47 rifle up the path to the building.

Donovan ran across the beach, holding his pants like a sack in his hand as the guard walked cautiously toward the lighthouse. He waded out, waist deep in the water, and tested the knot he had made with his belt around the loops in his pants. He tied the ends of the legs together and put them around his neck. He slipped his pocketknife between his teeth and then pushed himself into the water and breaststroked his way behind the speedboats.

The guard swept his assault rifle back and forth as he cautiously stepped onto the concrete patio of the lighthouse. He turned an ear, leaned in the direction he had heard the sounds coming from, and waited.

"¿Quien es?" he called out nervously. The selector made a loud plop as he released the safety. "Estoy armado." He heard a sliding sound coming from the hallway and swung the rifle barrel abruptly in that direction. "Who's there?" he exclaimed. "Come out. I have a gun."

After waiting for the intruder to come out, the guard took a step toward the hallway but stopped when the sliding noise became more pronounced. He let out a short burst when the body of the dead lighthouse keeper slid out of the hallway on the concrete patio.

As the men sleeping on the beach ran to check on the gunfire, armed with their assault rifles, Donovan eased himself out of the water behind the speedboats. He waited for the men to run up the path toward the lighthouse before he took the makeshift haversack from around his neck and untied the first leg. He removed a kilo brick and waded to the side of the nearest boat. He cut open the brick and poured the contents all along the inside of the boat. He removed the other brick from the remaining pant leg and likewise spread the illicit powder all along the inside of the other boat.

He heard laughter coming from the lighthouse and looked in that direction. The men had started back down the path to the beach. With no time to waste, Donovan went to the transom and cut the fuel hose. He snapped open the engine cover and hastily cut all the hoses and wires he could find before closing the cover and moving to the other boat.

Augie strained to find Donovan through the binoculars. The professor reclined against the steering box, looked at his watch, and went to join him on the starboard side of the afterdeck.

"It's been more than an hour," the professor said.

"One hour and thirteen minutes," Augie replied as he continued to look for his partner.

"Do you think he's all right?"

"I don't know." Augie lowered the binoculars. "If I knew what he was up to, I could better say."

The professor looked at Sandy and Poli, sitting on top of the main cabin by the mainmast. Poli had his hands out, palms up, while Sandy held his palm down over Poli's, barely touching. Poli suddenly brought his left hand over Sandy's right as Sandy drew them away in time to avoid having his hand slapped.

"The boys look bored," he said to Augie.

"Quit playing slapjack and stand by to get underway," Augie called to them in a low voice.

"Aye, aye, Mr. Fagan," they both replied.

The professor chuckled to himself and looked up the beach at the lighthouse as the beacon subtly flashed on for two seconds before fading. He scrunched his brows. "That's strange."

"What's strange?" Augie asked.

"Do you notice something different about the beacons on the island?" Dr. Ventura inquired.

Augie turned his head to look up the beach. After a few seconds, the beacon on the lighthouse flashed. Then darkness followed. "What happened to the strobe?"

The professor nodded. "That's what I was missing. The range beacon stopped flashing."

"What do you think caused it?"

"They don't work so good when you cut off the power source," Donovan said as he lifted himself over the transom of the ship.

Surprised by his sudden appearance, Augie and Doctor Ventura just stared at him as he came onboard.

His partner frowned at him. "What happened to your pants?"

CHAPTER

13

When morning came, Itzél went about her daily routine like any other day. She rose well before dawn to prepare for the breakfast rush as usual. She swept and mopped the floors, wiped down all the tables and countertops, and set out what she would need to serve breakfast. She had always enjoyed performing these simple but essential tasks. Like most people, she found comfort in routine. Routine enables people to reflect on their lives. She thought she had a good one. However, much had happened recently to upset that belief.

Normally, by the end of the morning rush, Benício would have already come in from his day fishing at the Seyba Playa Reef. He had yet to come downstairs, a fact that did not go unnoticed by the town's leading busybodies, Señora Gutiérrez and her sister-in-law, Tencha María, who made it their practice to come to the Cocina Maya in the waning minutes before noon.

Itzél liked the elderly ladies and enjoyed serving them. They made pleasant conversation that normally amounted to harmless chitchat but could turn into a relentless inquisition if something piqued their interest. Like sharks, they kept their distance unless they smelled blood in the water. She had learned how to fend them off politely and had done so quite skillfully that morning. After they finished their breakfast, she walked with them to the door.

"Gracias, señoritas." The bell over the entrance jingled as she opened the door for them. "See you tomorrow."

"I hope Don Benício is feeling better." Señora Gutiérrez walked through the door. "He's getting to that age when a cold can easily turn into pulmonia. Make sure that he sits up at least once an hour for ten minutes and remind him to cough. He has to cough to keep his lungs from filling up."

"Give him some mezcal with a twist of limón," her comadre, Tencha María, added. "That always worked for mí Juanito, que en paz descanse." She crossed herself in respect for her late husband. "Don't forget."

"Mezcal con limón." Itzél nodded. "Muchas gracias."

Señora Gutiérrez looked at her watch. "¡Díos mío!" She pulled her comadre through the door by the arm. "We're going to be late for your checkup."

"Mind your driving, Señora Gutiérrez," Itzél cautioned her. "Don't forget to wear your glasses."

Everyone in Seyba Playa knew that Señora Gutiérrez did not drive well. The dents on her car stood as a testament to her lack of skill and depth perception. People literally steered clear of her car as she overshot curves, crossed the center line, or bounced her tires off the curb in a tight turn. Her inability to round a curve without climbing it or at least scraping her tires on it earned her the nickname "Comadre Matacurvas."

"Adíos, mijita," the elderly woman said as she rushed to her car with her comadre in tow.

Itzél closed the door and waved goodbye to them. She flipped the sign on the glass door, closing her restaurant so that she could begin preparing for la comida.

"Why did you tell them I was sick?" Benício asked from the hallway at the back of the restaurant.

The events of the previous evening had worn out the aging panguero, and he slept in past the morning rush. Benício rolled up his sleeves and sat at the counter by the register. Itzél went behind the counter to get a coffee cup and the coffeepot.

"What was I supposed to say to them?" She set the cup in front of him and poured coffee into it. "They know you're always back by this time of day. I couldn't tell them you were still out fishing with your panga tied out there where they might see it."

"Hmm." Benício nodded. He took a sip of coffee and raised his eyes to look at his wife. "Are you still upset with me?"

"Should I be?" Itzél put the pot back on the warmer.

"You know I had to go." He put his cup down. "Lázaro needed my help."

"Is that the real reason you went?" Itzél went to the sink to wash dishes. "Or did you feel you had to prove something?"

Benício shifted his eyes and then looked at her. "What's that supposed to mean?"

She turned to look at him. "Why didn't you let me go to Capitán Donovan for help?"

"We've troubled him enough."

"What would have happened if the armada caught you?"

He slowly took a sip of coffee, his eyes beaming defiantly at her. "They didn't." He put the cup down and turned away. "And they won't." He took a long, deep breath and released it. "Lázaro and I talked it over last night. We agreed that what we were doing was a mistake." He turned to her. "We're going to see the public ministry agent later today to tell his side of the story."

"You should have done that to begin with."

"I realize that now." He nodded. "You don't know how much I thank God for sending the storm to keep me from meeting that ship."

Itzél turned back around to resume washing dishes. "You should be thanking Capitán Donovan." She sprayed water on the plate in her hand. "He's the one who kept the ship from meeting you."

He slammed the heel of his fist on the counter, startling Itzél and spilling his coffee. "I asked you not to involve him!" he barked.

She stared at him in disbelief. She had never seen him lose his temper or heard him raise his voice like that before. After a moment, she turned back around to dry the plate she had just rinsed.

"I didn't." She set the plate on a stack next to the sink. "I went to see Don Macario."

"That's the same as going to him."

She turned to look at him and noticed the coffee spreading on the counter. She went to wipe it up with the dishrag in her hand. "It's a good thing I did. Don Macario told me the armada set a trap to catch the ship in the act," she said calmly. "Capitán Donovan went to warn the captain you were going to meet. That's why the ship never showed up." She put the dishrag on the back counter and got the coffeepot off the warmer. "The storm had nothing to do with it."

Indeed, had Donovan not warned Captain Santos, he would have had enough time to make the rendezvous west of the Seyba Reef before the storm. He deliberately took his time delivering his cargo to the Ta' Kuntah oil platform and then chose to wait for the storm before he headed back to Seyba Playa.

"You should thank Don Macario for going to him," she said as she poured coffee into his cup.

Benício stared at his cup as she poured. "In the long run, it really doesn't matter." He sat up, looked at her, and took a sharp breath through his nostrils. "El Demonio will be back."

She finished filling his cup. "Don Macario said that Capitán Donovan went to make sure that he doesn't come back."

Benício crumpled his brow. "How's he going to do that?"

She turned to put the pot back on the warmer and then looked at him. "I don't know."

As the Bell 205 Iroquois made a gradual approach to Cayo del Centro from the east, Lieutenant Baeza looked through the large square window at the CB90H combat boat anchored just south of the two smaller skiffs beached below the lighthouse. The blue-gray, fifty-two-foot all-aluminum assault craft of Swedish design not only looked fast; she looked mean. A small cadre of marines formed a perimeter on the beach around the fast attack boat and the two skiffs while the rest of the complement secured the rest of the island.

The armada directed the combat boat away from its patrol duties around the Cantarell offshore platforms to Cayo del Centro to check on the lighthouse keeper. The security officer stationed at the Ta'Kuntah platform called the lighthouse to report that the range beacon on the west side of the islet had gone out apparently due to the storm. When he failed to answer the radio, the security officer alerted the armada.

A lookout spotted a group of armed men running toward the lighthouse as the combat boat came up the shallow waters from the south between the reef and the east side of the islet. The complement of marines on board made a tactical landing, securing the island without meeting any resistance from the men. As the marines secured the island, they found the remains of the lighthouse keeper in a hastily dug grave behind the lighthouse. They also found a load of cocaine hidden poorly in the brush nearby and seven AK-47 rifles wrapped in a sleeping bag in the rubble of a building on the opposite side of the narrow islet.

The Seventh Naval Zone in Lerma dispatched the Iroquois to transport a judicial officer to investigate the crimes committed by the men, a forensic specialist to gather the evidence, and two technicians to repair the damaged range beacon. Lieutenant Baeza accompanied the team to debrief the marines and gather intelligence resulting from the incident.

The pilot slowed the helicopter considerably as he flew over the building behind the lighthouse. Several marines stood guard over six shirtless men, sitting on the slab behind the structure with their hands on the tops of their heads. Lieutenant Baeza tapped the naval judicial officer sitting next to him on the shoulder and pointed out the window at a mound of beige-colored packages in the brush behind the lighthouse. The judicial officer, a young woman in her late twenties, directed the petty officer sitting on her other side to take a photograph of the contraband.

A petty officer went to meet the Iroquois after it landed just north of the lighthouse, hunching his back to avoid the blades. He slid the door open, saluted the officers on board, and then led the passengers away from the helicopter. The two radio technicians went directly to the range beacon, taking their equipment bags with them. The judicial officer, forensic specialist, and Lieutenant Baeza followed the petty officer with their backs hunched until they had cleared the rotor blades.

"Teniente Cobarrubias ordered me to escort the legal team," the petty officer said.

Naval Lieutenant Elizondo, the judicial officer, stepped forward. "Take me to the body first, maestre." The lieutenant whipped her hand to the top of her head to keep the prop wash from blowing off her cover.

"A la orden, teniente."

Lieutenant Baeza went to join the technicians, who stood at the foot of the range beacon tower, watching the cold-humored judicial officer follow behind the petty officer. The prop wash fluttered through her loose-fitting olive drab utilities, accentuating her shapely form.

"Is it permissible for a lieutenant to look that good in her work clothes?" Cabo Peña commented to the other technician.

"The wind has no respect for military decorum, cabo," Petty Officer Esquivel replied. He looked at Lieutenant Baeza. "Isn't that right, mí teniente?"

"To what are you referring?" Lieutenant Baeza asked.

"The way female marines wear their utilities." Cabo Peña sighed in a dreamy tone.

The lieutenant looked over his shoulder and then back at the communications technicians. "I see only a lieutenant." He looked up the tower at the bottom of the crow's nest around the range beacon. "I think I see the problem," he said to the technicians, pointing at a severed cable, obviously cut with a sharp instrument."

"Piratas pendejos," Petty Officer Esquivel cursed the pirates under his breath. "Why cut power to the range beacon? Didn't they realize it would attract attention?"

"Maybe they're not the ones that cut it?" Cabo Peña suggested.

"Who then?" Petty Officer Esquivel asked. "They killed the lighthouse keeper."

"I wonder …" Lieutenant Baeza pondered aloud. He looked around the range beacon and then at the marine standing guard by a red-topped slab on the beach by the rubble of an abandoned building. "That must be where they found the assault rifles," he said to the technicians, who had climbed the crow's nest without him noticing.

He looked back at the collapsed building and spotted a narrow trail in the sand leading away from behind the red-topped slab. He went to stand on the slab to survey the area. He noticed a large hole below him and ran his eyes along the outline of the room that abutted the slab. He followed the narrow trail with his eyes from the edge of the large hole, past the edge of the room, and up the sandy ridge directly to the lighthouse.

"Is this where they found the rifles?" Lieutenant Baeza asked the marine standing guard.

"No, mí teniente." The marine pointed at a pile of rubble. "There, under those planks. That's where they found the rifles wrapped in a sleeping bag."

"Then what's this pit all about?" The lieutenant stepped down into the hole and ran his eyes along the bottom, looking for an explanation. He looked around his feet and then up the narrow path leading away from the pit to the sandy ridge. Then he spotted a beige-colored rectangular object in the high wild grasses that ran along the top of the ridge. He climbed out of the pit, stepped over the ruins of the foundation, and went to retrieve the object in the wild grass. He knelt on one knee and used both hands to push the grass aside.

"Don't let anyone move this, marinero," he called to the guard standing by the slab.

The warehouse Fausto López used to conduct his business belonged to Don Rodrigo of the Campechano Growers Association, who bought the building from the port authority after they moved to their new facility downtown. The warehouse stood in the middle of the dock area at the port of Seyba Playa, overlooking the docks and the other warehouses. It stood out among the sheet-metal and pitched-roof buildings that lined the north side of the dock area because of its white concrete finish construction and flat roof.

The building served as the principal warehouse for the Campeche Growers Association until they transferred their business to larger facilities in Ciudad del Carmen and Champotón to accommodate their growing container operation. The association's distinctive logo, a large circular shield with a conquistador's bearded silhouette and the association's name painted artistically around it still adorned the sides of the building. All the windows, save for the large plate glass window at the office, had the panes blackened to discourage curious eyes. No one, not even the Federal Preventive Police, charged with port security, dared to make an unannounced visit.

The sun bore down on José Luis as he walked toward the warehouse with his roan-colored leather sports jacket dangling from his finger over the back of his shoulder. He raised his sunglasses off his face and put them on top of his head before he knocked on the outer door to the office. After a moment, Beto opened the door.

"What did you find out?" Fausto asked José Luis from behind his desk.

"It's like Santos said." He hung his coat on the back of the chair. "The armada followed him to the platform and back."

"What else did the girl tell you?" Fausto leaned toward him. "Was there an informer involved?"

"She believes so."

"Believes so?" He pushed himself back and scoffed. "You spent an entire morning with her and that's all you got?"

"What do you expect from a secretary? She doesn't have access to that kind of information." José Luis lowered himself into the chair. "All she knows is that they were acting on Lieutenant Baeza's information."

"There's that name again." Fausto gritted his teeth. "We're going to have to do something about that guy."

"Do you want me to kill him?" Beto said dryly.

"No." Fausto sighed. "We don't want to stir the hornet's nest just yet," he said, echoing his cousin's fears. He looked at José Luis. "Did your girlfriend have any ideas who the informer might be?"

"She's not my girlfriend," José Luis said heartlessly.

"So she's a little gordita?" Fausto grinned. "Come on. A little fat is fun."

"That's more fun than I care for."

Fausto chuckled. "Do you think she can find out?"

"Probably not." José Luis rested his arms on his thighs. "But I have a good idea who it is."

"Not that again." Fausto stood and walked around the desk to the plate glass window.

"Who else could it be?" José Luis turned his head to follow him with his eyes. "If not Dario, it had to be one of the rest of us. Felipe, Nacho, or—" He turned to Beto standing by the door and stared at him suspiciously.

The skinny, long-haired sicario glared back at him. "I'm no dedo."

"Beto would never put the finger on anyone," Fausto said in his defense.

"What about Felipe or Nacho?"

"Them too," Fausto retorted.

"That leaves me or you." José Luis looked at him dubiously. "And I know I didn't say anything."

Fausto let out his breath and looked out through the blinds. "You're not making any sense."

"Am I not?" José Luis stood and faced him. "Tell me who else knew about the guns we lost at Punta Morro?" The heels of his low-top boots plopped on the concrete floor as he stepped around the chair. "Who else knew about the rendezvous yesterday?"

El Demonio split the blinds open with his fingers. "Dario would never do this to me."

"You said it yourself. He has no stomach for killing. Don't you think it's at least possible that he might do something like this to head off another drug war?"

"I refuse to believe he's an informer." He gazed out the window. "It has to be someone else." He released the blinds and stepped toward José Luis. "You sleep around. Maybe you let something slip."

"Oh no." José Luis chuckled. "I don't talk in my sleep, and I don't make pillow talk about work."

The two men were trying to stare each other down when a knock on the door broke their concentration. Beto stepped back and opened the door to let Don Rodrigo into the office.

Fausto glanced at José Luis. "We'll talk about this later."

"Am I interrupting something?"

"Just a little housekeeping we can take care of later," El Demonio told his benefactor.

"Does it concern the merchandise you lost today?"

Fausto looked at José Luis, who shrugged and shook his head. He turned to Don Rodrigo. "If you're referring to the aborted delivery yesterday afternoon—nothing was lost. Santos led the armada away from the rendezvous. We're going to have to find another way of getting it."

"I'm not talking about that." Don Rodrigo looked at him through his brows. "I mean the seizure this morning at Cayo del Centro."

José Luis took a step toward him. "What seizure?"

"It was in the midday news. The armada detained six men in two boats with about fifty kilos of cocaine on Cayo del Centro this morning. I assumed it was yours."

Fausto swallowed hard. "What makes you think it was my cocaine?"

"Did you have the cocaine buried near a metal tower?"

"You mean the beacon on the west side of the island?" José Luis inquired.

"I have no idea what side of the island it was on," Don Rodrigo snapped, irritated by the question. "I saw a picture of a stack of bricks hidden in some brush behind a lighthouse and a hole dug in the sand by an old building beneath a tower. The news said the men were trapped on the island by the storm after they dug up the cocaine."

The color washed from Fausto's face.

"I thought so," Don Rodrigo remarked. "The men must have found your cocaine, dug it up, and moved it behind the lighthouse." He chuckled. "A helicopter spotted the bricks from the air and contacted one of their boats patrolling the Cantarell oil platforms."

"Chinga su madre," José Luis cursed under his breath. "Did they say who the men were?"

"They believe they're the pirates who raped that young girl earlier this month," Don Rodrigo responded. "One of them was wearing a watch belonging to the girl's father," he explained. "They also found the lighthouse keeper with his throat cut in a shallow grave and a half dozen assault rifles wrapped in a sleeping bag. Very clumsy."

José Luis grunted. "Why didn't they run after they were spotted by the helicopter?"

"Apparently, their boats were damaged by the storm."

Fausto, visibly shaken by the news, walked to his desk and dropped himself into his chair. The heels of José Luis's low-cut boots resounded sharply as he went to stand in front of the desk.

"Don't worry, Fausto," he reassured him. He put his hands on his hips. "I'll talk to my contact in Honduras and get another load. We'll make up the loss." He put his hand on his shoulder. "You'll get your guns."

"I wouldn't count on anybody in Honduras," Don Rodrigo interposed. "Nor anybody else you're used to dealing with."

José Luis turned to Don Rodrigo. "What are you talking about?"

"Don Arturo found out that you're behind the surge in the supply of basuco in Campeche," he explained. "You've been blackballed."

"I told you it was risky trusting the gangs," Beto commented, a rare occurrence.

José Luis turned to Fausto. "What did you do?"

El Demonio glared at him bitterly and then looked away. "I wanted to show my appreciation to the comandantes for their loyalty," El Demonio explained. "They were supposed to get the cocaine out of Campeche." He looked at José Luis. "I suggested that they go back to their contacts with the Comisión." He exhaled forcefully. "How was I to know those idiots would give the bricks to their gangs to cut up and sell on the street?"

"Greed is a funny animal." Don Rodrigo commented. "The comandantes obviously wanted to squeeze every centavo they could out of what you gave them." He chuckled annoyingly. "You should have expected that."

José Luis lowered himself into the chair across the desk from Fausto. "I wish you hadn't done that."

As the two men sat in quiet reflection on their situation, an unsympathetic Don Rodrigo checked his watch and scoffed. "Time is running out. Comandante Sánchez is in Chiapas, meeting with the Comisión." He started for the door. "You'd better come up with something before Sánchez steals back the gangs from you."

On the west end of Tuxtla Gutiérrez, in the part of the city where men find diversion after a hard day's work in the consumption of refreshing alcoholic beverages and the company of loose women sat the Cantina La Soldadera. The cantina served appetizers, known as botanas, for free as long as the patron ordered a beer much like a Spanish tapas bar. In Mexico, such establishments are known as "cantinas botaneras," and the more a patron drinks, the more he eats. La Soldadera served its first botana nearly a hundred years ago. Since then, it had been visited by an assortment of personalities, some of them famous and many of them infamous, including revolutionaries, gunrunners, and narcotics traffickers.

La Soldadera occupied the corner of the old mercantile built just before the Mexican Revolution. The cantina looked much the same as it did in the times of Pancho Villa and Emiliano Zapata, except that windowpanes replaced the wooden shutters over the large rectangular openings, originally designed to let the breeze cool the inside of the bar. The massive native hardwood shutters, gray and scarred by the ravages of time, still hung faithfully to the sides of the windows, waiting dutifully for recall into service. All the businesses that originally occupied the old concrete building had long since passed and only La Soldadera marched stalwartly on, providing drink and diversion for the weary working man looking for repose.

The inside of the bar had changed very little since the cantina opened its doors. The tables and chairs, crafted crudely but functionally and painted in the colors of the Mexican flag, still filled the sprawling red concrete floor as they had for decades. The floor had faded and cracked in spots over the years as had the white plaster walls, adorned by a century's worth of patched-up bullet holes. The exposed beams supporting the second floor and painted a dark brown now had broad-bladed ceiling fans, hanging strategically from them to help cool the room.

La comida had yet to begin, and only a few patrons partook of the greasy but delicious appetizers brought to them by the busty waitresses wearing the white, low-cut, shoulderless blouses and short red skirts that fanned out like umbrellas. At a small table at the back of the cantina, away from the growing crowd of midafternoon diners, sat a dark-headed, stocky man wearing an expensive blue suit. The bartenders behind the long, rustic bar silently acknowledged the man's presence among themselves with their eyes, avoiding looking in his direction. They went about preparing the bar for the afternoon rush, waiting to see which one of them would step up and tend to the man at the back of the cantina. Finally, the bar manager threw down his clipboard in disgust and began pouring a Negra Modelo from the tap into a heavy mug as he glared bitterly at the reluctant bartenders around him. He motioned one of the bare-shouldered waitresses to the bar and handed the busty young woman with the pouty red lips the dark beer, throwing his eyes in the direction of the well-dressed man.

The young waitress, either undaunted by or ignorant of the man's significance, delivered the beer to his table without hesitation. Comandante Tercero of the Chiapas State Police thanked her with a simple tip of his head as she delivered his beer. She may or may not have known that the man with the pockmarked face, thin eyebrows, and neatly trimmed mustache worked not only as a state police commander but also for the band of corrupt Chiapas State Police officers who made up the Comisión drug-trafficking organization. As she turned to leave, a tall, robust man pulled out the chair across from the comandante and sat.

"¿Algo para tomar?" the busty waitress offered him a drink.

"Vino tinto," the man responded, removing his wide-brimmed straw golfing hat. He turned to admire her bouncy gait as she went to fetch his red wine.

"Te gusta?" Comandante Tercero asked his colleague from the Campeche State Police.

"What's not to like?" Comandante Sánchez replied. He looked over his shoulder to watch the waitress bounce her way back to the bar. "Muy guapa."

"She's one of the plain ones." Tercero chuckled.

"Madre de díos," Sánchez muttered under his breath. He turned to Tercero with a serious look in his eyes. "When can I expect the first shipment of guns?"

The smile left Tercero's face. He dropped his eyes and cleared his throat. "I'm sure by now you've heard that the Norteño cartel is coming."

"Precisely why I need the guns," Sánchez retorted.

Tercero looked across the table at the comandante like a poor poker player holding a mediocre hand. "Alejandro wants to know where the gangs stand."

"With the Comisión, of course."

"Alejandro doesn't believe you speak for them," Tercero said pointedly.

"The task force controls the gangs, and I control the task force," Sánchez responded sharply. "They'll do what I tell them."

Tercero eased back into his chair. "That's not our understanding."

Sánchez turned his head slightly and looked at Tercero through the side of his eyes, "What are you getting at?"

"We hear that the comandantes found a new leader."

"Nonsense," Sánchez scoffed and looked away.

"Do you deny that Fausto López has joined the gangs?"

"Just as an adviser," he said through his teeth. "I'm still their leader."

Tercero crossed his arms. "Now that the northern border war is over, it's become harder to jump their shipments coming from Guatemala. We're losing revenue." He leaned toward him. "Alejandro needs to know that you can deliver like before."

Sánchez put his elbow on the back of his chair and undid the buttons on his short-sleeve tropical jacket. He removed a pack of cigarettes from the pocket of his powder-blue shirt and put one between his lips. "Tell Alejandro not to worry." He whipped his

Ronson lighter open and lit his cigarette. "I'll keep up my end of the bargain if he keeps up his."

"Alejandro doubts that you can," Tercero retorted. "Since you ended the arrangement, we understand that the comandantes and their gangs have become self-sufficient and are no longer interested in renewing the arrangement."

"It's like I said." Sánchez exhaled a long stream of smoke in Tercero's direction. "The gangs will do as I say. They need guns and will do whatever they have to to get them."

"We heard that López promised to get them new guns from the gringos."

The end of the cigarette Sánchez held between his lips glowed brilliantly as he drew on it. He scoffed. "Did you hear about the guns he lost at Punta Morro?" He forced the smoke out his nostrils.

Tercero shrugged. "I'm sure it's just a temporary setback."

"That's as close as he's ever going to get. All his supply sources have dried up." He flicked the ashes from his cigarette onto the floor. "The Norteños control the corridors in and out of Texas." He chuckled arrogantly. "His supply line has been cut."

"And you believe the comandantes will follow you if you can keep them supplied with guns?"

"The comandantes have become quite comfortable since taking over the gangs." Sánchez pulled another drag from his cigarette. "They're convinced that the Norteños plan to take their plazas from them." He slid the ashtray in the center of the table toward him. "They share a common enemy with the Comisión." He released the smoke from his lungs as he smashed the cigarette into the ashtray. "Can Alejandro afford to turn away a potential ally?"

The underboss for the Comisión glowered at him for a moment and then stood as the pouty-lipped waitress came to the table with Sánchez's glass of wine. "That's for Alejandro to decide." Tercero handed several peso notes to the waitress. "Bring him another glass of wine." He waited for the waitress to leave before he continued, "You'll get your guns after you prove you can keep up your end of the bargain." He tipped his head at Sánchez and then left.

RANCHO NOCHE BUENA, NEAR MONTERREY, NUEVO LEON

Anastasio Noches Treviño, the head of the Norteño cartel, made his home on a ranch not far from the city of Monterrey, a mere two-hour drive southwest of the Rio Grande Valley of Texas. It sat on a rise on a canyon floor, surrounded by a pine forest high above the desert in the foothills of the Sierra Madre Oriental mountain range with a view of the saddle-shaped Cerro de la Silla Mountain to the west and a breathtaking view of a waterfall spilling over a flat canyon wall to the east. At times, fog rose along the canyon floor, and the sprawling Mediterranean-style stone house with a Spanish-style red-clay tile roof and sweeping archways seemed to sit on a cloud. The cobblestone drive leading to the imposing home spilled through an archway into a large courtyard surrounded by a high stone wall with a fountain at the center.

Unlike others in his profession, Anastasio did not flaunt his immense wealth by surrounding himself with expensive if not opulent material possessions. He did, however, indulge his taste for fine wines and fine horses. He had a grotto found beneath his house converted into a wine cellar where he stored expensive wines from all over the world. Across the courtyard from the ranch house, he built a long stable also made of stone where he kept a string of expensive Colombian Paso Fino horses. He bred the elegantly gaited horses for show and kept a small remuda of quarter horses for riding through the trails that wound through the canyon around his ranch. He spent much of his free time with his horses and often sat under a shade tree by the stable in the late afternoons.

Anastasio enjoyed drinking iced tea or a cool glass of lemonade after the sun had slipped beyond the top of the canyon and the air cooled down. When he could, he entertained his guests, most often his business associates, under the shade tree. From time to time, he'd sit chatting amicably with Señor Fuentes, the old wrangler who looked after his horses. Often, he'd just sit alone, listening to the thunder rolling through the canyon.

He did not consider himself a violent man, although he had no qualms about using it to enforce his business dealings or defend what he had built. He started the business in the mountains of Durango where he grew and processed marijuana and later opium. As his business flourished, he found it necessary to expand and did so in a no-nonsense, businesslike manner, inviting other traffickers to join him, using his business model to entice them. He got his drugs to market in the United States via a narrow corridor through Coahuila and southern Chihuahua, the use of which he negotiated with the relatively small-time entrepreneurs operating there. When the Frontera cartel tried to seize control of the corridor, Anastasio found it necessary to come to their assistance and in doing so brought the weight of his organization against the greedy Dominguez brothers and their cartel. The Dominguez brothers escalated the conflict by bringing in El Demonio, the notoriously violent vigilante paramilitary, who gained notoriety during the drug war in Michoacán with his depraved usage of decapitations and mutilations. Anastasio responded by luring the legendary special forces commander, Aníbal Barca Rayos, the Thunderbolt, away from a promising military career to counter El Demonio.

He had not intended to instigate a wholesale drug war for control of the northern border drug-trafficking corridors. His only interest in engaging the Frontera cartel centered on keeping his trafficking corridor into the United States. His associates, however, saw an opportunity to use the Dominguez brothers' aggression to take it all, and he reluctantly abided by their will. However, the victory had come at a price. The cartel's business had suffered a serious financial setback.

The drug war had cost his organization dearly. The intervention of the Mexican Army in the war had stemmed the cartel's supply of narcotics, seriously reducing profits. The theft of their loads coming up from Central America by the Comisión exacerbated matters, and the members of the Norteño cartel demanded satisfaction. Anastasio Noches Treviño knew that he had to address this wrong if he hoped to maintain the leadership of the cartel. Much as he dreaded the prospect, he had no choice but to authorize another campaign to adjust accounts with the Comisión.

The northern border drug war had done more than bring his organization to the verge of financial ruin. It has also taken its toll physically on him. His brown eyes looked tired and his skin gray. His face had aged and looked gaunt. The hair on top of his head had begun to seriously thin out. He had always carried his weight well, but now he seemed thin, like a man consumed by illness.

He sat under the shade tree outside the stables next to Francisco Cisneros Cienfuegos, a young man who had made a name for himself salvaging the cartel's trafficking operation through the muck of the drug war. The cartel owed its financial survival to the young man not yet thirty who had entered into a love affair with himself.

Cisco, the name he preferred, had little he could be proud of regarding his physical appearance. He had a small frame, unnaturally pale skin, and a ferret-like face. He shamelessly adorned himself with thick gold chains, expensive rings, and a variety of high-priced Rolex watches. He kept his hands immaculately manicured and his hair combed back so heavily saturated with hair cream that it always looked wet. The exorbitant amount of high-dollar cologne he applied to his person preceded him like a cloud of pungent gas, negating the intended effect. His lack of imagination also nullified the high price tag on the clothes he wore.

He had a high opinion of himself when it came to the ladies despite his tacky appearance, unkempt demeanor, tawdry style, and absolute absence of social grace and sophistication, all evidence of his ignoble upbringing. He knew very little outside of managing the criminal affairs of a drug-trafficking organization. He compensated for his shortcomings with cruelty, sarcasm, and a decidedly Napoleonic disposition. Like the diminutive wonder of the Western world, Cisco's arrogance was only exceeded by his paranoia.

"I don't understand," Cisco said in a raised voice. "Why don't we just use my sicarios to take out the Comisión?"

"Because, mí querido Cisco, it was agreed that Colonel Barca would execute the plan."

Anastasio turned his ear to the distant sound of horse hooves clip-clopping on the cobblestone and smiled as he listened to the rhythmic cadence of his daughter's Paso Fino mount.

"My halcones did all the work."

"Only because it was agreed to use your spies instead of Colonel Barca's," Anastasio countered. "His men deserve a rest."

The piston-like pounding of the horse's hooves on the smooth cobblestone drive echoed into the courtyard as his sixteen-year-old daughter rode her mount under the high archway toward the stable. Cisco turned his attention to the young lady dressed in English riding clothes.

"Natasha is blossoming into quite a beautiful young woman, Don Anastasio," Cisco commented, unable to completely disguise his lascivious tone. "You'll have to be careful who you allow to date her."

Anastasio glowered distastefully at his lustful underling. "Natasha is a strong-minded woman. She'll decide for herself who she wants to date." He turned to look at Señor Fuentes taking the reins from her as she dismounted. She smiled at her father and waved before going to the ranch house. "I imagine she'll pick a man who likes the outdoors like she does and runs horses at full gallop along the edge of the canyon." He smirked at the young narco. "Maybe you should go out riding with her sometime … Oh, I forgot. You're afraid of horses."

The humiliated young narco raised his head when he heard the sound of a car driving through the archway into the courtyard. The black BMW rolled across the cobblestone drive and stopped by the shade tree. A well-built man dressed in a black short-sleeved, square-bottomed shirt, black slacks, and wearing sunglasses stepped out of the right front door and opened the door behind him for Colonel Aníbal Barca Rayos while the driver, who dressed similarly, opened the opposite door for Major Antonio Zamora Toledo.

Both former special forces officers wore business suits, the colonel dressed entirely in black while the major dressed in a dark-gray suit with a lighter gray shirt and tie. Both men stood over six feet tall, their bodies fit and trim, and they sported conservative haircuts. The colonel carried himself with the grace of an aristocrat and had the same type of sculpted face as the French actor Louis Jordan. The major had a simpler way about him and did not share the facial characteristics of any actor. He had a hard face, handsome by some standards, and eyes like a jaguar on the hunt. He did share the colonel's dark hair, eyes, and cream-colored skin.

Anastasio rose to his feet to greet the leaders of the cartel's elite paramilitary unit, Los Rayos, the Thunderbolts. "Welcome

Colonel Barca." Anastasio shook the colonel's hand and then Major Zamora's. He turned to the wimpy narco standing beside him. "You remember Cisco."

The colonel ignored the puny narco. "I thought your man was sending his halcones to the isthmus to collect intelligence?"

Anastasio glared at Cisco, whose dumbfounded expression signaled his ignorance of what the colonel meant. "His people have been checking in regularly," he said in defense of his underling. Embarrassed, he cleared his throat. "To what are you referring?"

"Did they report that the Campechanos have organized a military wing?"

"That's impossible," Anastasio insisted. "I spoke with Arturo. He turned me down when I offered to help him stop Comandante Sánchez and his task force from hijacking their drug shipments. He assured me he could handle it with a payoff and that he didn't need a security force. I don't see Arturo lying to me like that."

"If your man was doing his job correctly, he would have known that Don Arturo is losing control of the Campechanos. He would have known that Sánchez's task force comandantes have seized control of the Campeche gangs and that they are being turned into a military force." The colonel gazed intently at the Norteño cartel leader. "I hear that even now Sánchez is on his way to Chiapas to forge an alliance with Alejandro and the Comisión."

"Impossible." Cisco scoffed. "Sánchez is a buffoon. He doesn't have the first idea of how to raise an army."

"Who is this Sánchez?" Anastasio asked.

"He's a nobody," Cisco said disparagingly.

The colonel continued to ignore Cisco. He drew a breath calmly before answering Anastasio's question. "Comandante Sánchez is the head of the Campeche governor's antinarcotics task force. He and his comandantes recruited the gangs operating in their plazas to help them sell the drugs they seized from the Campechanos to the Comisión. The Campechanos stopped the arrangement by hiring Sánchez's task force to handle their security."

"And you believe that the Campechanos are turning them into an army," Anastasio concluded.

The colonel turned to Major Zamora, who had until that moment kept silent. The stone-faced major, his eyes as clear as a rocky-bottomed brook, turned to Anastasio. "The marina seized a shipment of AK-47 rifles and M9 pistols at Punta Morro south of Campeche City from two known members of the Frontera cartel."

"So?" Cisco commented defiantly. "They were obviously selling off the guns, now that they don't need them." He scoffed. "They were probably going to sell them to farmers."

Like the colonel, the major did not acknowledge Cisco and directed his response at Anastasio. "The men were the primary gunrunners used by Fausto López during the drug war."

"We believe that El Demonio is helping the Campechanos raise an army to strike an alliance with la Comisión," the colonel added.

"And you're basing this on one gun seizure?" Anastasio inquired skeptically.

"There are other indicators," the major responded. "The gangs in Campeche have evolved overnight into sophisticated criminal organizations since they were taken over by Sánchez's task force. It's not likely that the comandantes are responsible for the gang's astonishing leap forward in sophistication. Nor is it likely that the comandantes have the expertise to train the gangs in military tactics."

"Clearly, another hand has been mixing the pot," the colonel concluded.

"It doesn't take a genius to organize a gang," Cisco dismissed the argument.

Uncharacteristically, the major broke ranks and glared sarcastically at Cisco. "Obviously," he remarked derisively. "A final point regarding the guns at Punta Morro." He turned to Anastasio. "Farmers prefer shotguns and twenty-two rifles to shoot game and varmints, not military-style weapons."

CHAPTER

14

The leather-skinned sailor sat in his perch high above the deck near the top of the mainsail mast above the spar with nothing but the sharpness of his eyes to perform the duties of a lookout. His turn in the perch came as a welcome respite to the heat and thick, humid air on the deck below. The wind blowing cooled his tortured, mosquito-bitten skin as the ship rounded the point at Varaderos above the Sabancuy estuary under full sail.

He had barely taken his post and settled himself into the cramped confines of the perch when he spotted a vessel sitting in the waters off the estuary with her sails down. He cupped his hands around his mouth to call down to the poop deck.

"Ship off the port bow!"

The quartermaster went to port side of the afterdeck and shaded his eyes to look for the ship. "She's a caravel, Captain," the quartermaster reported. "Sitting high with her sails down."

The captain reached into his bucket-top boot for his spyglass and joined the quartermaster on the port side. He scanned the deck of the ship from the high-angled bowsprit to the raised afterdeck and massive rudder astern. He grinned with delight as he watched the small crew frantically trying to hoist her sails.

"That she is, Mr. Brown," the captain replied as he focused his glass on the caravel's captain. The Spaniard stood over the helmsman with his hand pointing toward the coast. "Looks like her captain's going to make a run for the shallows."

"He'll run her aground first."

"Not likely, Mr. Brown." The captain lowered his spyglass and turned to his second-in-command. "I'll wager that rascal knows these waters well."

"Should we put one across her bow, Captain?"

"Don't waste the shot. Her captain's made his intentions clear." He focused his glass on the stern of the little ship. He grinned when he saw the Spanish captain looking back at him through his own glass. He lowered his glass. "Clear for quarters, Mr. Brown."

"Clear for quarters!" the quartermaster yelled down to the crew on the main deck. "Action stations!"

The ship came alive in a cacophony of cursing men, some repeating the order at the top of their lungs over the sound of thumping feet running across the main deck. Mr. Brown looked forward to the prow where the gunners calmly loaded the swivel guns and the gunner's mates their muskets. Each man looked aft to Mr. Brown after loading his weapon to wait for his order to fire.

"Forward gun crew ready to fire on the bridge, Captain," Mr. Brown reported.

"We won't be able to get close enough to use the swivel guns," he told the quartermaster. He trained his glass on the oversized rudder and then lowered it. "Disable the rudder."

"Aye, Captain." The quartermaster turned to the helmsmen. "Hard to port, Mr. Jennings."

"Aye. Hard to port, Mr. Brown." The helmsman spun the ship's wheel sharply to the left.

"Clear the starboard beam," Mr. Brown yelled down to the main deck. "Prepare to disable the rudder, Mr. O'Shay."

The thunderous roar of heavy wooden cannon wheels rumbling across the deck drowned out the sound of yelling men. The gun crew rolled the heavy cannon into place, extending the muzzle over the starboard gunwale as several mates threw buckets of sand on the deck around the cannon to aid the gun crew's footing.

The captain sighted his spyglass on the massive rudder behind the caravel. "Fire when ready, Mr. Brown."

"Take her rudder, Mr. O'Shay!" the quartermaster yelled to the master gunner.

"Aye, Mr. Brown!" He turned to his men and squatted behind the cannon. "Steady, laddies," the master gunner said softly to his crew. Mr. O'Shay hunched behind the cannon to line his shot and judge the pitch-and-roll of the carrack. He closed an eye as he watched the end of the cannon rise over the caravel's poop deck and then drop to the waterline before rising again in perfect line with the large rudder. "Prepare a bomb," he called to his mates.

The gun crew worked quickly. The loader poured six pounds of gunpowder into the muzzle and stuffed a cotton rag into it. He stepped aside to allow another crewman to pack the shot down the bore with a ramrod. The loader then held a four-pounder close to the bore, rotating the black iron sphere until he got the fuse in position for the master gunner to light.

Mr. O'Shay, never taking his eye off the target, muttered an indistinct cadence to himself as he timed his shot. He slowly extended the fire stick and touched the tip of the fuse on the bomb.

A brilliant flash preceded a dull pop followed by a hissing noise. "Load!" he yelled.

The loader dropped the hissing four-pounder down the muzzle as Mr. O'Shay moved to his left, behind the cannon, where he crouched down, quietly muttering his cadence as he waited on the pitch-and-roll of the ship. He lowered the end of the fire stick over the touch hole and waited for the muzzle to come down, in line with the caravel's poop deck. He eased the flame down to the cannon just as the caravel made an unexpected turn to port.

The cannon belched out the hissing iron ball with a hollow, booming thud. A dense cloud of gray smoke spread over the deck as the four-pound ball whistled across the water toward the caravel. A plume of water shot vertically into the air after the bomb blew a hole below the caravel's waterline at the stern.

"Damn that gunner!" the captain cursed.

"An unfortunate decision by the Spaniard, Captain," Mr. Brown said calmly.

The caravel began to list drastically as the sea raced into the gaping wound made by the gunner's cannonball.

"Damn! Damn! Damn!" the captain cursed.

The white linen shirt he had cross-tucked in his loose-fitting wine-colored breeches filled with the wind as he collapsed his spyglass with a pop and slipped it into his right brown leather bucket-top boot. The caravel listed to port, her bow rising in a sharp angle as her stern slipped into the briny. The crew stood up from their stations to watch the struggling sailors disappear one by one under the gentle waves. There was no empathy in their eyes, only wonder about what it might be like and how soon before they met a similar end.

"What a shame. We could have used her shot and powder," the captain said with regret.

"Do you want me to organize a salvage party?"

"No, there's not enough daylight left and the water's too deep."

Mr. Brown looked at the bobbing heads among the flotsam of the once proud little coastal patrol vessel. "What do you want to do about the crew? We might be able to ransom them."

"I doubt that the governor would part with a single real for the lot of them." The captain took his spyglass out of his boot and extended it to take a closer look at the beleaguered crew. "I want to take on fresh water before dark. Take us to the river up the coast."

"Aye, Captain." He turned to the helmsman. "Prepare to come about."

"Aye, Mr. Brown."

"After we fill our casks, take us to See Ho beach, Mr. Brown. It'll be the last night the men sleep ashore for a while. Make sure they enjoy it."

"Aye, Captain Morgan."

Below the desperately thrashing limbs of her crew, the mortally wounded caravel slowly sank to the seafloor. The stern struck the bottom first, breaking her keel and then sending the mainsail mast crashing on the mizzenmast and the aftercastle. A cloud of sand enveloped the wreck as the loose gear that had rolled off her deck rained down on the wreck, disappearing into the murky maelstrom of misfortune. There she would rest, lost and forgotten, for nearly four hundred years.

Over time, the strong current and the shifting sands of the bottom consumed the wreck as it decayed into rot and rust. The sand and silt shifted relentlessly as the years passed into decades and the decades into centuries until all that remained visible of the caravel was the outline of her hull. When she went down, she had almost made it to the shoals around the Sabancuy estuary and somehow missed discovery when the engineers dredged the channel leading to the lagoon at the mouth of the estuary. It took a fisherman snagging his net on the wreck to finally give the caravel a chance to tell her story.

The current at the mouth of the Sabancuy Channel rocked the Siete Mares like a mother lovingly rocking her child in a cradle. The gentle, rhythmic lapping of the water against the hull made it difficult for either Sandy or Poli to keep his eyes open. Neither had slept much since they set sail from the Arcas. It had taken them most of the day to get to the channel, and they hardly had a chance to steal more than a wink or two, here and there. The clear skies, the bright sun's rays bouncing off the water, and the soft breeze added to their drowsiness as they sat on the deck watching Dr. Ventura on the television monitor.

The professor pulled on a measuring tape, looked at his watch, and then noted the results on a dive slate before swimming to another location and repeating the process. For most of the last two hours, the boys watched the professor and Augie swim back and forth across the monitor, taking measurements and taking pictures.

The wreck lay in about sixty-eight feet of water on a sandy bottom. They watched Augie swimming in the background with an underwater digital camera dangling from his side as the professor repeated the monotonous routine. Fish of every variety, size, and color imaginable swam in and around the site among the limestone and coral outcroppings, including a barracuda hovering over the bottom between a group of rocks and the wreck.

"Poli." Sandy nudged him. "Look at this!" Sandy laughed at the sight of his uncle swimming out of a cloud of sediment.

"Are they coming up?" Poli wiped the drowsiness from his eyes. "What happened?"

"You missed it." Sandy chuckled. "Uncle Augie surprised a barracuda."

Poli chuckled along with him, although he had completely missed the spectacle. He stared at the monitor and then leaned closer and frowned. "Where's the skipper?"

"He's on the other end of the tape the professor's holding."

"Oh," Poli muttered. He sat back, using the heels of his hands for support as he looked at the monitor sitting on top of the main cabin under the main mast. He yawned and looked at the mast, running his eyes up the spar to the top. He sighed and then returned his tired eyes to the screen. "What did you say they were doing?"

"They're conducting a three-dimensional site survey of the shipwreck."

"How do they do that?"

"Well ..." Sandy paused. "They begin by laying out the bottom, identifying structures to use as fixed points."

"Fixed points?"

Sandy hunched his shoulders. "Coral outcroppings. Rocks. Stuff that doesn't move." He turned to the screen and pointed at it. "Once they do that, they use the fixed points to plot the wreck and the debris field."

"What's a debris field?"

"The stuff that rolls off the deck or falls out of the ship as it breaks up," Sandy explained.

"What do you mean by 'breaks up'?"

"Sometimes a ship breaks into two or more parts when it sinks."

"What causes that?"

Sandy thought about it for a moment before answering. "Ships don't always sink straight down." He held his hands out on an even plain. "A ship is held together by the keel, which is supported by the water. If the water rushing into the ship doesn't go in evenly"—he slowly lowered his left hand—"the part with the most water gets heavier than the rest of the ship, causing that part to sink first." He suddenly dropped his left arm to his side. "Breaking the keel and splitting the ship in two." He looked at Poli. "Depending at what point the ship breaks up as it's sinking, how deep the water is, and the current—the parts of the ship can be far apart." He pointed at the screen. "It looks like the keel didn't break until it hit the bottom. That's why the debris field is small and close to the wreck."

As the two boys looked at the screen, Augie drifted into the picture, holding the underwater camera up to his mask. Poli paid close attention to him as he took several pictures of an elongated, heavily barnacled structure partially buried in the sand.

"Why's your uncle taking a picture of a rock?" Poli asked.

"Something about the rock got his interest." Sandy leaned closer to the monitor. "Looks like it could be a cannon."

"A cannon?" Poli took a harder look. "Are you sure? It looks kind of small?"

"It could be a swivel gun," Sandy suggested.

"What's a swivel gun?"

"It's kind of a small cannon that worked sort of like a shotgun." He sat up and formed a circle with his hand to demonstrate. "They'd load it with iron pellets, nails, rocks, glass—anything that could be used to tear into the enemy crew," he explained. "They were usually mounted on the gunwale."

"What's a gunwale?"

"You know…" Sandy pointed at the ship's rail. "The part of the ship that keeps drunk sailors from walking off the deck."

As the two boys laughed at the thought of a drunken sailor walking off the deck, Sandy glanced at the screen and saw the professor motioning frantically to his uncle. "Looks like the professor found something interesting."

The boys watched Augie swim over to him, holding his camera at the ready. The professor pointed at a very large rock half buried in the sand. Augie took several photos of it from varying angles as Dr. Ventura pulled on the tape measure. He looked at the depth meter on his watch, noted it on his slate, and then made a thumbs-up to his uncle. As Augie swam off, the professor flipped the dive slate over and began to sketch it.

"What is Dr. Ventura doing now?"

"Making a sketch of what they found."

Poli strained to make out the coral-covered structure. "I don't know," he mumbled. "I kind of could see how that other rock looked like a little cannon, but this just looks like a rock to me."

Sandy chuckled. "It probably is." He rested a hand on the deck as he stared at the monitor. "It takes a trained eye to recognize an artifact after it's been underwater for a long time. Barnacles and other junk build up over time, changing the lines until it looks like just any other rock." He looked at Poli. "It's not unusual to think you've found something real cool and wind up with just another piece of coral." He let the air out of his lungs as he stared into the monitor. "Then sometimes you get lucky and you find an important clue that can help identify the wreck."

"What kind of clue?"

"Anything that might have the ship's name on it. A ship's bell. A cannon." He hunched his shoulders. "Sometimes they put the ship's name on the dishes—or the forks and spoons." He leaned forward to watch his uncle take another photograph.

"Why's your uncle taking so many pictures?"

"That's the thing about a site survey." Sandy cocked his head to the side. "You have to take advantage of the time you're here. You can't always get back to take a second look. So you take a lot of pictures. If you see something you think might be important, you take a picture of it and plot where you found it. Later, an underwater archeologist will go over the pictures and look at the notes you made of where you found it. It'll be up to him to determine if there is something worth coming back to get." Sandy raised his brow. "If you don't take a picture of what you're looking at, you might miss something and lose out in making an important discovery."

Poli looked at Sandy. "How do you know so much about this stuff?"

"Uncle Augie got me a job on a marine research vessel one summer," Sandy said, looking back at the screen. Dr. Ventura and his uncle were gathering their equipment and heading for the anchor line. "Looks like they've started back up." He switched the monitor to a different camera to watch the divers start up the anchor chain.

Poli got up and stretched his back. "Did you like working on a research boat?"

"Yeah," Sandy said with his breath. "That's what I want to do for the rest of my life."

He looked back into the monitor and at the divers stopping periodically on their ascent to allow their bubbles to beat them to the surface. He drew a sharp breath and let it out slowly. "When I was little, Benício would sometimes take me fishing with him in his panga." He turned to Sandy. "He's a good fisherman and never quit until he had a good catch."

"I bet that was fun." Sandy smiled.

"Not really." He scoffed. "The sun was always hot, and the glare off the water made it hard to see sometimes." He looked out at the ocean. "I felt sorry for the fish."

"But you learned something, didn't you?"

Poli gazed thoughtfully at Sandy and then smiled. "I learned I didn't like fishing."

Like most stepfathers who sincerely accept another man's child, Benício tried to bond with his wife's son. Naturally, he took him to the park to watch him play on the merry-go-round, slide down the slide, and climb the monkey bars. However, when it came to kicking a fútbol with Poli, who loved soccer, he simply did not have the stamina. For that matter, he didn't even enjoy watching the sport. His father never indulged him with such frivolous things, and it didn't matter to Benício. He had always imagined himself as a panga fisherman and had hoped that Poli would too. Sadly for him, that never happened. Poli had inherited his father's adventurous spirit and had no interest in fishing, especially fishing in a panga.

It came as no surprise to his mother that Poli took so readily to crewing on the Siete Mares. Though her husband never got the chance, she believed that he would have taken to sailing as well as Poli had. His mother had unwittingly told him stories about his father, some that she made up or at least told to him in a different setting; they must have inspired Poli's sense of adventure. The events of the previous evening had roused that sense of adventure.

"What do you think the skipper went to do last night on the island?" Poli asked Sandy.

"Beats me." Sandy turned to Poli. "All I know is that whatever it was he went to do, my uncle and the professor weren't happy with it."

Seventh Naval Zone, Lerma, Campeche

The keyboard sounded like a pair of woodpeckers pounding their rock-hard beaks on opposite sides of the same tree in a mocking competition—one burst of heavy thumps, followed by another burst of softer clacks in a back-and-forth, up-and-down, seesaw exchange. Lieutenant Baeza stared at the computer screen as he first enlarged and then reduced the image he attempted to enhance with intense concentration. Across the desk from the lieutenant sat Captain Mendiola, waiting for the intelligence officer to show him what he called him to his office to see.

"Have you almost got it?" Captain Mendiola asked.

The frustrated lieutenant exhaled sharply and sat back. "The cameras on the oil platform are too far to get a clear image." He moved the mouse to the printer button on the screen and clicked on it. The printer came to life, squeaking and groaning as it printed the image on the screen. He turned to the captain. "I can't get a clear image of the ship."

"Can you at least tell what it is?"

The lieutenant took the printout out of the printer and handed it to the captain. "Considering the image was taken in moonlight, the angle, the distance ..." He sighed. "All I can say is that it is some type of sailing vessel with at least two sails."

"It's a good thing the hull and sails are light-colored," the captain remarked. "Otherwise, you might not've been able to even say that."

"Um-hmm," he agreed as he stared at the screen. "We should consider updating the cameras we have mounted on top of the Ta'Kuntah platform."

"That takes money, my friend." He held up the printout and took another look at it. "Why are you so interested in this mystery ship?" He handed the photo back to the lieutenant.

"After I went to bed last night, I started thinking about the operation."

"Don't dwell on it, Teniente," Captain Mendiola remarked. "It's like I told you. You can't believe everything an informer tells you." He shook his head. "They embellish the truth to make up for gaps in what they know. I don't doubt that your informer heard something about a delivery of cocaine being made west of the Seyba Reef, but he didn't know who was involved. I've heard the rumors myself about the Pemex supply ship making cocaine runs, but that's all they are—rumors." He scoffed. "He was wrong about the panguero we detained with the handgun, and he was wrong about the Pemex supply ship. He probably threw that part in to persuade you to go back to the Seyba Reef, hoping you would stumble on the real traffickers and get a handsome reward."

"I understand all that, mí capitán." Baeza set the surveillance photo aside and opened a drawer in his desk. "But that's not what was keeping me awake." He pulled out a file and spread a group of pictures across his desk. "These are the pictures taken by the forensic expert regarding the incident today on Cayo del Centro." He picked up a photo of a Rolex watch and another of a close-up of the serial number and handed them to the captain. "We know that the men on Cayo del Centro are the pirates who attacked that Canadian pleasure boater off Holbox Island. One of them was wearing his watch."

"They as much as admitted it." The captain handed the photos back to him.

"They also admitted slitting the lighthouse keeper's throat," the lieutenant added. He picked up a picture of the sleeping bag spread on some broken planks with six AK-47 rifles resting on it and handed it to the captain. "Here is a picture of the guns they also didn't deny were theirs."

"What's your point?" He handed the picture back to the lieutenant.

"If they admit to murder, rape, and possession of illegal weapons, why deny possessing the cocaine?"

"What are you suggesting?"

"What if the cocaine was planted on them?"

"You're reaching, Teniente," the captain replied. "I read Teniente Elizondo's report. The men brought the cocaine with them. The forensic technician found traces of cocaine in both skiffs."

Lieutenant shuffled through the pictures on his desk and picked up several photos of the interior of both boats. He glanced at them before handing them to the captain. "If you take a close look at these photos, you'll notice that only the starboard side of the skiffs show traces of powder." He looked at the pictures on his desk and picked up several other photos.

The captain rolled his lip out. "It looks like someone poured the cocaine from the outside of the boats."

"Here are pictures of the skiffs' outboard motors." Baeza handed him the photos. "Notice anything unusual."

"The hoses have been cut." He handed the photos back to him.

"Exactly." He gave him more pictures to look at. "Here are the packages of cocaine recovered from the brush behind the lighthouse. Look at the way the bricks are wrapped."

The captain shuffled through them. "I've never seen bricks wrapped this way. It's like a weave."

"Look at the markings on the top and bottom of the bricks."

"It looks like a pentagram with an upside-down cross in it?"

"The sign of the devil," he added. He took another group of photos and gave them to the captain.

"What are these?"

"I had the forensic expert take a picture of a large hole I found behind a slab in the ruins of the house where the marineros found the rifles. Notice the broken plank sitting on the edge of the pit."

"It looks like it was used to dig the hole." The captain tried handing him back the picture.

He gave the captain another picture. "Here's a picture taken from the slab looking from the pit up to the sand dune. Notice the trail." As the captain looked over the picture, Baeza opened the center drawer of his desk to get a magnifying glass. "Now, look closely to the left of the trail where the grass has been pushed down." He handed the magnifying glass to him. "See anything?"

The captain studied the picture using the magnifying glass and then raised his eyes. "It looks like an old brick."

"It's not an old brick." He handed the captain another picture. "Here's a close-up."

"More cocaine."

"The wrapping and the stamp are identical to the ones found behind the lighthouse." He shuffled through the pictures until he found the one he wanted and gave it to the captain. "We found two more bricks in the pit they must've missed. The wrappings and stamps are the same."

He gave the pictures and the magnifying glass back to the lieutenant. "I see where you're going with this, Teniente."

"I believe the cocaine behind the lighthouse came from that pit on the west side of the island. Somebody, not the pirates, dug up the load and hid it in the brush behind the lighthouse. They salted the skiffs to connect the pirates to the load, sabotaged their outboard motors to strand them on the island, and then disabled the range beacon to get us to come there."

"Let me look at that first picture again, the wide angle of the trail." Captain Mendiola took it from the lieutenant. "Looks like the work of one man." He handed the picture to him. "The trail is narrow. If it had been more than one man, the trail would be broader."

"That's a good observation, mí capitán." He took the picture from the captain and made a note on the back of it. "Gracias."

"Have you told the judicial officer about your theory?"

"Not yet," Lieutenant Baeza replied. "I'm still trying to work out who's behind setting up the pirates."

The captain put the photos in his hand on the desk and sat back. "Do you think this is the same fifty pounds of cocaine we were trying to intercept last night?"

"I'm almost sure of it." Lieutenant Baeza gathered the photos, returned them to the file, and set it aside next to the enhanced surveillance photo.

"What makes you think so?"

He opened the desk drawer to get another file and looked at the captain. "I believe my informer was deliberately fed bad information to keep us away from where the delivery was going to be made."

"Your informer again?" The captain scoffed. "If it was me, I'd forget about ever using him again."

"Bear with me, mí capitán." He opened the file and handed the captain a picture of the hapless panguero holding a weathered revolver standing between two marines. "Knowing what we know now, I believe my informer was right about the panguero you caught with the gun. He wasn't out west of the Seyba Reef to go fishing. He had no tackle. He had extra gas cans to make a long voyage, and his hold was empty." He scoffed. "And he wasn't there to commit an act of piracy. Not with that gun."

The captain studied the picture for a moment. "All right. I'll concede that he might have been en route to collect a load of cocaine." He gave the picture back. "But I still say your informer made up the part about the Pemex ship."

"I respectfully disagree, mí capitán." He took the picture and held it in his hand. "If you will recall, Capitán Santos took his time unloading his cargo at the Ta'Kuntah platform and left just as the storm was coming." He looked the captain directly in the eye. "He had to know about the storm. He's an experienced captain. He had plenty of time to unload his cargo and make it back to Seyba Playa, way ahead of the storm." He threw the picture on the desk. "Yet he didn't."

"I will agree that his behavior was unusual," the captain conceded. "But I'm sure there's probably an explanation why he waited to leave when he did, as bad a decision as it was."

"Santos must have known we were on to him," Lieutenant Baeza adduced. "I believe he was providing a diversion while another ship went to fetch the load."

Intrigued but not entirely convinced, the captain sat back and folded his arms. "I'm listening."

He looked at the picture on his desk of the panguero standing between the two marines. "If the panguero you caught with the gun was working for a drug trafficker, wouldn't it make sense that they would presume he talked and might have told us who he was going to meet?"

The captain thought about it for a moment. "I'll give you that."

"And wouldn't it make sense that the traffickers wouldn't risk losing fifty kilos of cocaine by using a ship that might have been compromised?" He nodded at the captain. "Your presence west of the Seyba Reef the day you detained the panguero might be viewed by the traffickers as more than just coincidental, causing them to believe that an informer might have been involved."

The captain nodded. "I can see that."

"Does it make sense, then, given Santos's unusual behavior yesterday at the platform that he might have acted as a decoy while another ship went to get their fifty kilos?"

"Your argument deserves consideration," the captain remarked. "However, you're just stringing facts together. Most of it on conjecture alone." He gazed at the lieutenant. "If we accept that another ship was sent to get the load and that the fifty kilos recovered behind the lighthouse are the same fifty kilos your informer told us about, how do you explain why the traffickers would sacrifice a load to frame the pirates? By your own argument, they obviously went to great lengths to protect the load by setting up a diversion using the Pemex ship."

"That's what's been bothering me," the lieutenant admitted. "Let's say that whoever went to retrieve the cocaine was interrupted by the sudden appearance of the pirates."

"Are you saying now that the pirates stole the cocaine from the traffickers?"

"No, I'm convinced the pirates were ignorant of the cocaine that was planted on them." Lieutenant Baeza sat back and gripped the ends of the armrests of his chair. "They never knew the people sent to get the load were there."

"You're losing me."

"Consider this." The lieutenant put his elbows on the desk. "What if whoever went to get the cocaine was being forced to get it and saw the pirates as a way out?"

"You're saying they framed the pirates to make it look like it was stolen from them?" The captain turned his head and then looked at him. "From what I know about drug traffickers, they don't accept excuses for losing a load. They would've expected them to die before giving up the load to the pirates."

"Unless they didn't consider the consequences," the lieutenant countered. He let out his breath. "We'll know for sure if their bodies turn up."

"Hmm." The captain nodded. "You make a good case, but unless we're able to come up with proof, the pirates will have to take responsibility for the fifty kilos."

He picked up the surveillance photo he had enhanced and stared at it. He gazed at the grainy image of the ship. "If there was only a way to identify this ship."

"You're assuming that the ship was involved," the captain commented. "What if there was another—a speedboat or shrimper, perhaps?"

"No," the lieutenant said softly as he set the surveillance photo on the desk. "A cigarette boat, cabin cruiser, or shrimper might have been noticed by the pirates. The ship had to slip in and slip out quietly."

"Like a sailboat," the captain concluded. "Now I understand your interest in the mystery ship—but it's still a reach."

The lieutenant took one last look at the ship in the grainy image of the sailboat caught in the surveillance camera. "If we can identify this ship, we might be able to find out who did it … and why."

Captain Mendiola took the surveillance photo from him and studied it. "The ship appears to be sailing from the southwestern tip of the island." He raised his eyes. "What time was this footage taken?"

Baeza looked at the screen on his computer and then clicked on the mouse, reducing the image until he found the dateline. He turned the computer monitor toward the captain. "Here you go."

"Oh-four-eleven this morning." He took another glance at the enhanced photo. "The ship appears to be on a southeasterly heading."

The lieutenant swiveled his chair around to look at the chart on the wall behind his desk. "That would take it to Isla Aguada. Maybe Sabancuy."

"That's where I'd start looking for your mystery ship." The captain tossed the photo on the lieutenant's desk. "If they're still in the area, look for a ship with a light-colored hull and at least two sails." The captain rose to his feet. "Whoever framed the pirates had a pair on him—I'll give him that."

Lieutenant Baeza picked up the picture and stared at it. "I have a good idea who that might be."

EPILOGUE

There's something about the twilight that quiets the anxious mind, especially after a beautiful sunset, like the sunsets in Seyba Playa. The twilight never disappoints and varies from day to day. Problems seem to fade into the afterglow backlighting the clouds. Even on those evenings when a storm lurks beyond the horizon, solace awaits in the brilliant display of light and color raging silently through the hearts of the thunderheads rising into the coming night and in the soft rumbling of the thunder dissipating into the distance. Twilight in Seyba Playa not only quiets the anxious mind; it soothes the troubled soul.

The twilight always comforted Itzél. Sometimes she liked to walk across the street to the malecon and sit on the seawall, waiting for the stars to come out or marveling at the colorful flashes of lightning dancing in the storm clouds. She liked to sit and let the calm of the twilight and the coolness of the night air do its work. After a day like she had the day before, she needed the twilight more than ever.

"The great artists," Don Macario said to Itzél as he lowered himself to sit next to her. "Monet. Van Gogh. Tried to capture the true magnificence of a sunset." He took in the panoramic beauty unfolding before him and inhaled sharply. "They were never satisfied that they had."

She smiled and then leaned over to kiss him on the cheek. "Thank you, Don Macario, for everything."

"I was glad to do what little I could." He chuckled softly.

She took his hand in hers. "Benício told me how you helped Lázaro with the public ministry."

"It was no great undertaking. The head of the PGR is a close friend." He put his free hand on hers. "When Lázaro told me what happened, I couldn't believe that the PGR would handle a murder investigation in such a manner. I also found it odd that there was no mention of the murder in the paper." He smiled at her. "As it turns out, his office was very familiar with the woman he supposedly murdered. He showed Lázaro a picture of a woman detained last night trying to do the same thing to a wealthy businessman." Don Macario scoffed. "I've never seen anyone so relieved."

"I wish Benício had gone to you first." She raised her head. "When I think of what could have happened to him ..." She turned to him. "Thanks for sending Capitán Donovan to help my husband."

"I can't take credit for that either," Don Macario said. "All I did was mention to Simon that Benício was in trouble, and he sprang into action without hesitation." He inhaled deeply and then released the air from his lungs. "He even found a way to keep El Demonio from bothering him about making another trip."

She looked at him curiously. "How did he do that?"

"It's better that you don't know the details."

Itzél looked beyond the horizon, her eyes lost in thought. The last rays of the sun glowed on the water like the embers of a dying fire. She raised her eyes to look at the first stars breaking through the blue of the sky as night began to fall.

She turned to Don Macario. "What kind of man is Capitán Donovan?"

Don Macario chuckled softly. "He's like any other man, I suppose. Maybe a little more daring. A little too reckless." A large meteoroid streaked across the sky, catching his eye. "And perhaps a bit foolish when it comes to chasing a dream."

"Look!" Augie called out as he helped Dr. Ventura remove his diving equipment. "A shooting star."

The meteoroid glided along the edge of the upper atmosphere, leaving behind a long, brilliant tail. Poli pointed it out to Sandy, who would have missed it had it punched directly into the atmosphere, burning itself out in an instant. The two boys gazed at the unusually long-lasting spectacle from the stern of the ship.

Donovan watched the streak fade into the darkest part of the sky, ending its brief visit to the earth's upper atmosphere. He handed his tank to Augie, who stacked it in the rack next to the one he took off the professor.

"Aren't you gonna make a wish?" Augie asked him.

"What kind of wish?"

"I don't know." He took a long, slow breath. "Another shot at romance."

"Some believe that a shooting star is a soul being released from purgatory," the professor commented.

"Lucky guy," Donovan muttered cynically.

"They're supposed to be good luck," the professor added. "What do you think, Simon?"

Donovan looked at where the meteoroid had dissipated into the night, leaving a faint streak in its wake. Then he looked at the first stars breaking through the sky and how they sparkled like diamonds.

"It's just a rock."